my LITTLE PONY

FRIENDS FOREVER

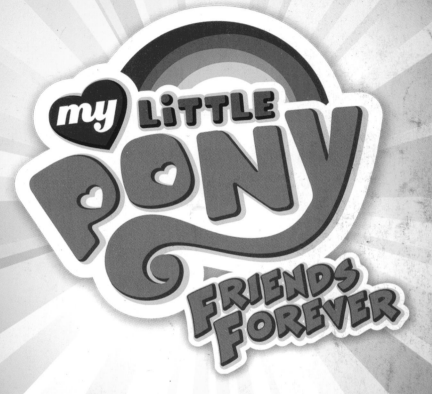

MY LITTLE PONY
FRIENDS FOREVER

TWILIGHT SPARKLE & BIG MAC

Written by
Ted Anderson

Art by
Brenda Hickey

Colors by
Heather Breckel

Letters by
Neil Uyetake

RAINBOW DASH & FLUTTERSHY

Written by
Christina Rice

Art by
Jay Fosgitt

Colors by
Heather Breckel

Letters by
Neil Uyetake

Special thanks to Erin Comella, Robert Fewkes, Joe Furfaro, Heather Hopkins, Pat Jarret, Ed Lane, Brian Lenard, Marissa Mansolillo, Donna Tobin, Michael Vogel, and Michael Kelly for their invaluable assistance.

For international rights, please contact licensing@idwpublishing.com

ISBN: 978-1-63140-488-7

18 17 16 15   1 2 3 4

Ted Adams, CEO & Publisher
Greg Goldstein, President & COO
Robbie Robbins, EVP/Sr. Graphic Artist
Chris Ryall, Chief Creative Officer/Editor-in-Chief
Matthew Ruzicka, CPA, Chief Financial Officer
Alan Payne, VP of Sales
Dirk Wood, VP of Marketing
Lorelei Bunjes, VP of Digital Services
Jeff Webber, VP of Licensing, Digital and Subsidiary Rights

www.IDWPUBLISHING.com

Licensed By: Hasbro

Facebook: facebook.com/idwpublishing
Twitter: @idwpublishing
YouTube: youtube.com/idwpublishing
Tumblr: tumblr.idwpublishing.com
Instagram: instagram.com/idwpublishing

RaRiTY & THE CaKES

Written by
Christina Rice

Art by
Brenda Hickey

Colors by
Heather Breckel

Letters by
Neil Uyetake

PRinCESS LUNa & DiSCORD

Written by
Jeremy Whitley

Art by
Brenda Hickey

Colors by
Heather Breckel

Letters by
Neil Uyetake

Cover by
Amy Mebberson

Series Edits by
Bobby Curnow

Collection Edits by
Justin Eisinger & Alonzo Simon

Collection Design by
Neil Uyetake

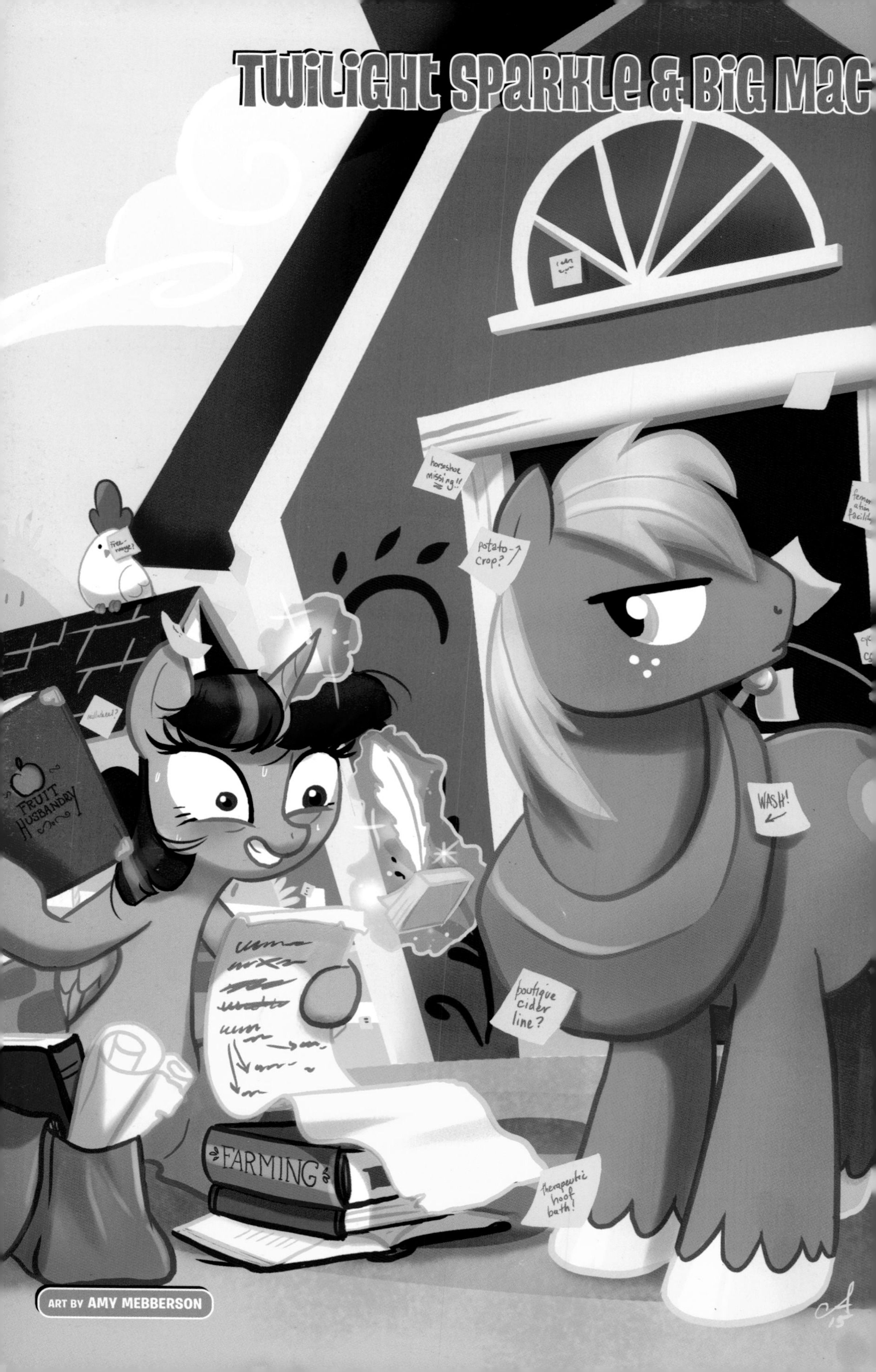
TWILIGHT SPARKLE & BIG MAC
horseshoe missing!!
potato-crop?
WASH!
FRUIT HUSBANDRY
boutique cider line?
FARMING
therapeutic hoof bath!
ART BY AMY MEBBERSON

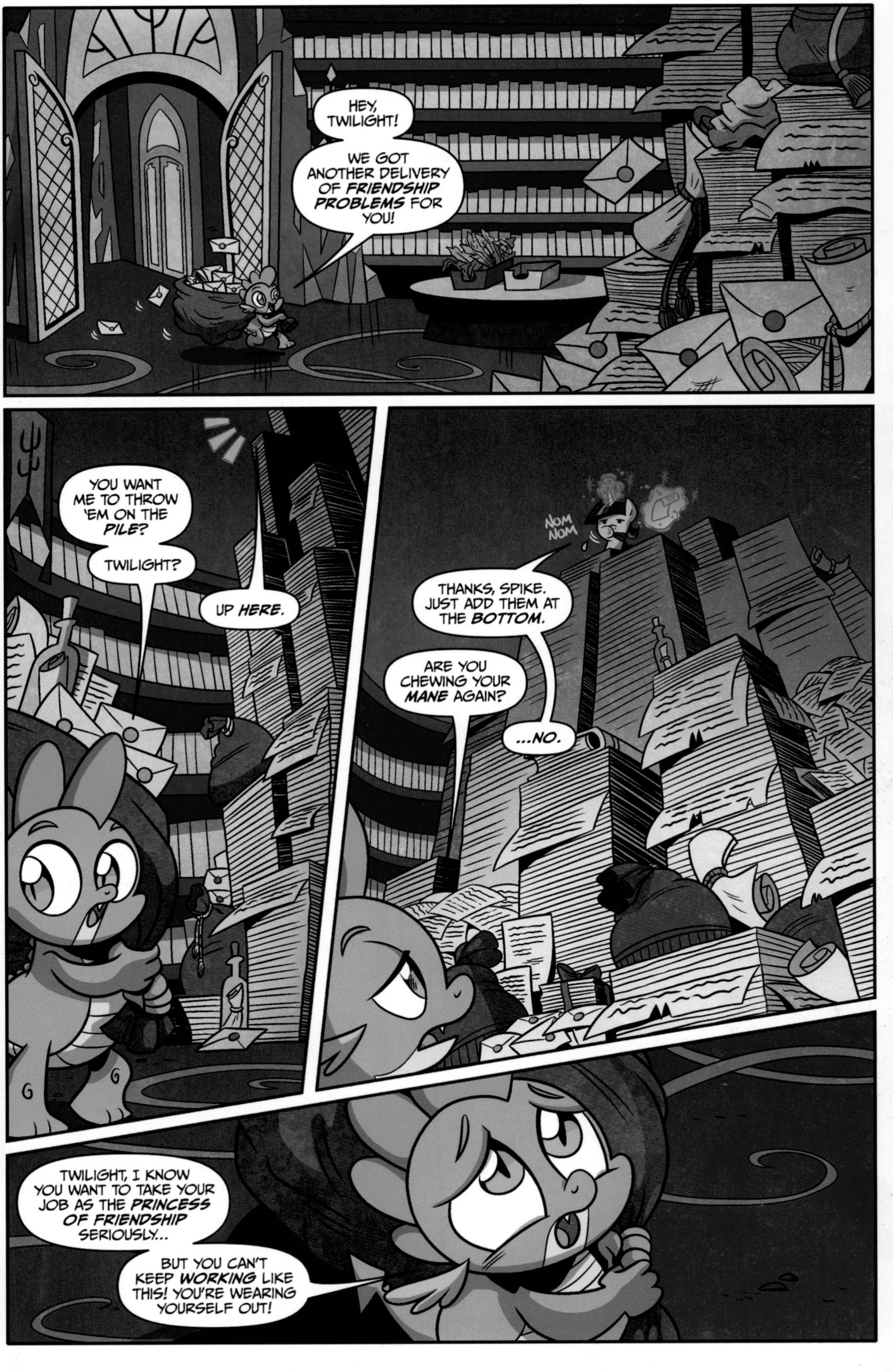

HEY, TWILIGHT!
WE GOT ANOTHER DELIVERY OF FRIENDSHIP PROBLEMS FOR YOU!
YOU WANT ME TO THROW 'EM ON THE PILE?
TWILIGHT?
UP HERE.
NOM NOM
THANKS, SPIKE. JUST ADD THEM AT THE BOTTOM.
ARE YOU CHEWING YOUR MANE AGAIN?
...NO.
TWILIGHT, I KNOW YOU WANT TO TAKE YOUR JOB AS THE PRINCESS OF FRIENDSHIP SERIOUSLY...
BUT YOU CAN'T KEEP WORKING LIKE THIS! YOU'RE WEARING YOURSELF OUT!

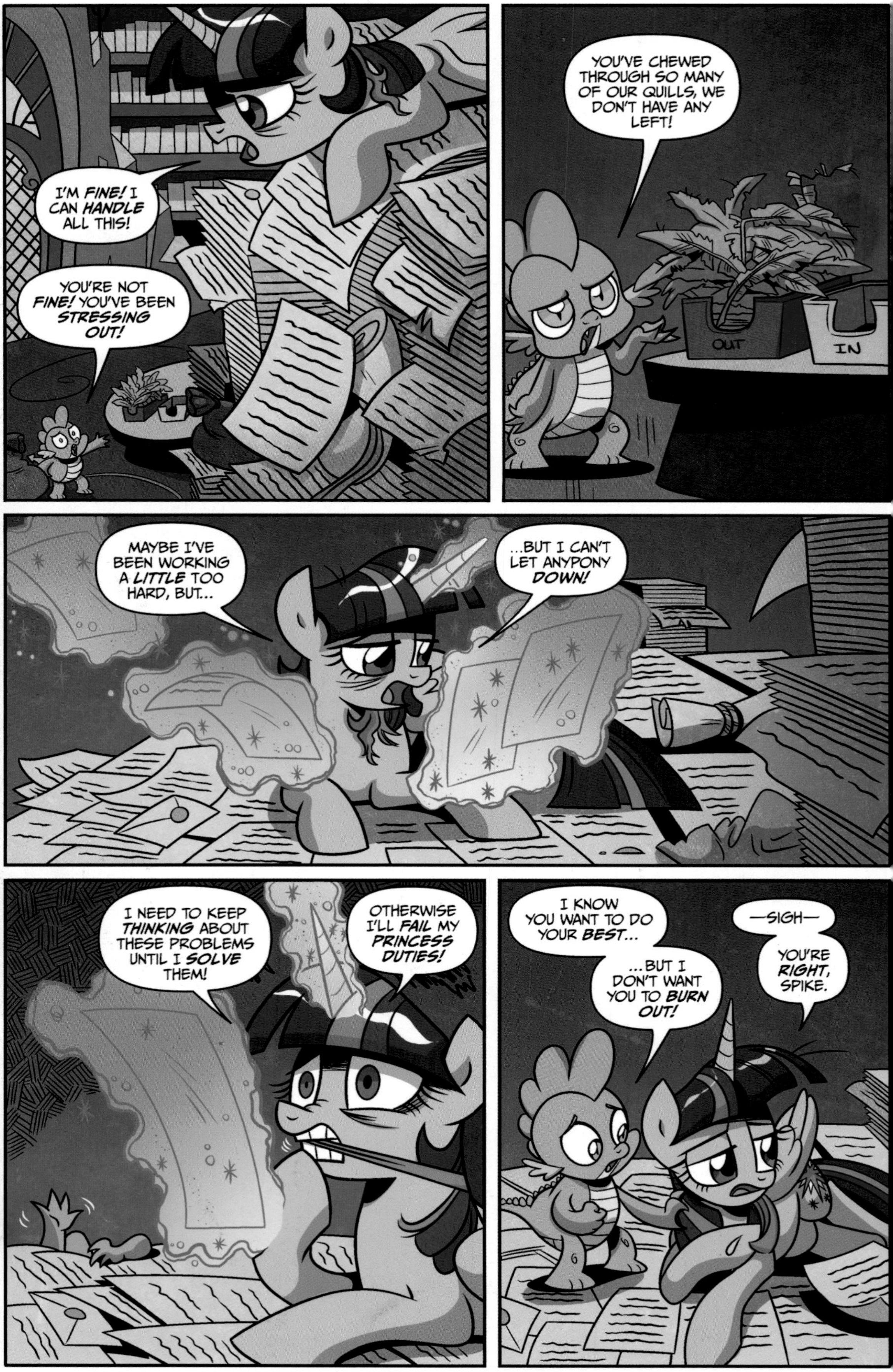
I'M FINE! I CAN HANDLE ALL THIS!
YOU'RE NOT FINE! YOU'VE BEEN STRESSING OUT!
YOU'VE CHEWED THROUGH SO MANY OF OUR QUILLS, WE DON'T HAVE ANY LEFT!
OUT
IN
MAYBE I'VE BEEN WORKING A LITTLE TOO HARD, BUT...
...BUT I CAN'T LET ANYPONY DOWN!
I NEED TO KEEP THINKING ABOUT THESE PROBLEMS UNTIL I SOLVE THEM!
OTHERWISE I'LL FAIL MY PRINCESS DUTIES!
I KNOW YOU WANT TO DO YOUR BEST...
...BUT I DON'T WANT YOU TO BURN OUT!
—SIGH—
YOU'RE RIGHT, SPIKE.

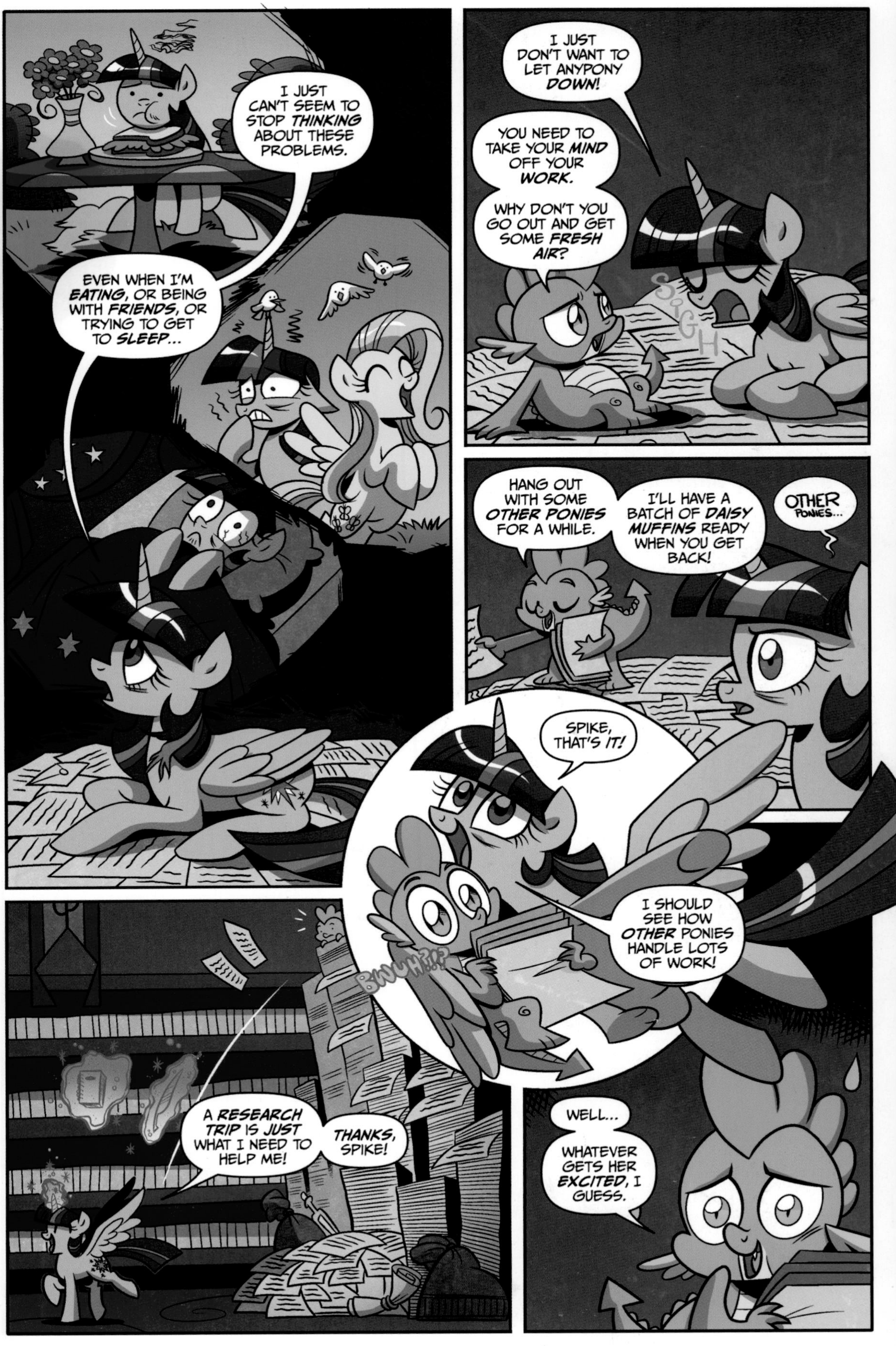
I JUST CAN'T SEEM TO STOP THINKING ABOUT THESE PROBLEMS.
EVEN WHEN I'M EATING, OR BEING WITH FRIENDS, OR TRYING TO GET TO SLEEP...
I JUST DON'T WANT TO LET ANYPONY DOWN!
YOU NEED TO TAKE YOUR MIND OFF YOUR WORK.
WHY DON'T YOU GO OUT AND GET SOME FRESH AIR?
SIGH
HANG OUT WITH SOME OTHER PONIES FOR A WHILE.
I'LL HAVE A BATCH OF DAISY MUFFINS READY WHEN YOU GET BACK!
OTHER PONIES...
SPIKE, THAT'S IT!
I SHOULD SEE HOW OTHER PONIES HANDLE LOTS OF WORK!
A RESEARCH TRIP IS JUST WHAT I NEED TO HELP ME!
THANKS, SPIKE!
WELL...
WHATEVER GETS HER EXCITED, I GUESS.

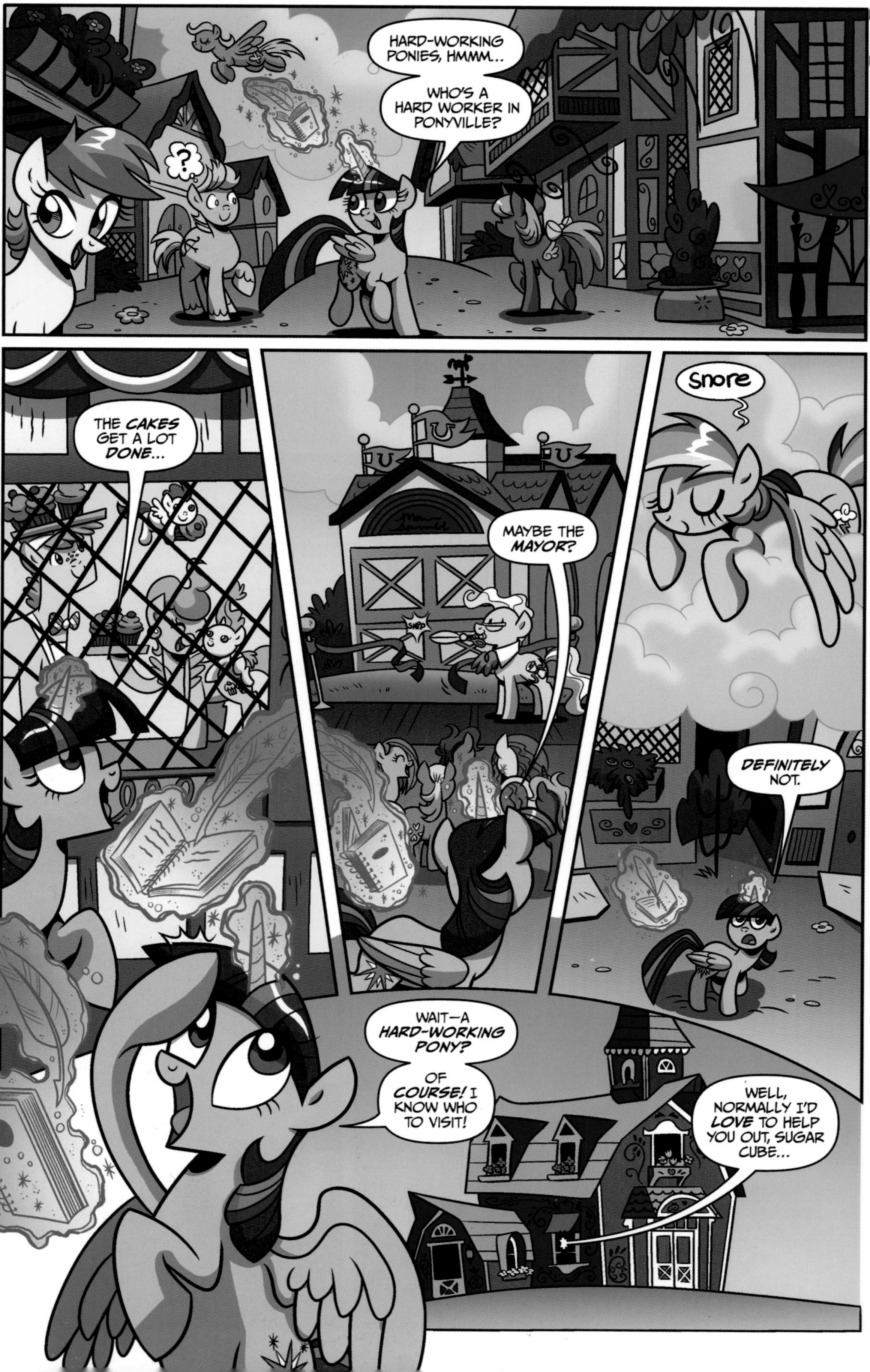
HARD-WORKING PONIES, HMMM...
WHO'S A HARD WORKER IN PONYVILLE?
THE CAKES GET A LOT DONE...
MAYBE THE MAYOR?
SNIP
Snore
DEFINITELY NOT.
WAIT—A HARD-WORKING PONY?
OF COURSE! I KNOW WHO TO VISIT!
WELL, NORMALLY I'D LOVE TO HELP YOU OUT, SUGAR CUBE...

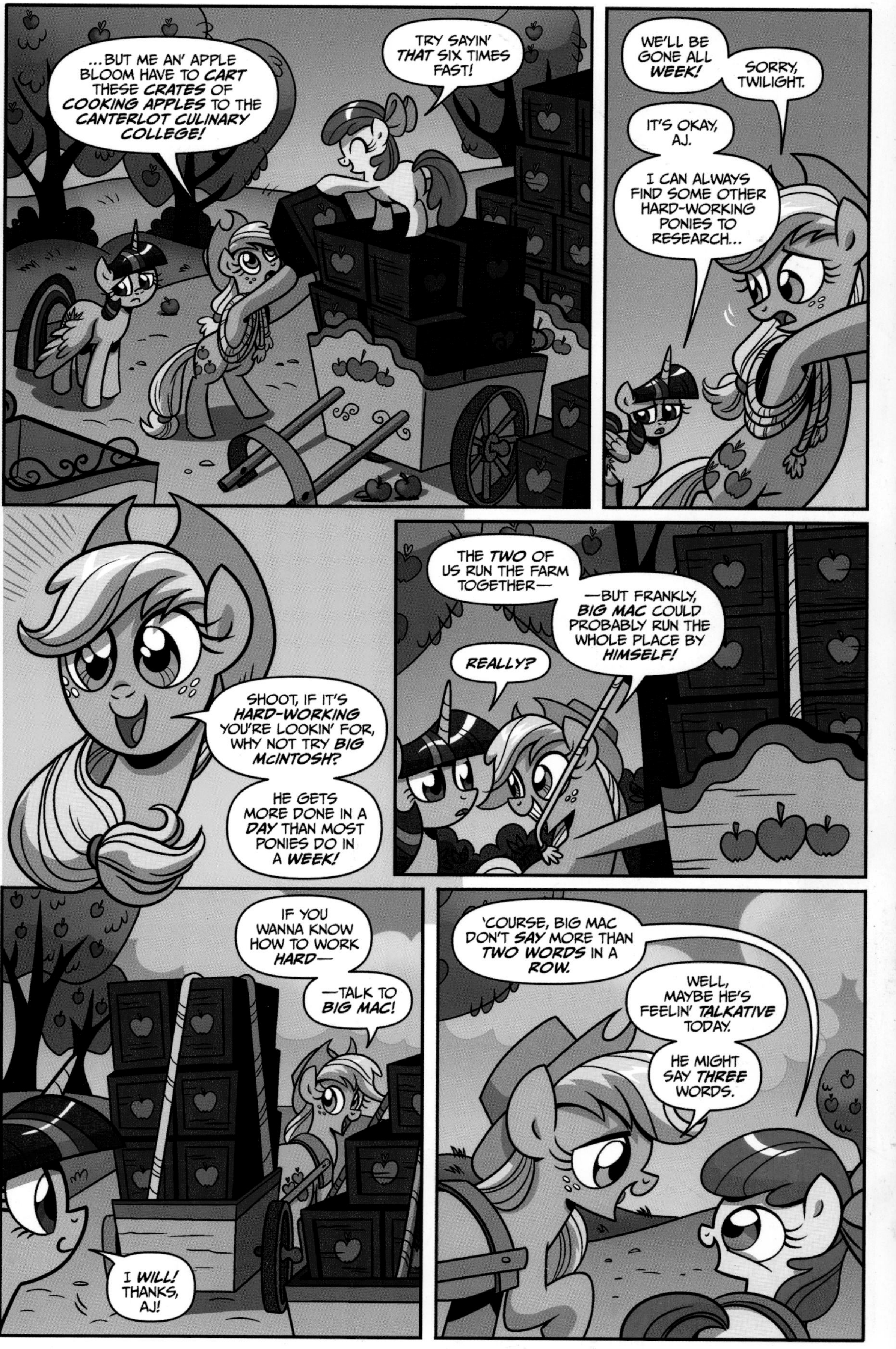
...BUT ME AN' APPLE BLOOM HAVE TO CART THESE CRATES OF COOKING APPLES TO THE CANTERLOT CULINARY COLLEGE!
TRY SAYIN' THAT SIX TIMES FAST!
WE'LL BE GONE ALL WEEK!
SORRY, TWILIGHT.
IT'S OKAY, AJ.
I CAN ALWAYS FIND SOME OTHER HARD-WORKING PONIES TO RESEARCH...
SHOOT, IF IT'S HARD-WORKING YOU'RE LOOKIN' FOR, WHY NOT TRY BIG McINTOSH?
HE GETS MORE DONE IN A DAY THAN MOST PONIES DO IN A WEEK!
THE TWO OF US RUN THE FARM TOGETHER—
—BUT FRANKLY, BIG MAC COULD PROBABLY RUN THE WHOLE PLACE BY HIMSELF!
REALLY?
IF YOU WANNA KNOW HOW TO WORK HARD—
—TALK TO BIG MAC!
I WILL! THANKS, AJ!
'COURSE, BIG MAC DON'T SAY MORE THAN TWO WORDS IN A ROW.
WELL, MAYBE HE'S FEELIN' TALKATIVE TODAY.
HE MIGHT SAY THREE WORDS.

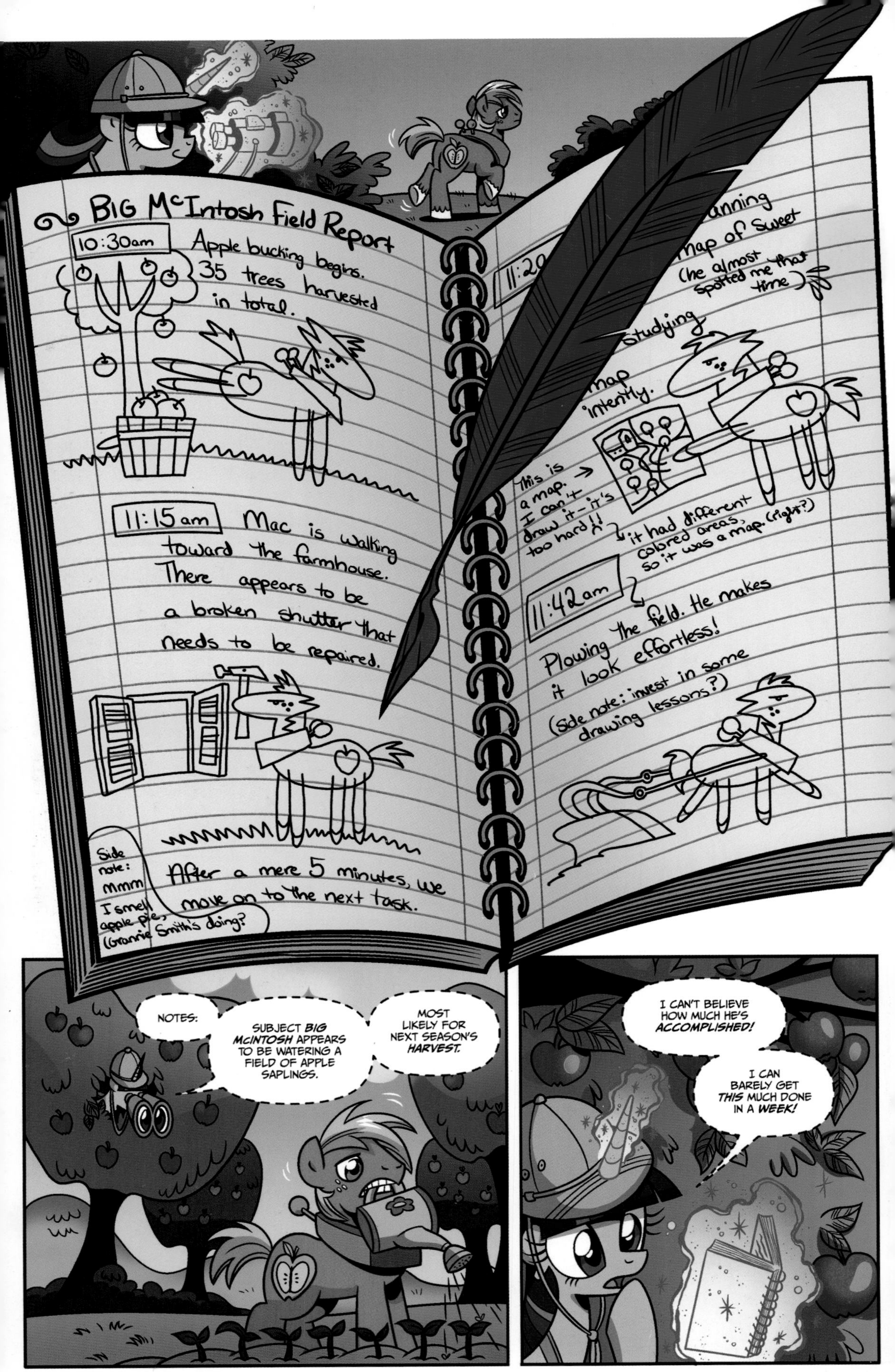

BIG McIntosh Field Report
10:30am
Apple bucking begins. 35 trees harvested in total.
11:15 am
Mac is walking toward the farmhouse. There appears to be a broken shutter that needs to be repaired.
Side note: mmm I smell apple pie, (Grannie Smith's doing?
After a mere 5 minutes, we move on to the next task.
anning
map of Sweet
(he almost spotted me that time)
studying
map intently.
This is a map. I can't draw it - it's too hard!!
it had different colored areas, so it was a map. (right?)
11:42 am
Plowing the field. He makes it look effortless!
(Side note: invest in some drawing lessons?)
NOTES:
SUBJECT BIG McINTOSH APPEARS TO BE WATERING A FIELD OF APPLE SAPLINGS.
MOST LIKELY FOR NEXT SEASON'S HARVEST.
I CAN'T BELIEVE HOW MUCH HE'S ACCOMPLISHED!
I CAN BARELY GET THIS MUCH DONE IN A WEEK!

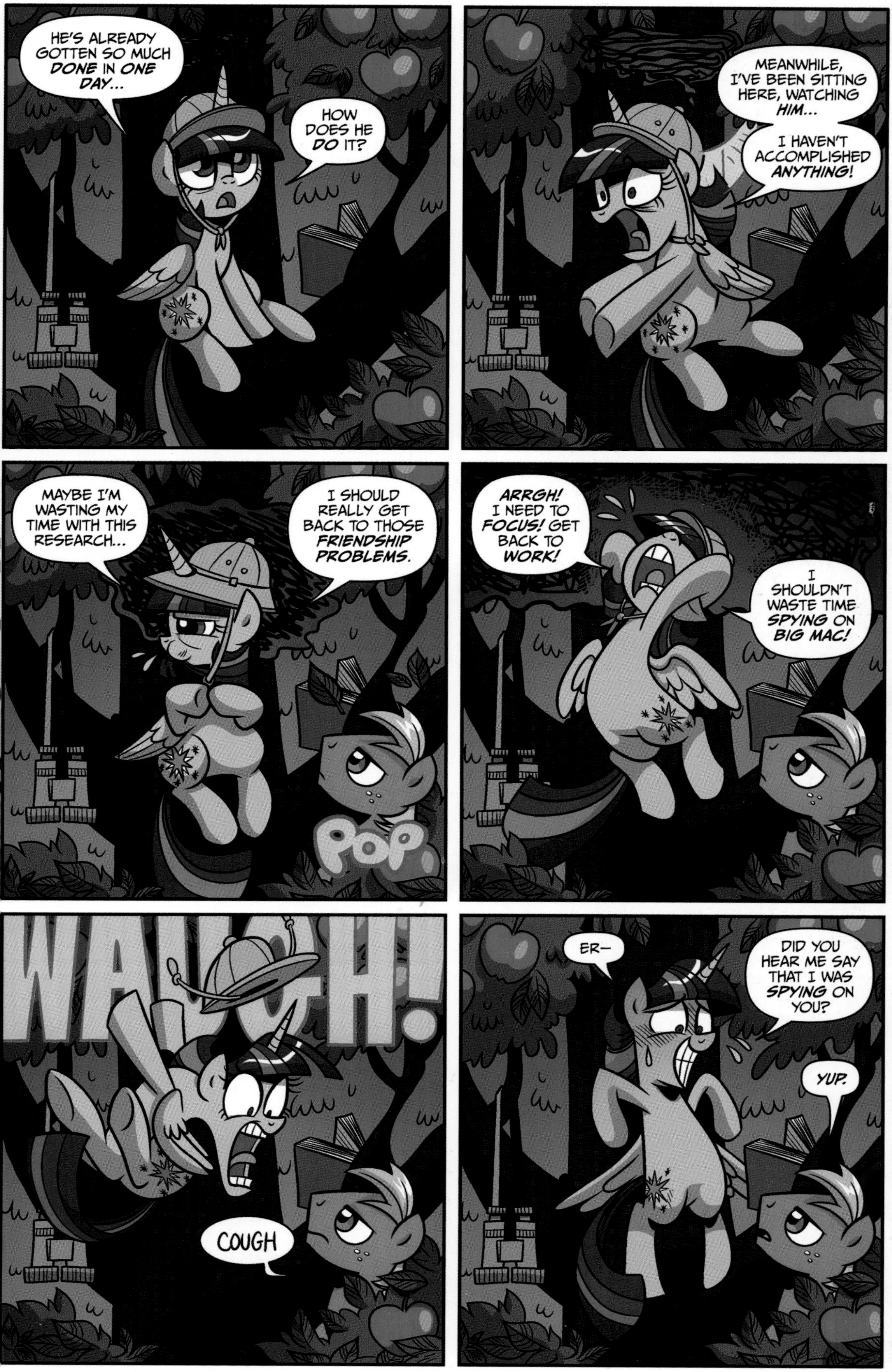
HE'S ALREADY GOTTEN SO MUCH *DONE* IN *ONE* DAY...
HOW DOES HE *DO* IT?
MEANWHILE, I'VE BEEN SITTING HERE, WATCHING *HIM*...
I HAVEN'T ACCOMPLISHED *ANYTHING!*
MAYBE I'M WASTING MY TIME WITH THIS RESEARCH...
I SHOULD REALLY GET BACK TO THOSE *FRIENDSHIP PROBLEMS.*
POP
ARRGH! I NEED TO *FOCUS!* GET BACK TO *WORK!*
I SHOULDN'T WASTE TIME *SPYING* ON *BIG MAC!*
WAUGH!
COUGH
ER—
DID YOU HEAR ME SAY THAT I WAS *SPYING* ON YOU?
YUP.

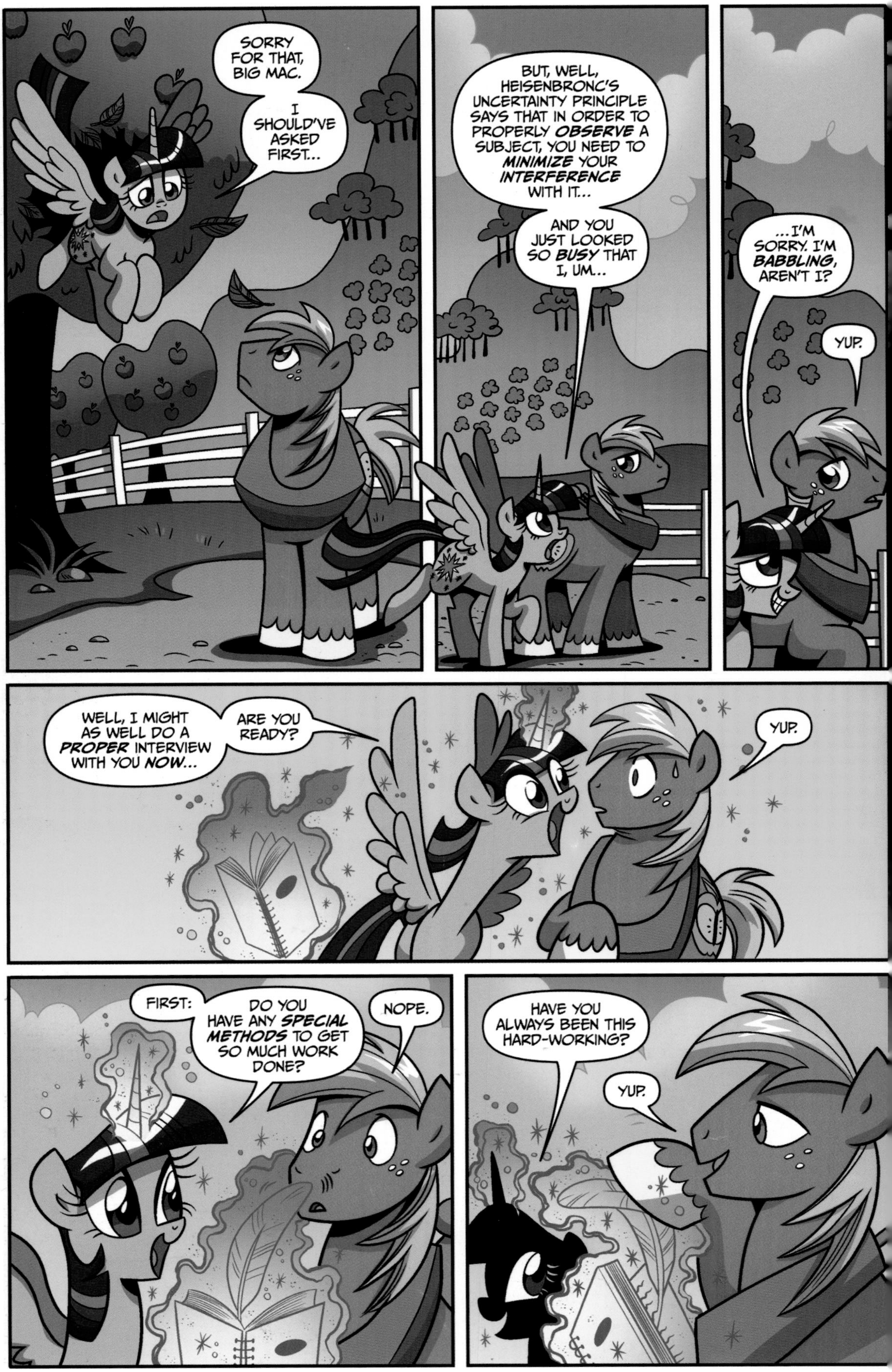
SORRY FOR THAT, BIG MAC.
I SHOULD'VE ASKED FIRST...
BUT, WELL, HEISENBRONC'S UNCERTAINTY PRINCIPLE SAYS THAT IN ORDER TO PROPERLY OBSERVE A SUBJECT, YOU NEED TO MINIMIZE YOUR INTERFERENCE WITH IT...
AND YOU JUST LOOKED SO BUSY THAT I, UM...
...I'M SORRY. I'M BABBLING, AREN'T I?
YUP.
WELL, I MIGHT AS WELL DO A PROPER INTERVIEW WITH YOU NOW...
ARE YOU READY?
YUP.
FIRST:
DO YOU HAVE ANY SPECIAL METHODS TO GET SO MUCH WORK DONE?
NOPE.
HAVE YOU ALWAYS BEEN THIS HARD-WORKING?
YUP.

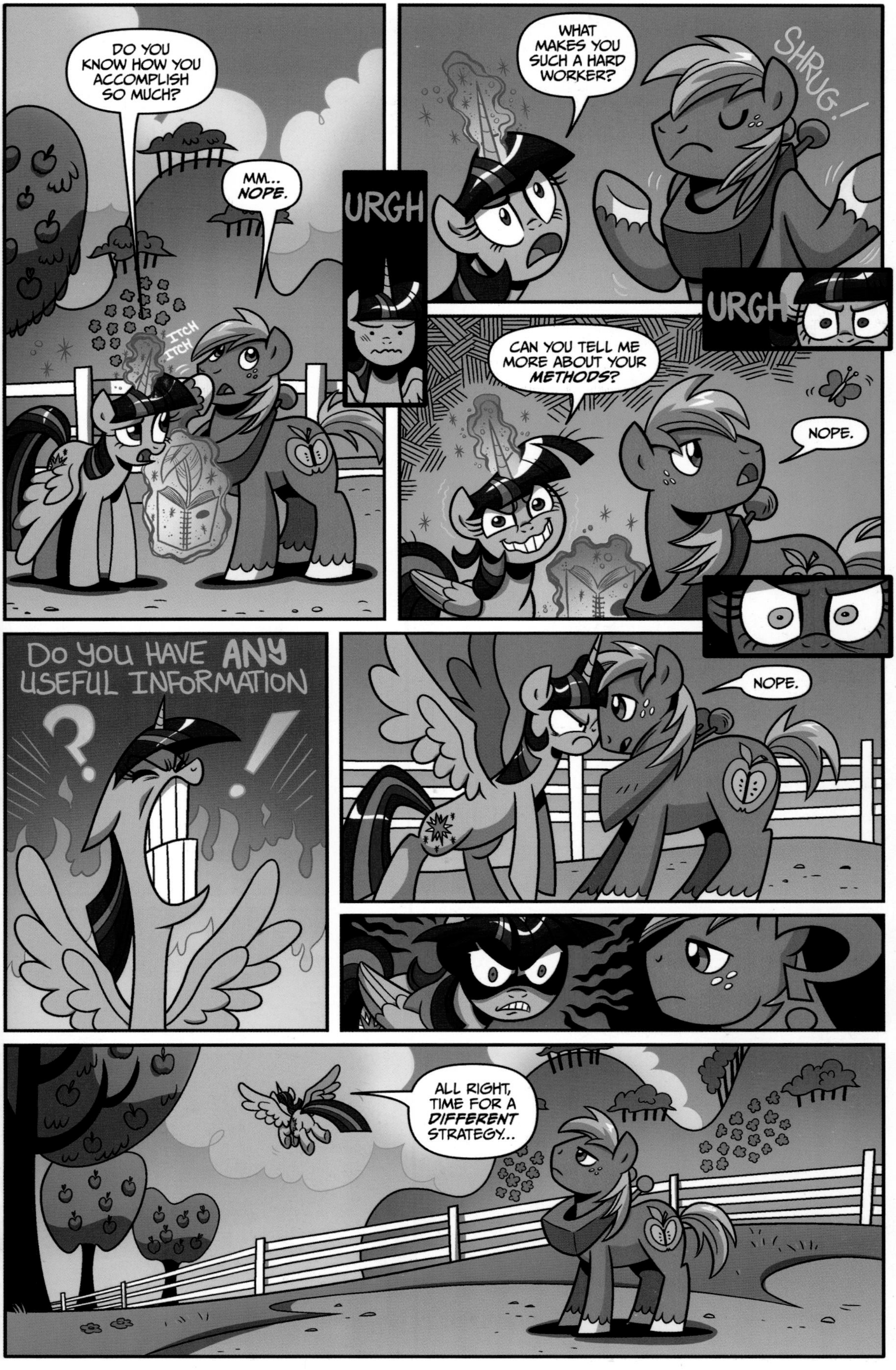
DO YOU KNOW HOW YOU ACCOMPLISH SO MUCH?
MM... NOPE.
ITCH ITCH
URGH
WHAT MAKES YOU SUCH A HARD WORKER?
SHRUG!
URGH
CAN YOU TELL ME MORE ABOUT YOUR METHODS?
NOPE.
Do YOU HAVE ANY USEFUL INFORMATION
?!
NOPE.
ALL RIGHT, TIME FOR A DIFFERENT STRATEGY...

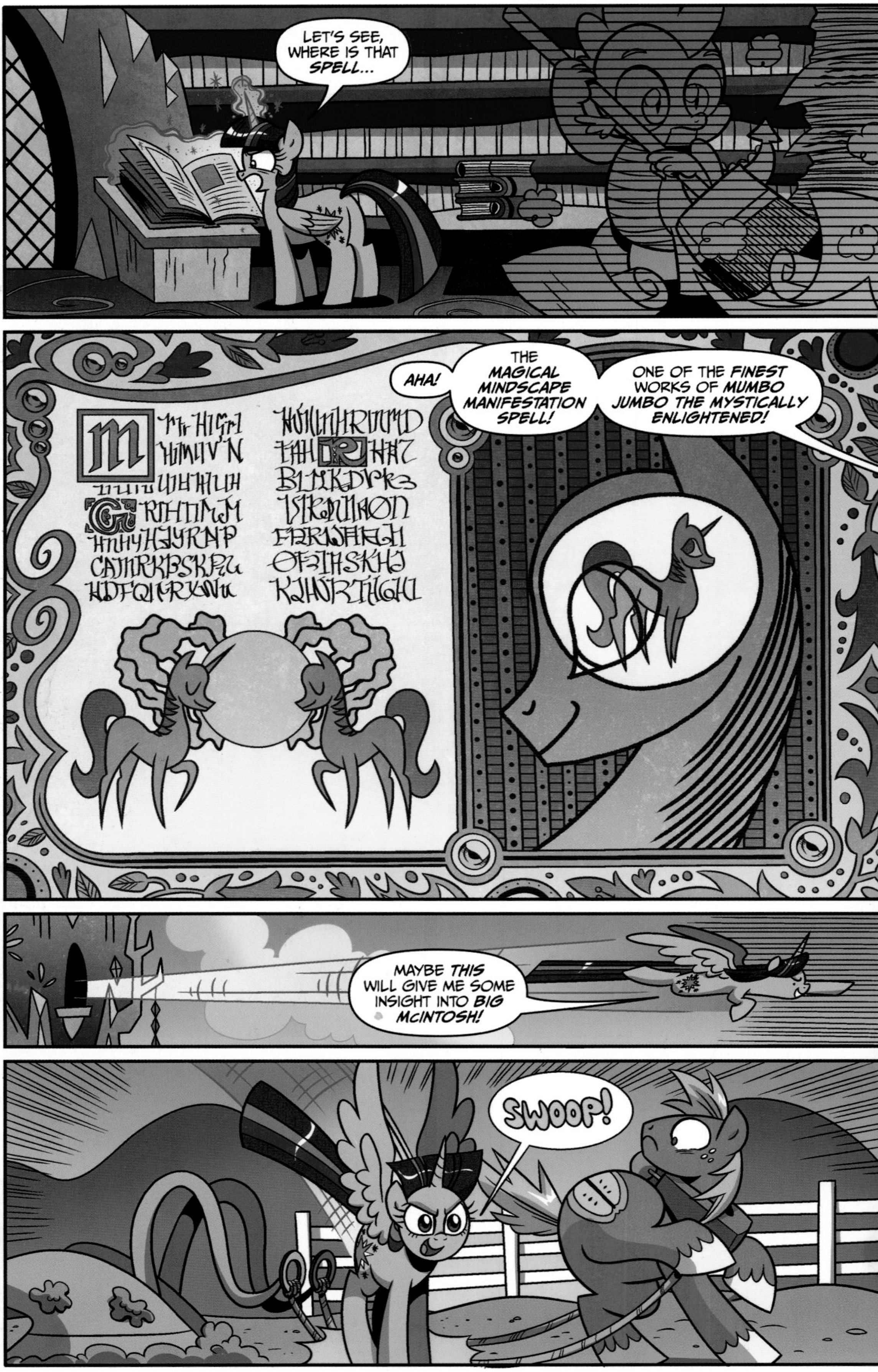
LET'S SEE, WHERE IS THAT SPELL...
AHA!
THE MAGICAL MINDSCAPE MANIFESTATION SPELL!
ONE OF THE FINEST WORKS OF MUMBO JUMBO THE MYSTICALLY ENLIGHTENED!
MAYBE THIS WILL GIVE ME SOME INSIGHT INTO BIG McINTOSH!
SWOOP!

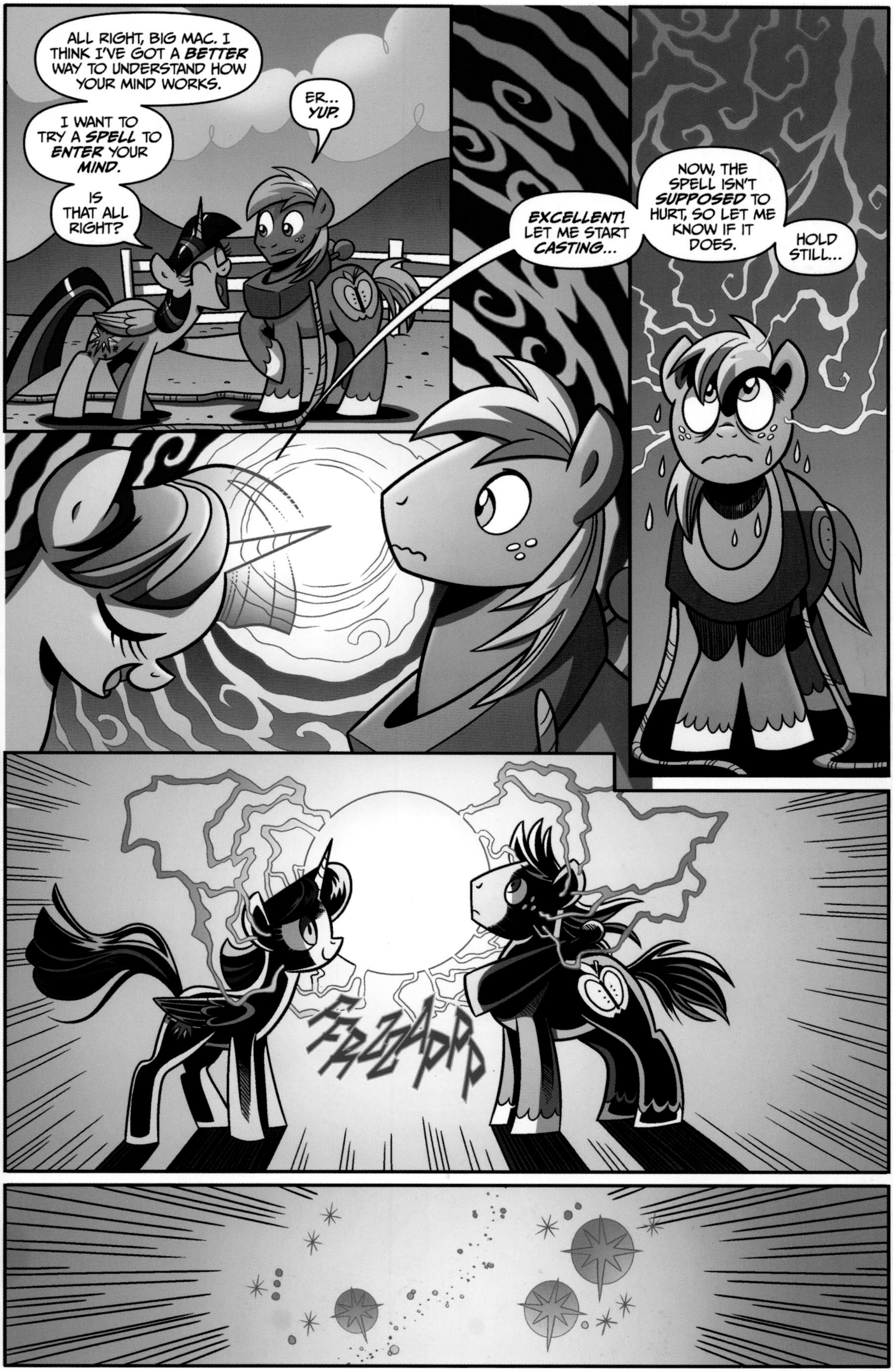
ALL RIGHT, BIG MAC. I THINK I'VE GOT A *BETTER* WAY TO UNDERSTAND HOW YOUR MIND WORKS.
I WANT TO TRY A *SPELL* TO *ENTER* YOUR *MIND*.
IS THAT ALL RIGHT?
ER... *YUP.*
EXCELLENT! LET ME START *CASTING...*
NOW, THE SPELL ISN'T *SUPPOSED* TO HURT, SO LET ME KNOW IF IT DOES.
HOLD STILL...
FFRZZZAPPP

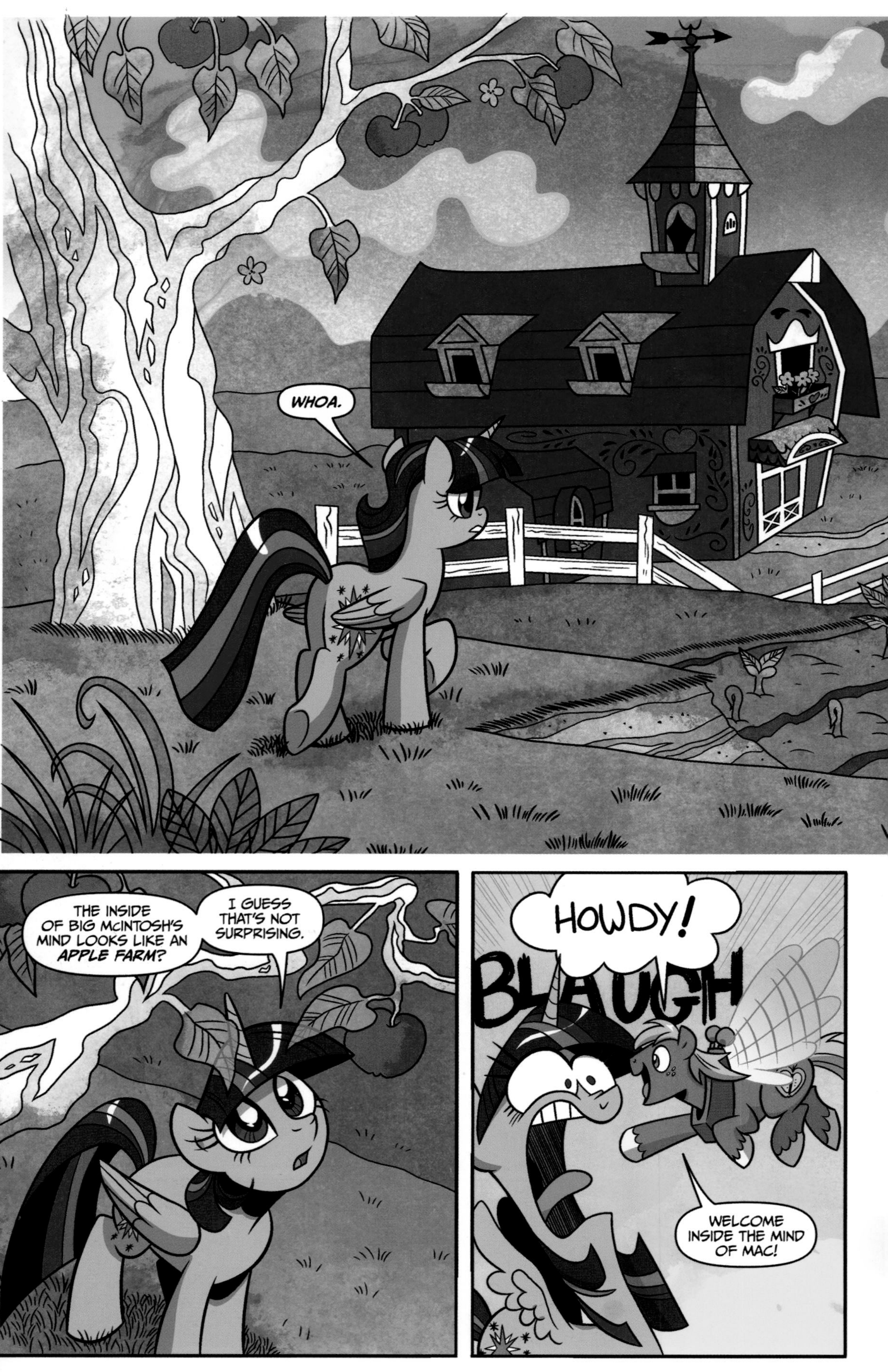
WHOA.
THE INSIDE OF BIG McINTOSH'S MIND LOOKS LIKE AN APPLE FARM?
I GUESS THAT'S NOT SURPRISING.
HOWDY!
BLAUGH
WELCOME INSIDE THE MIND OF MAC!

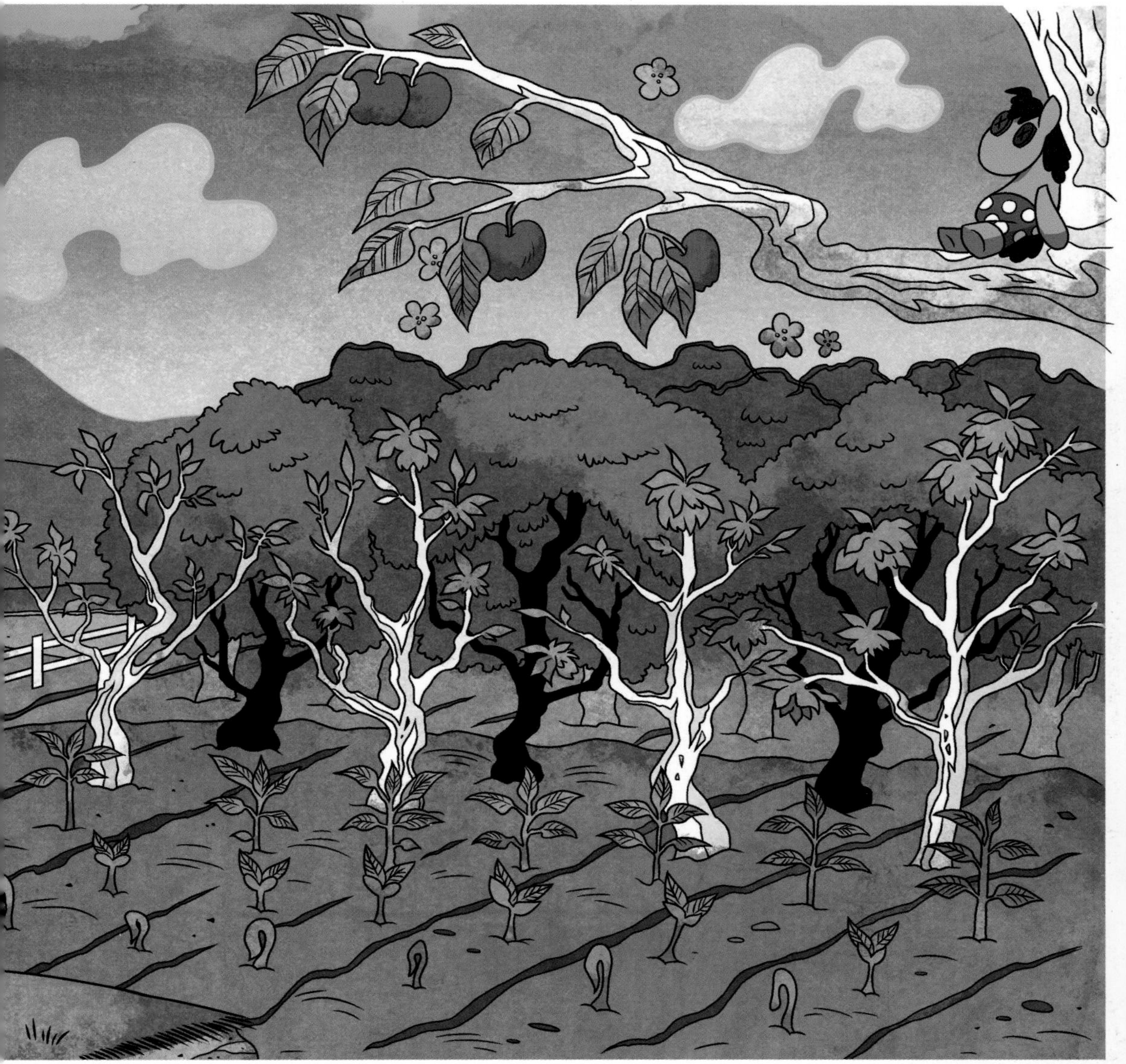

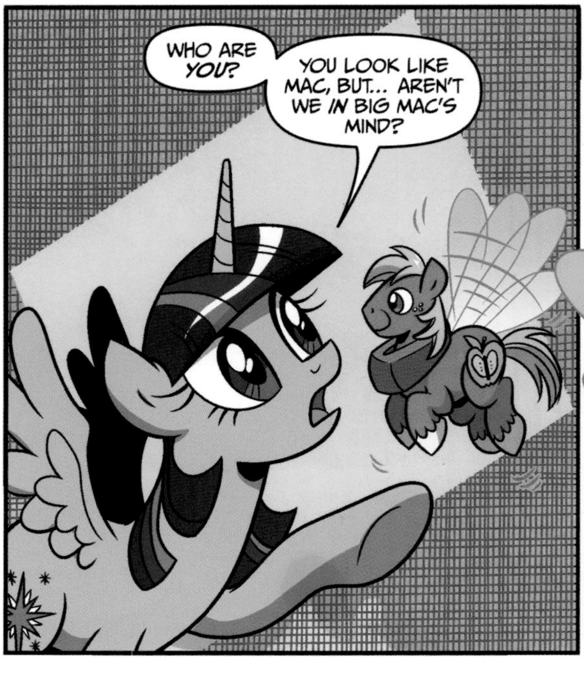
WHO ARE YOU?
YOU LOOK LIKE MAC, BUT... AREN'T WE IN BIG MAC'S MIND?

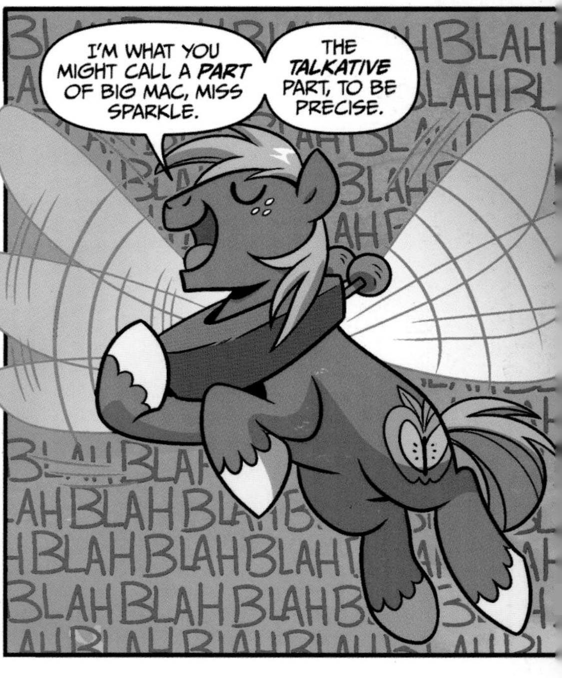
I'M WHAT YOU MIGHT CALL A PART OF BIG MAC, MISS SPARKLE.
THE TALKATIVE PART, TO BE PRECISE.
BLAH BLAH BLAH BLAH

EVERYPONY HAS DIFFERENT *SIDES* OF THEMSELVES, Y'KNOW.

EVEN THOUGH BIG MAC DOESN'T TALK MUCH...

...THERE'S A PART OF HIM THAT *WANTS* TO TALK A LOT.

AND THAT'S *ME!*

SORRY, I'M *BABBLING*, AREN'T I?

IT'S ALL RIGHT! I DIDN'T KNOW BIG MAC *HAD* A TALKATIVE SIDE.

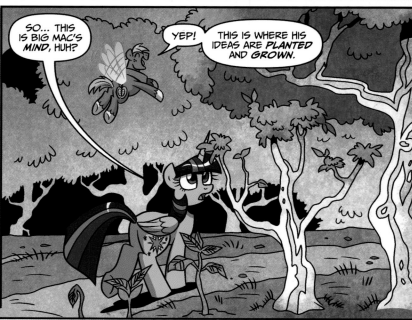

SO... THIS IS BIG MAC'S *MIND*, HUH?

YEP! THIS IS WHERE HIS IDEAS ARE *PLANTED* AND *GROWN.*

"PLANTED"? "GROWN"?

I DIDN'T KNOW IDEAS WERE *PLANTS.*

THEY ARE *HERE!*

ALL THESE FIELDS REPRESENT THE THINGS THAT BIG MAC IS THINKIN' ABOUT.

OVER *THERE*, FOR EXAMPLE, HE'S CONSIDERIN' WHAT TO DO WITH THAT OLD *SHED* THAT'S FALLING APART.

IN *THAT* FIELD, HE'S THINKING ABOUT WHAT TO MAKE FOR APPLE BLOOM'S *BIRTHDAY* NEXT MONTH...

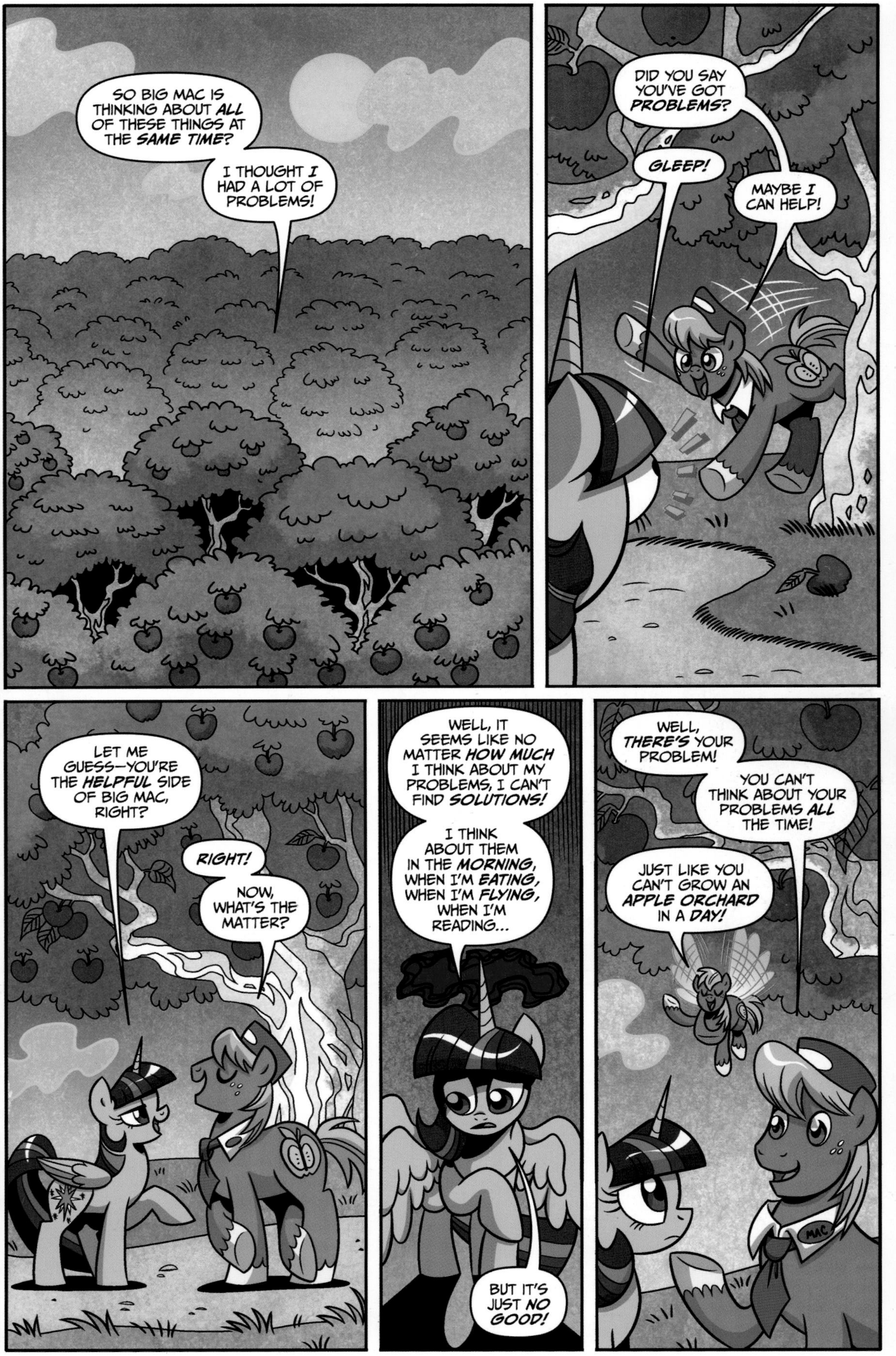
SO BIG MAC IS THINKING ABOUT ALL OF THESE THINGS AT THE SAME TIME?
I THOUGHT I HAD A LOT OF PROBLEMS!
DID YOU SAY YOU'VE GOT PROBLEMS?
GLEEP!
MAYBE I CAN HELP!
LET ME GUESS—YOU'RE THE HELPFUL SIDE OF BIG MAC, RIGHT?
RIGHT!
NOW, WHAT'S THE MATTER?
WELL, IT SEEMS LIKE NO MATTER HOW MUCH I THINK ABOUT MY PROBLEMS, I CAN'T FIND SOLUTIONS!
I THINK ABOUT THEM IN THE MORNING, WHEN I'M EATING, WHEN I'M FLYING, WHEN I'M READING...
BUT IT'S JUST NO GOOD!
WELL, THERE'S YOUR PROBLEM!
YOU CAN'T THINK ABOUT YOUR PROBLEMS ALL THE TIME!
JUST LIKE YOU CAN'T GROW AN APPLE ORCHARD IN A DAY!
MAC

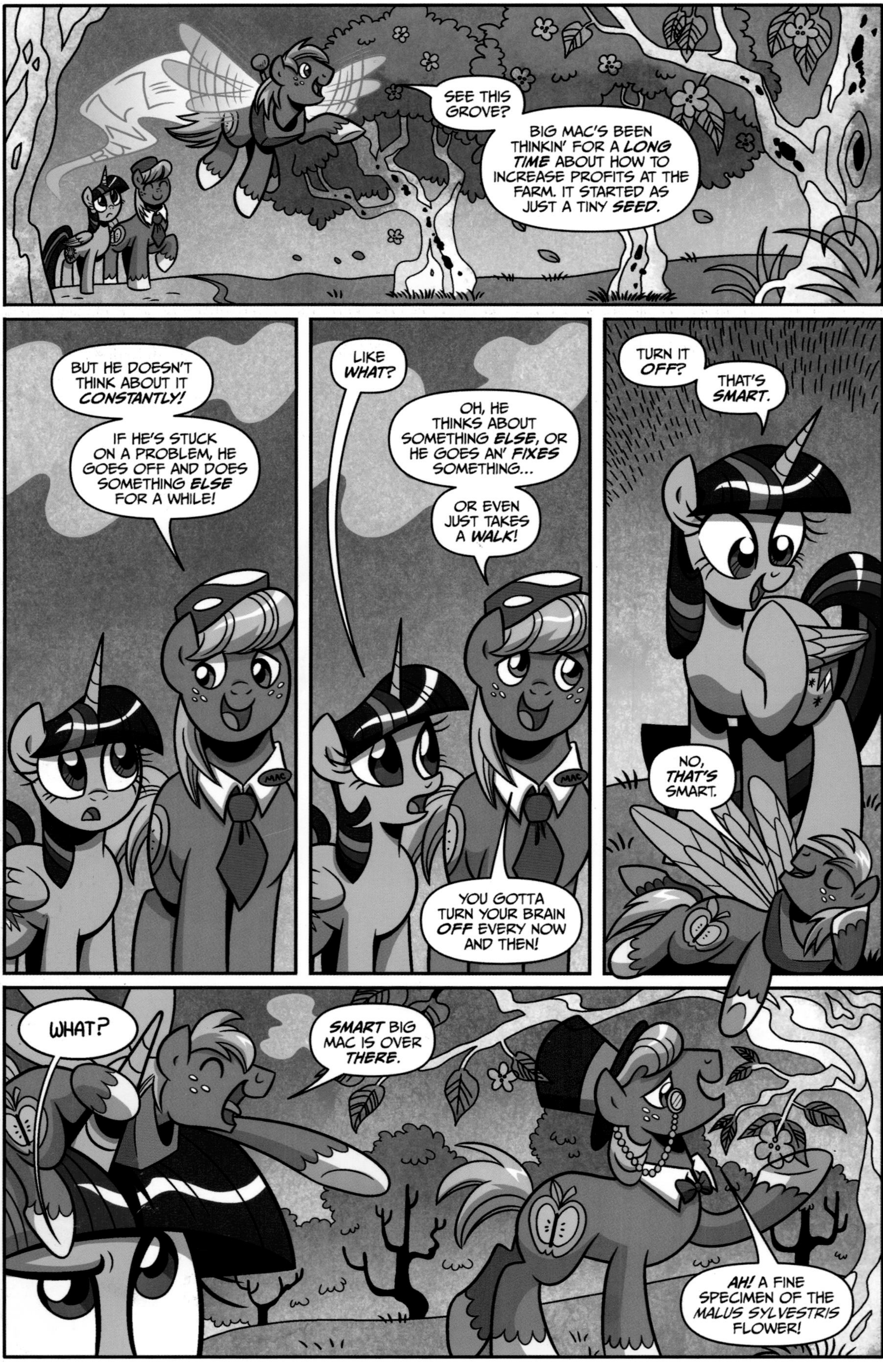
SEE THIS GROVE?
BIG MAC'S BEEN THINKIN' FOR A LONG TIME ABOUT HOW TO INCREASE PROFITS AT THE FARM. IT STARTED AS JUST A TINY SEED.
BUT HE DOESN'T THINK ABOUT IT CONSTANTLY!
IF HE'S STUCK ON A PROBLEM, HE GOES OFF AND DOES SOMETHING ELSE FOR A WHILE!
LIKE WHAT?
OH, HE THINKS ABOUT SOMETHING ELSE, OR HE GOES AN' FIXES SOMETHING...
OR EVEN JUST TAKES A WALK!
YOU GOTTA TURN YOUR BRAIN OFF EVERY NOW AND THEN!
TURN IT OFF?
THAT'S SMART.
NO, THAT'S SMART.
WHAT?
SMART BIG MAC IS OVER THERE.
AH! A FINE SPECIMEN OF THE MALUS SYLVESTRIS FLOWER!

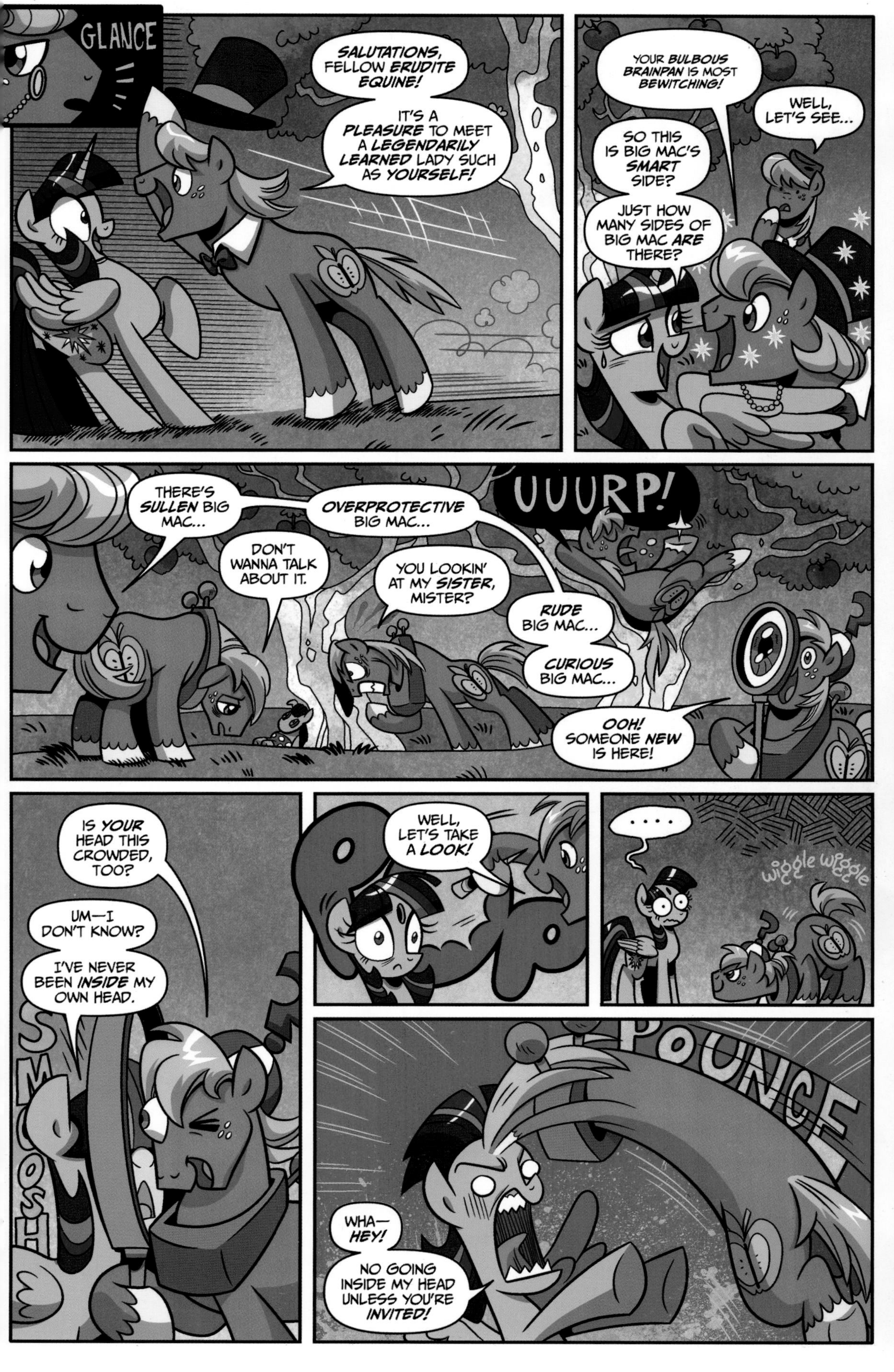
GLANCE
SALUTATIONS, FELLOW ERUDITE EQUINE!
IT'S A PLEASURE TO MEET A LEGENDARILY LEARNED LADY SUCH AS YOURSELF!
YOUR BULBOUS BRAINPAN IS MOST BEWITCHING!
WELL, LET'S SEE...
SO THIS IS BIG MAC'S SMART SIDE?
JUST HOW MANY SIDES OF BIG MAC ARE THERE?
THERE'S SULLEN BIG MAC...
DON'T WANNA TALK ABOUT IT.
OVERPROTECTIVE BIG MAC...
YOU LOOKIN' AT MY SISTER, MISTER?
UUURP!
RUDE BIG MAC...
CURIOUS BIG MAC...
OOH! SOMEONE NEW IS HERE!
IS YOUR HEAD THIS CROWDED, TOO?
UM—I DON'T KNOW?
I'VE NEVER BEEN INSIDE MY OWN HEAD.
SMOOSH
WELL, LET'S TAKE A LOOK!
....
wiggle wiggle
POUNCE
WHA—HEY!
NO GOING INSIDE MY HEAD UNLESS YOU'RE INVITED!

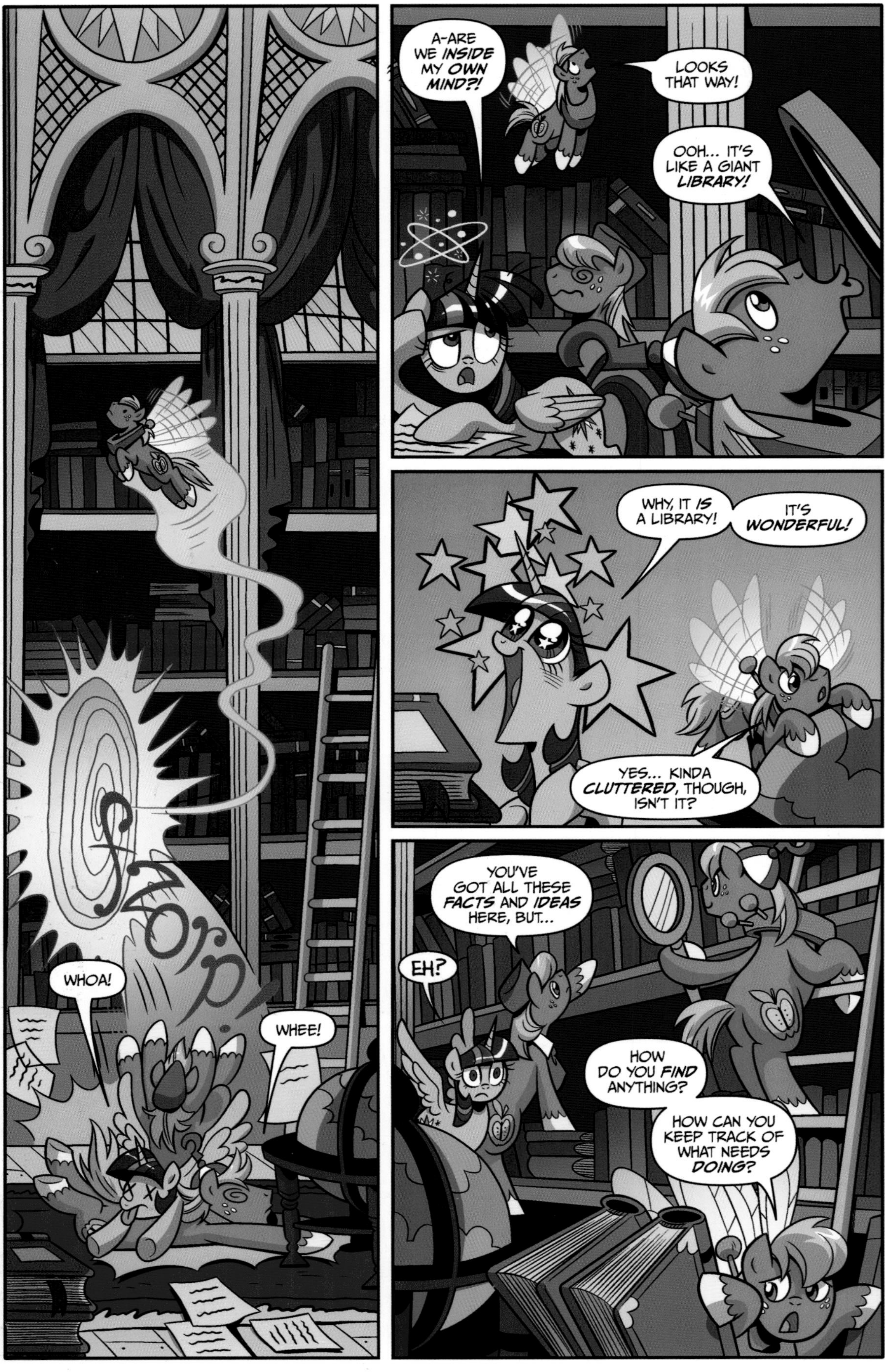
ZZOP!
WHOA!
WHEE!
A-ARE WE INSIDE MY OWN MIND?!
LOOKS THAT WAY!
OOH... IT'S LIKE A GIANT LIBRARY!
WHY, IT IS A LIBRARY!
IT'S WONDERFUL!
YES... KINDA CLUTTERED, THOUGH, ISN'T IT?
YOU'VE GOT ALL THESE FACTS AND IDEAS HERE, BUT...
EH?
HOW DO YOU FIND ANYTHING?
HOW CAN YOU KEEP TRACK OF WHAT NEEDS DOING?

IF YOU'RE WORKING ON EIGHT PROBLEMS AT ONCE, IT'S HARD TO KEEP TRACK OF WHAT YOU'RE DOING.
WHY IS THERE A BEEKEEPING MANUAL IN THE SAME PILE AS THE HISTORY OF HAIRCUTS?
I THINK YOU NEED SOME FOCUS, TWILIGHT.
AND SOME TIME OFF!
I THINK YOU'RE RIGHT, BIG MAC.
BIG MACS.
I NEED TO STOP OBSESSING OVER MY PROBLEMS...
...AND START MAKING TIME TO RELAX!
I CAN'T GET SO STRESSED!
YOU GET STRESSED?
OH, YES!
I'VE BEEN CHEWING MY MANE, LOSING SLEEP, NOT EATING...
BUT DON'T WORRY!
THANKS TO YOU THREE, I THINK MY STRESS IS A THING OF THE...
...PAST?
MBLRMBLRM

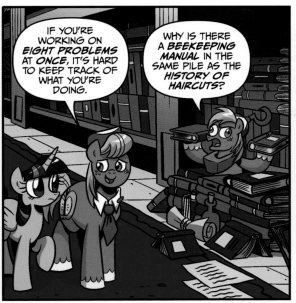

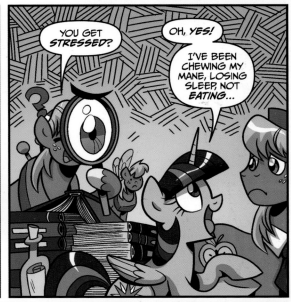

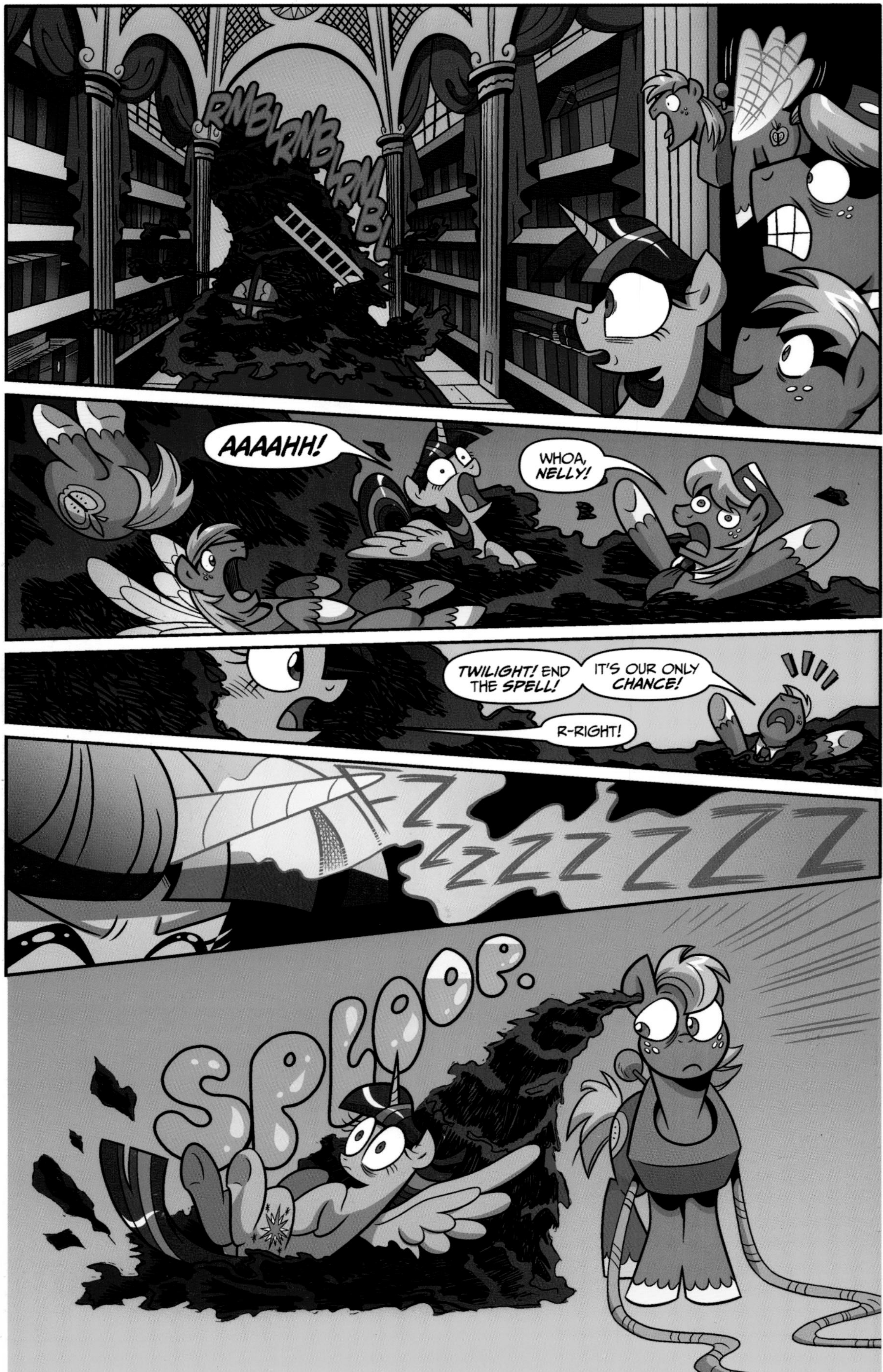
RMBLRMBLRMBLRMBL
AAAAHH!
WHOA, NELLY!
TWILIGHT! END THE SPELL!
IT'S OUR ONLY CHANCE!
R-RIGHT!
SPLOOP.

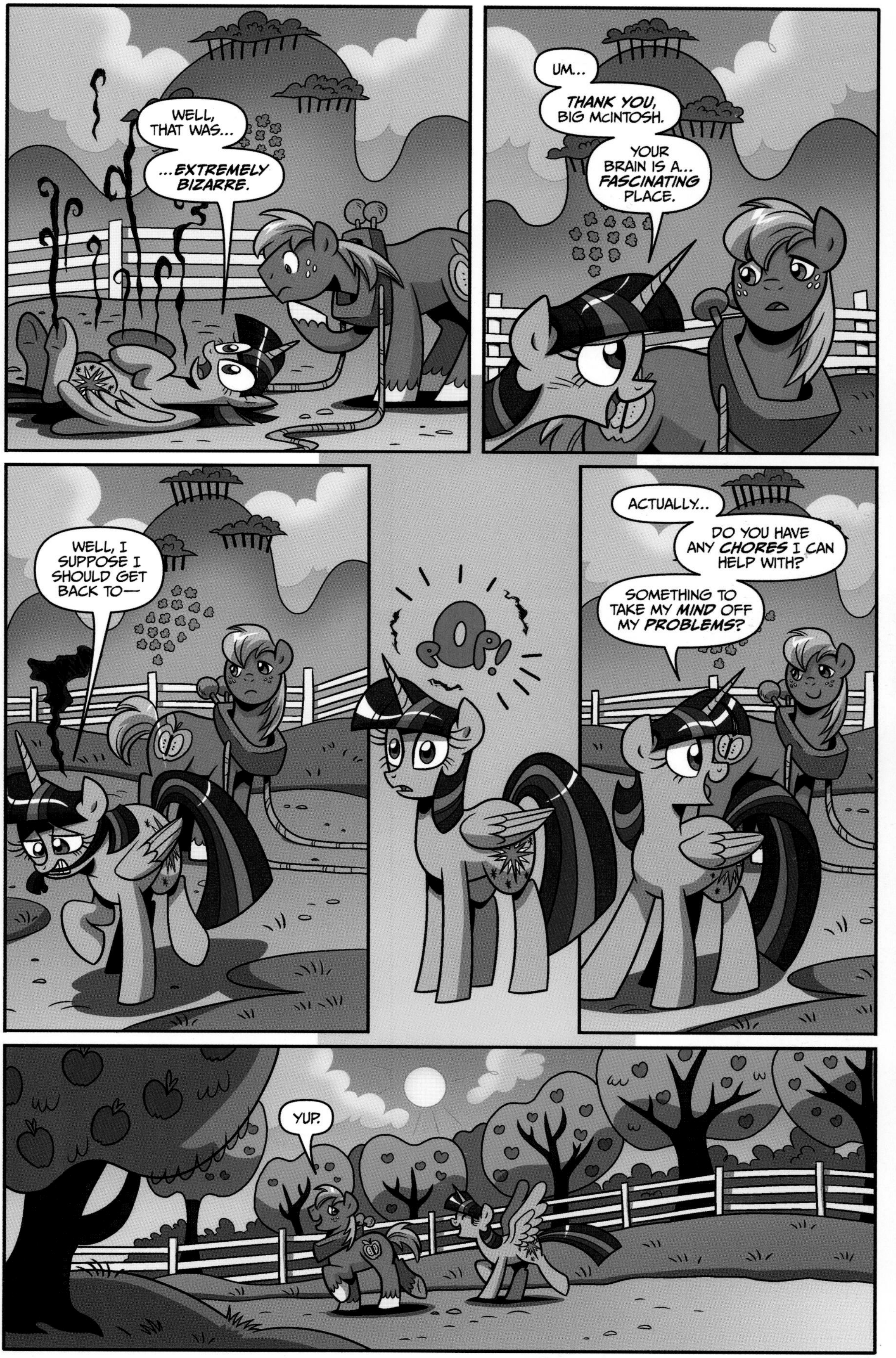
WELL, THAT WAS...
...EXTREMELY BIZARRE.
UM...
THANK YOU, BIG McINTOSH.
YOUR BRAIN IS A... FASCINATING PLACE.
WELL, I SUPPOSE I SHOULD GET BACK TO—
POP!
ACTUALLY...
DO YOU HAVE ANY CHORES I CAN HELP WITH?
SOMETHING TO TAKE MY MIND OFF MY PROBLEMS?
YUP.

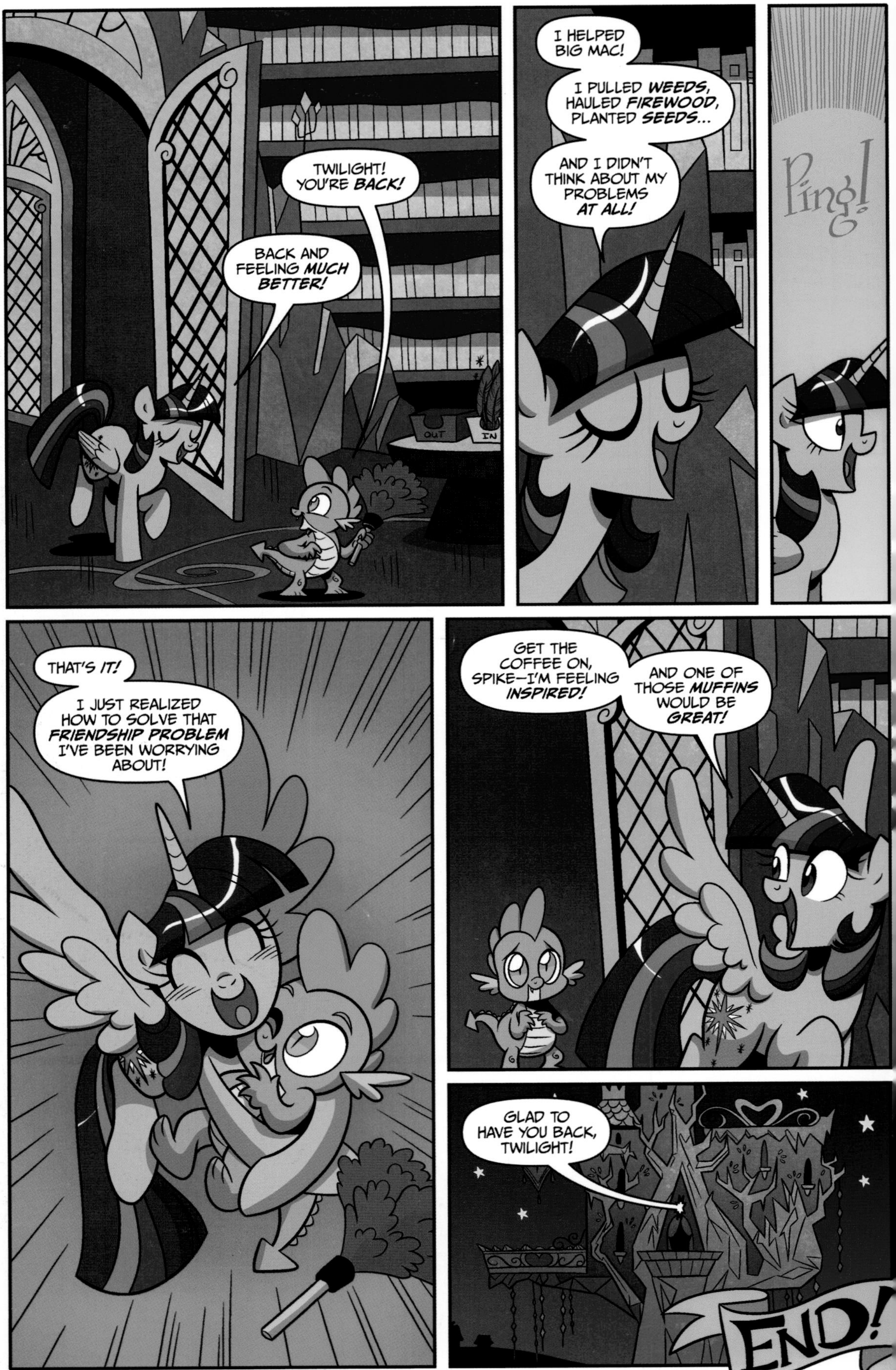
TWILIGHT! YOU'RE *BACK!*
BACK AND FEELING *MUCH BETTER!*
OUT
IN
I HELPED BIG MAC!
I PULLED *WEEDS*, HAULED *FIREWOOD*, PLANTED *SEEDS*...
AND I DIDN'T THINK ABOUT MY PROBLEMS *AT ALL!*
Ping!
THAT'S *IT!*
I JUST REALIZED HOW TO SOLVE THAT *FRIENDSHIP PROBLEM* I'VE BEEN WORRYING ABOUT!
GET THE COFFEE ON, SPIKE—I'M FEELING *INSPIRED!*
AND ONE OF THOSE *MUFFINS* WOULD BE *GREAT!*
GLAD TO HAVE YOU BACK, TWILIGHT!
END!

My Little Pony

Friends Forever

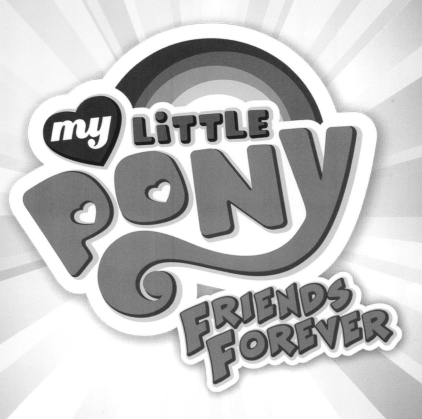

Rainbow Dash & Fluttershy

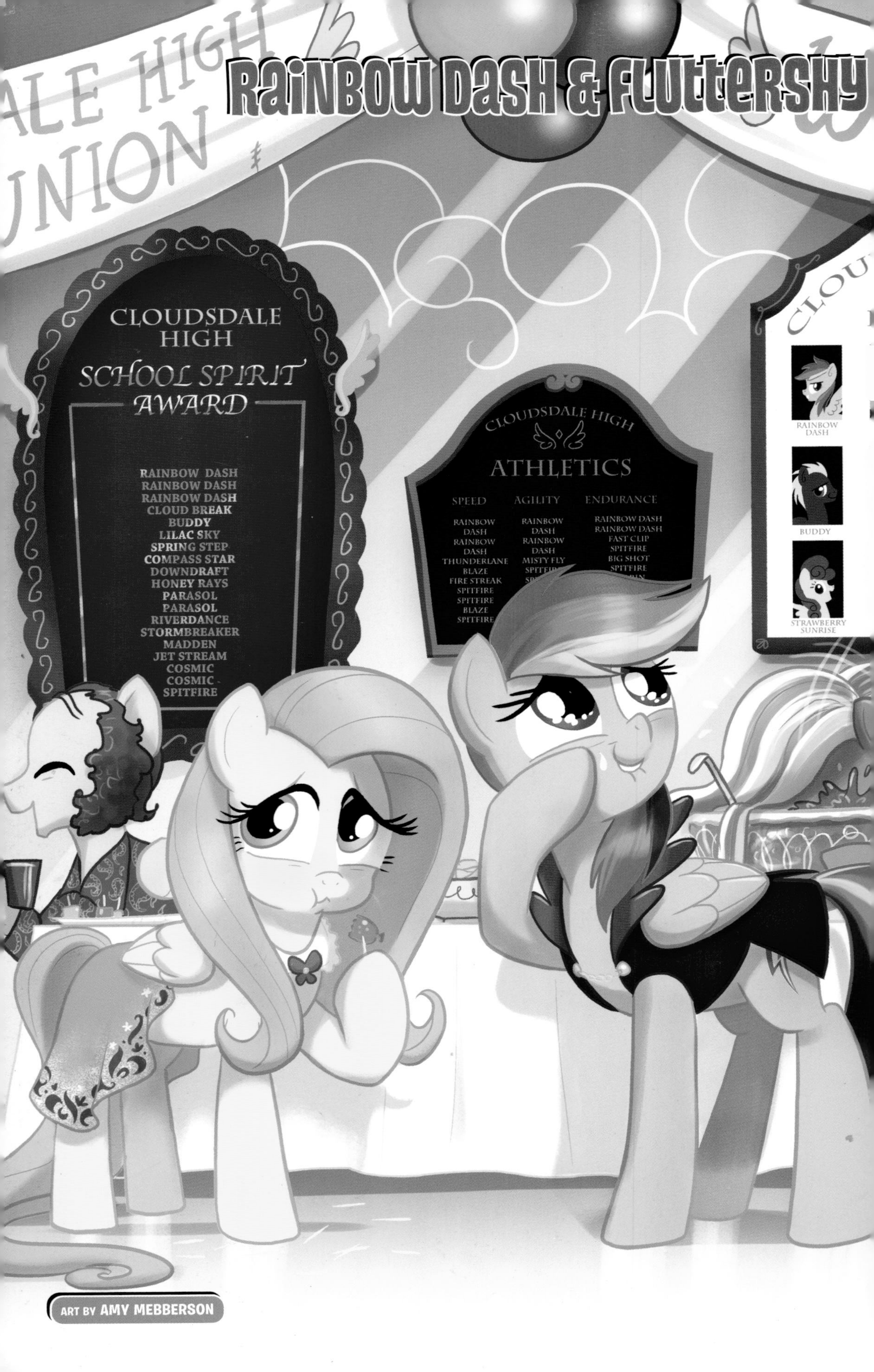

CLOUDSDALE HIGH
SCHOOL SPIRIT AWARD
RAINBOW DASH
RAINBOW DASH
RAINBOW DASH
CLOUD BREAK
BUDDY
LILAC SKY
SPRING STEP
COMPASS STAR
DOWNDRAFT
HONEY RAYS
PARASOL
PARASOL
RIVERDANCE
STORMBREAKER
MADDEN
JET STREAM
COSMIC
COSMIC
SPITFIRE
CLOUDSDALE HIGH
ATHLETICS
SPEED
RAINBOW DASH
RAINBOW DASH
THUNDERLANE
BLAZE
FIRE STREAK
SPITFIRE
SPITFIRE
BLAZE
SPITFIRE
AGILITY
RAINBOW DASH
RAINBOW DASH
MISTY FLY
ENDURANCE
RAINBOW DASH
RAINBOW DASH
FAST CLIP
SPITFIRE
BIG SHOT
SPITFIRE
RAINBOW DASH
BUDDY
STRAWBERRY SUNRISE

ART BY AMY MEBBERSON

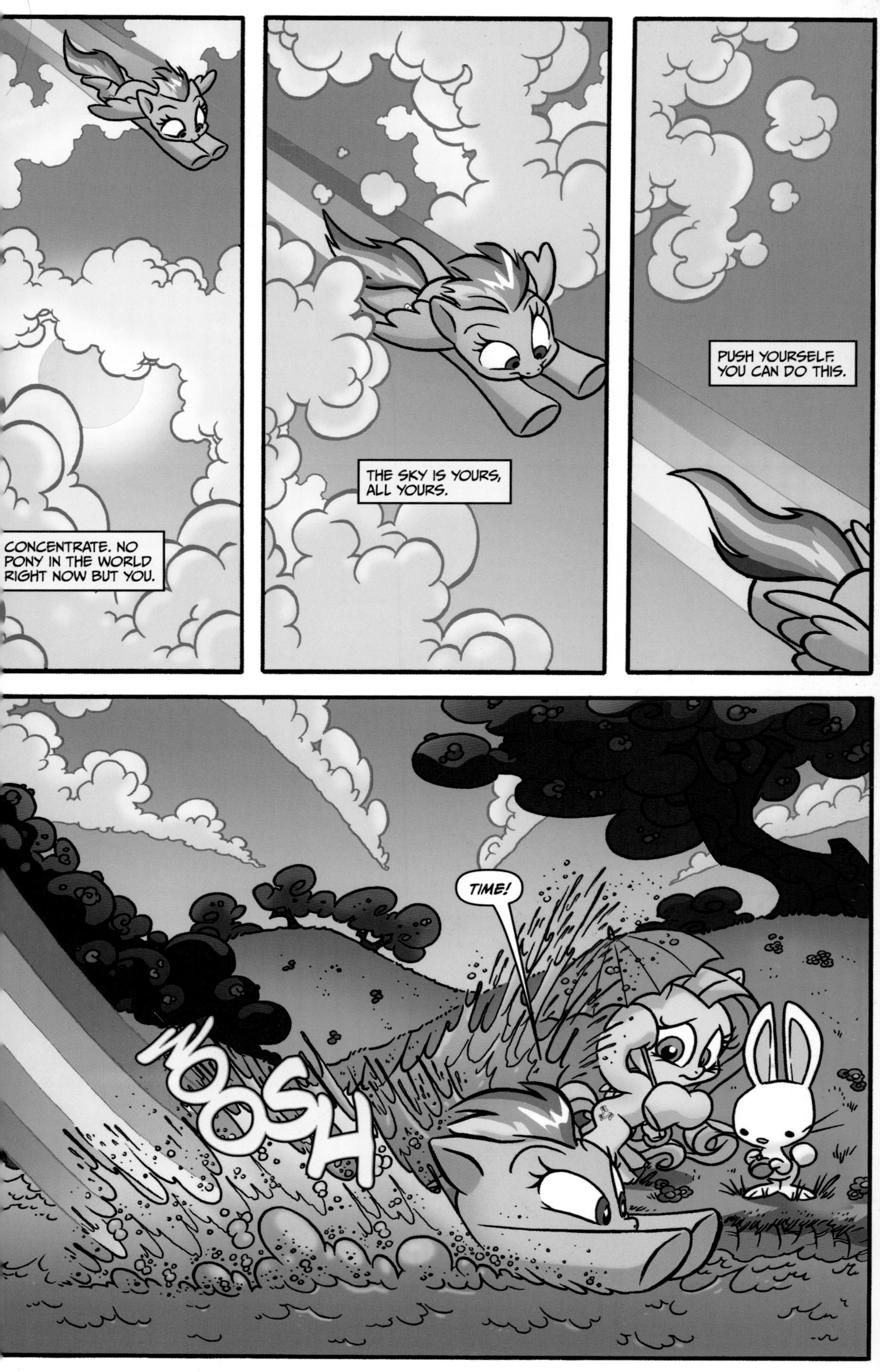
CONCENTRATE. NO PONY IN THE WORLD RIGHT NOW BUT YOU.
THE SKY IS YOURS, ALL YOURS.
PUSH YOURSELF. YOU CAN DO THIS.
TIME!
WOOSH

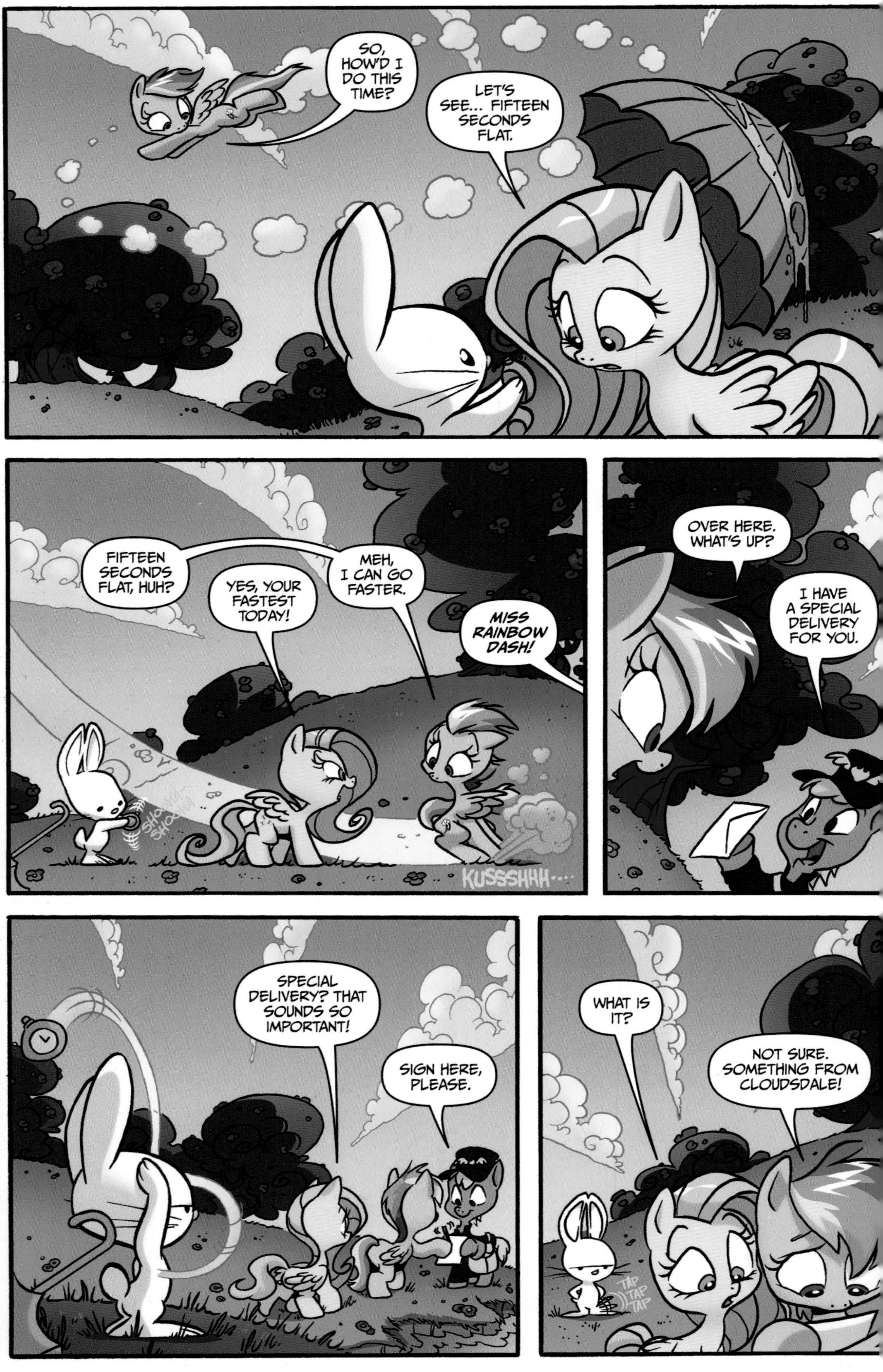
SO, HOW'D I DO THIS TIME?
LET'S SEE... FIFTEEN SECONDS FLAT.
FIFTEEN SECONDS FLAT, HUH?
YES, YOUR FASTEST TODAY!
MEH, I CAN GO FASTER.
MISS RAINBOW DASH!
SHOOKA SHOOKA
KUSSSHHH....
OVER HERE. WHAT'S UP?
I HAVE A SPECIAL DELIVERY FOR YOU.
SPECIAL DELIVERY? THAT SOUNDS SO IMPORTANT!
SIGN HERE, PLEASE.
WHAT IS IT?
NOT SURE. SOMETHING FROM CLOUDSDALE!
TAP TAP TAP

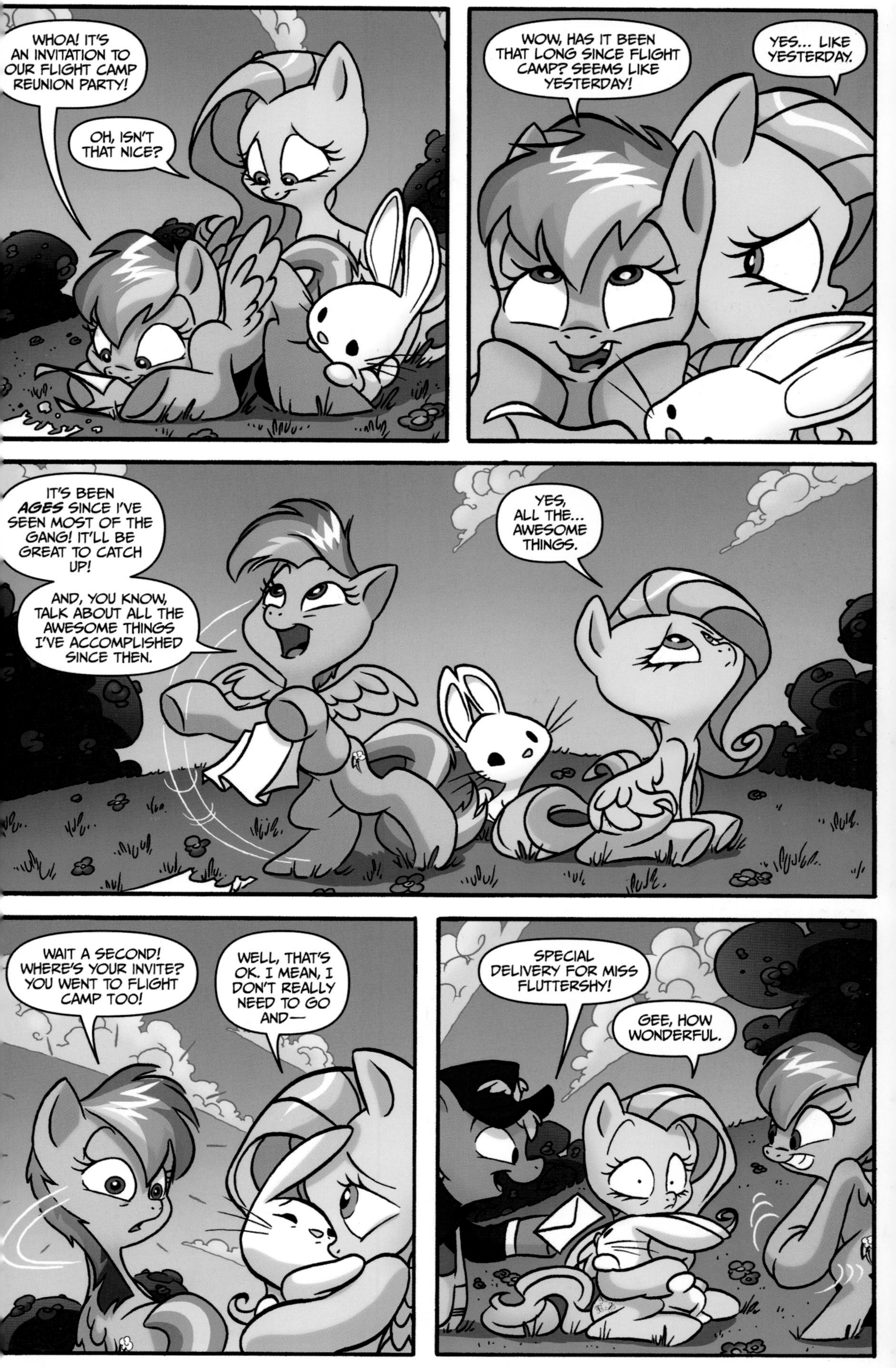
WHOA! IT'S AN INVITATION TO OUR FLIGHT CAMP REUNION PARTY!
OH, ISN'T THAT NICE?
WOW, HAS IT BEEN THAT LONG SINCE FLIGHT CAMP? SEEMS LIKE YESTERDAY!
YES... LIKE YESTERDAY.
IT'S BEEN AGES SINCE I'VE SEEN MOST OF THE GANG! IT'LL BE GREAT TO CATCH UP!
AND, YOU KNOW, TALK ABOUT ALL THE AWESOME THINGS I'VE ACCOMPLISHED SINCE THEN.
YES, ALL THE... AWESOME THINGS.
WAIT A SECOND! WHERE'S YOUR INVITE? YOU WENT TO FLIGHT CAMP TOO!
WELL, THAT'S OK. I MEAN, I DON'T REALLY NEED TO GO AND—
SPECIAL DELIVERY FOR MISS FLUTTERSHY!
GEE, HOW WONDERFUL.

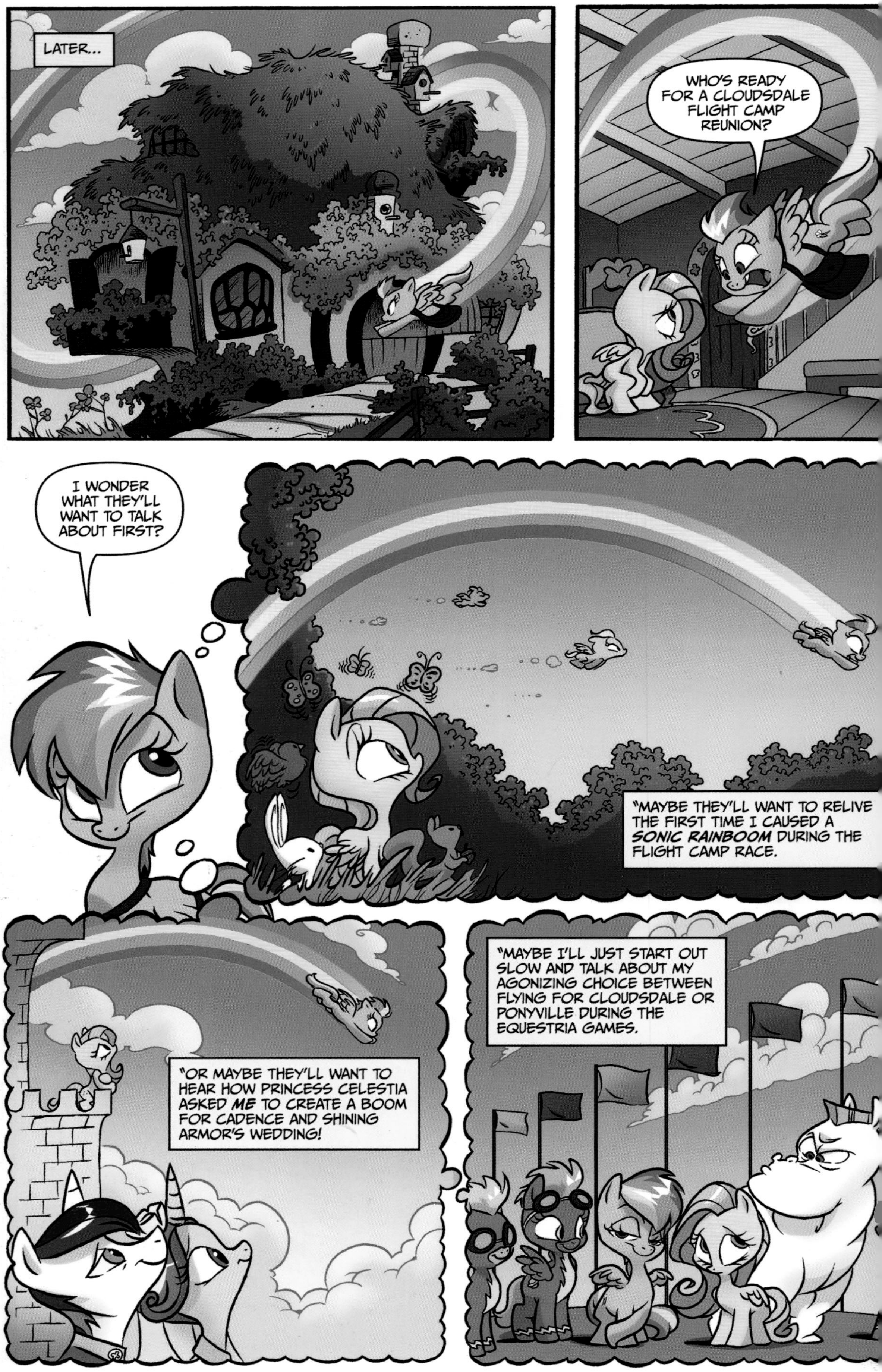
LATER...
WHO'S READY FOR A CLOUDSDALE FLIGHT CAMP REUNION?
I WONDER WHAT THEY'LL WANT TO TALK ABOUT FIRST?
"MAYBE THEY'LL WANT TO RELIVE THE FIRST TIME I CAUSED A SONIC RAINBOOM DURING THE FLIGHT CAMP RACE.
"OR MAYBE THEY'LL WANT TO HEAR HOW PRINCESS CELESTIA ASKED ME TO CREATE A BOOM FOR CADENCE AND SHINING ARMOR'S WEDDING!
"MAYBE I'LL JUST START OUT SLOW AND TALK ABOUT MY AGONIZING CHOICE BETWEEN FLYING FOR CLOUDSDALE OR PONYVILLE DURING THE EQUESTRIA GAMES.

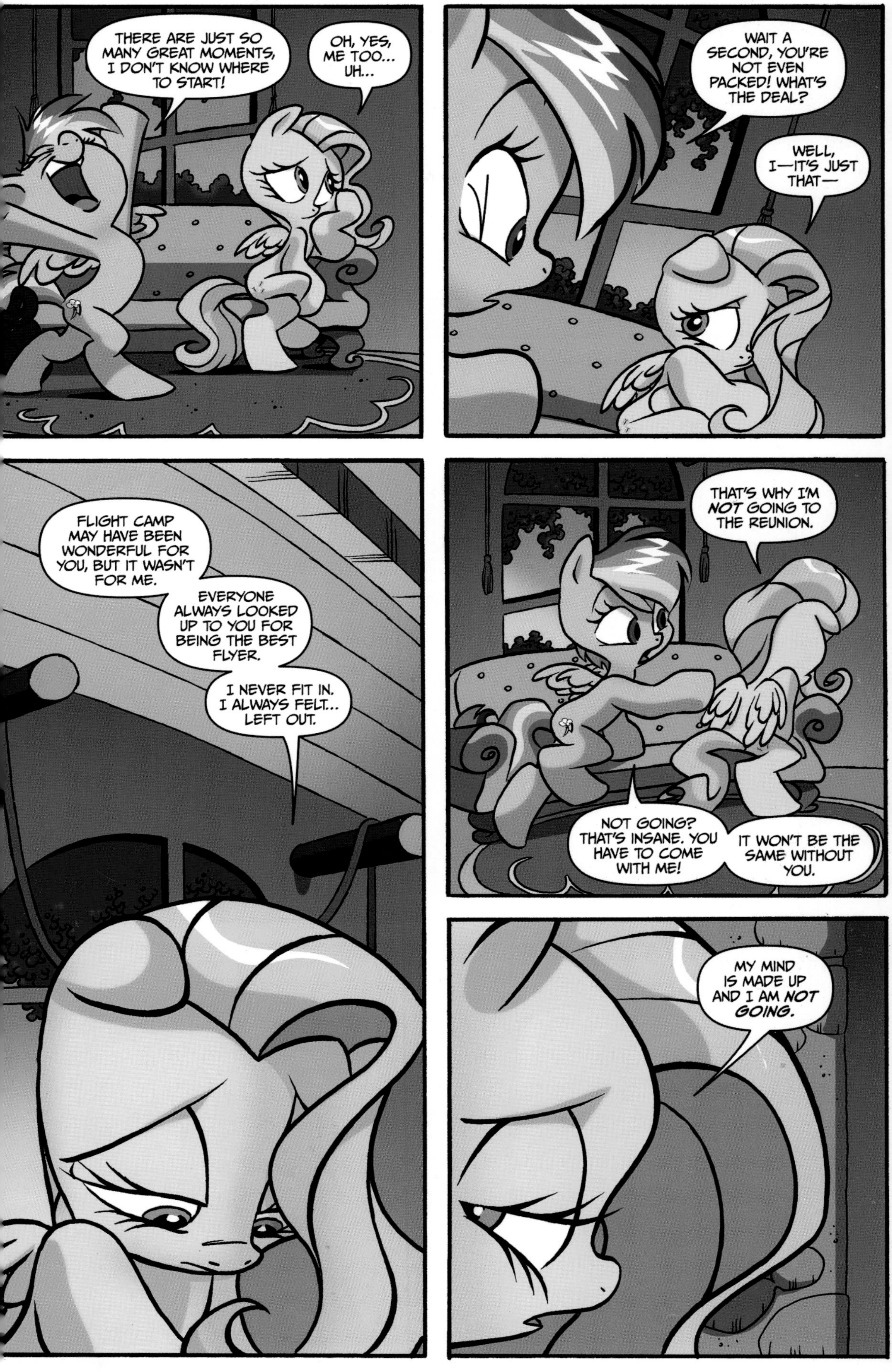
THERE ARE JUST SO MANY GREAT MOMENTS, I DON'T KNOW WHERE TO START!
OH, YES, ME TOO... UH...
WAIT A SECOND, YOU'RE NOT EVEN PACKED! WHAT'S THE DEAL?
WELL, I—IT'S JUST THAT—
FLIGHT CAMP MAY HAVE BEEN WONDERFUL FOR YOU, BUT IT WASN'T FOR ME.
EVERYONE ALWAYS LOOKED UP TO YOU FOR BEING THE BEST FLYER.
I NEVER FIT IN. I ALWAYS FELT... LEFT OUT.
THAT'S WHY I'M *NOT* GOING TO THE REUNION.
NOT GOING? THAT'S INSANE. YOU HAVE TO COME WITH ME!
IT WON'T BE THE SAME WITHOUT YOU.
MY MIND IS MADE UP AND I AM ***NOT GOING.***

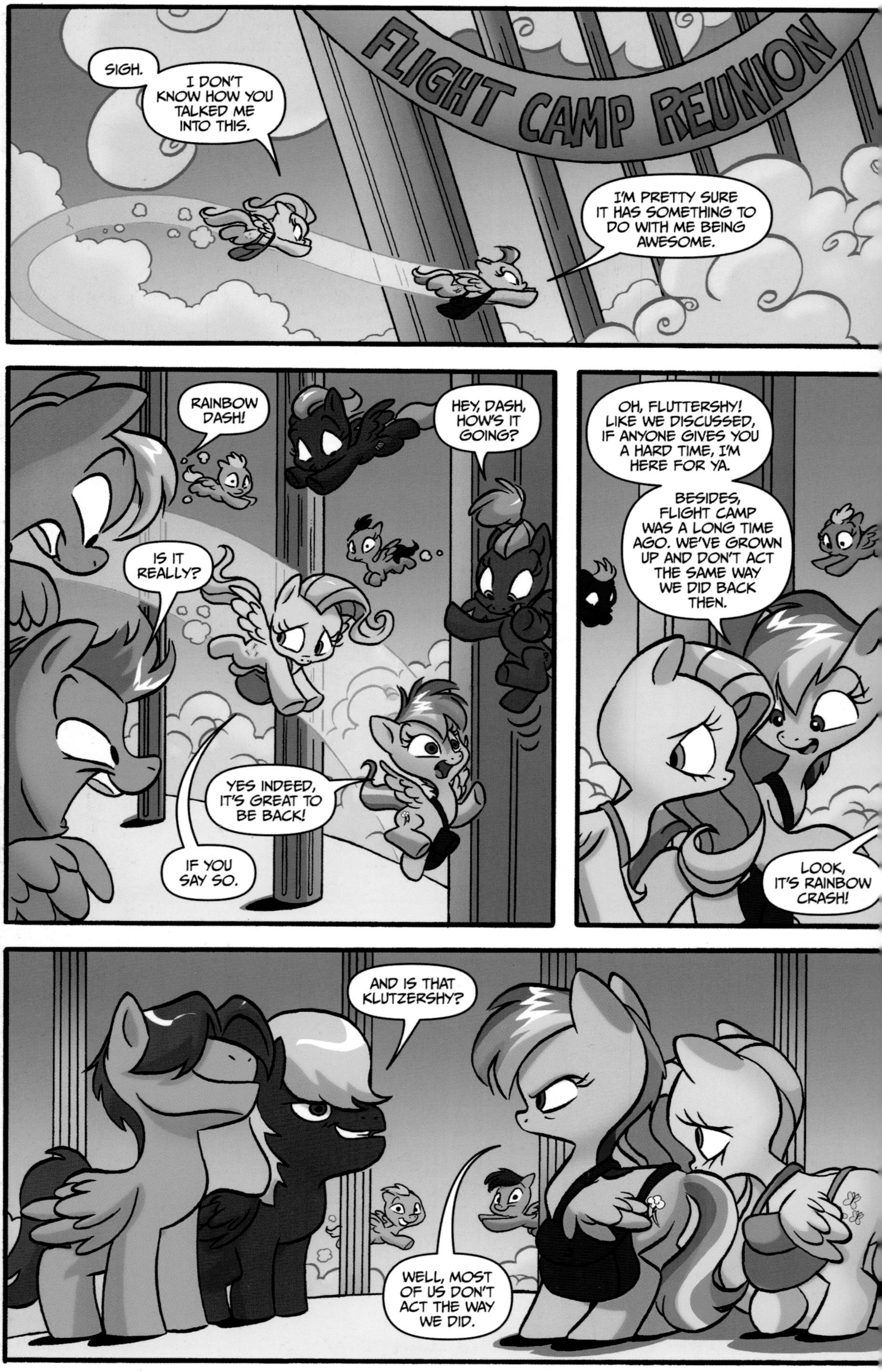
FLIGHT CAMP REUNION
SIGH.
I DON'T KNOW HOW YOU TALKED ME INTO THIS.
I'M PRETTY SURE IT HAS SOMETHING TO DO WITH ME BEING AWESOME.
RAINBOW DASH!
HEY, DASH, HOW'S IT GOING?
IS IT REALLY?
YES INDEED, IT'S GREAT TO BE BACK!
IF YOU SAY SO.
OH, FLUTTERSHY! LIKE WE DISCUSSED, IF ANYONE GIVES YOU A HARD TIME, I'M HERE FOR YA.
BESIDES, FLIGHT CAMP WAS A LONG TIME AGO. WE'VE GROWN UP AND DON'T ACT THE SAME WAY WE DID BACK THEN.
LOOK, IT'S RAINBOW CRASH!
AND IS THAT KLUTZERSHY?
WELL, MOST OF US DON'T ACT THE WAY WE DID.

WHAT DO YOU SAY, CRASH? UP FOR A LITTLE RACE?

SERIOUSLY? DON'T YOU TWO EVER LEARN?

WE'VE BEEN PRACTICING.

AND WAITING FOR THIS MOMENT FOR A LONG TIME.

OH PLEASE, YOU TWO DON'T STAND A CHANCE!

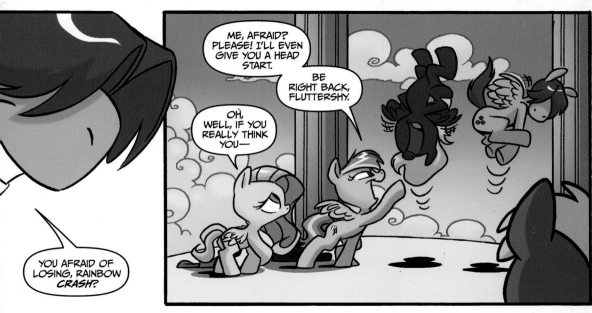

ME, AFRAID? PLEASE! I'LL EVEN GIVE YOU A HEAD START.

BE RIGHT BACK, FLUTTERSHY.

OH, WELL, IF YOU REALLY THINK YOU—

YOU AFRAID OF LOSING, RAINBOW CRASH?

—HAVE TO.

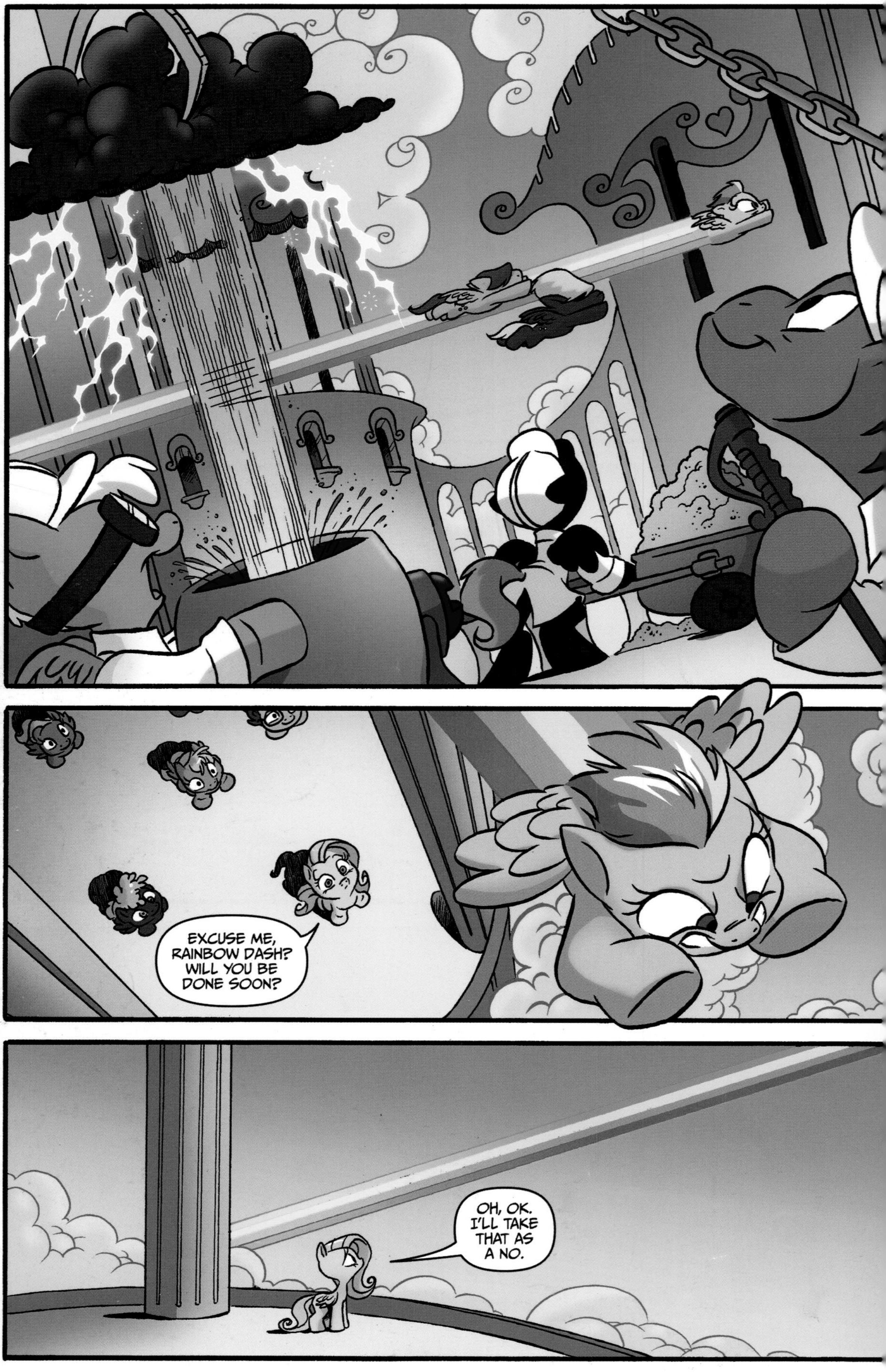
EXCUSE ME, RAINBOW DASH? WILL YOU BE DONE SOON?
OH, OK. I'LL TAKE THAT AS A NO.

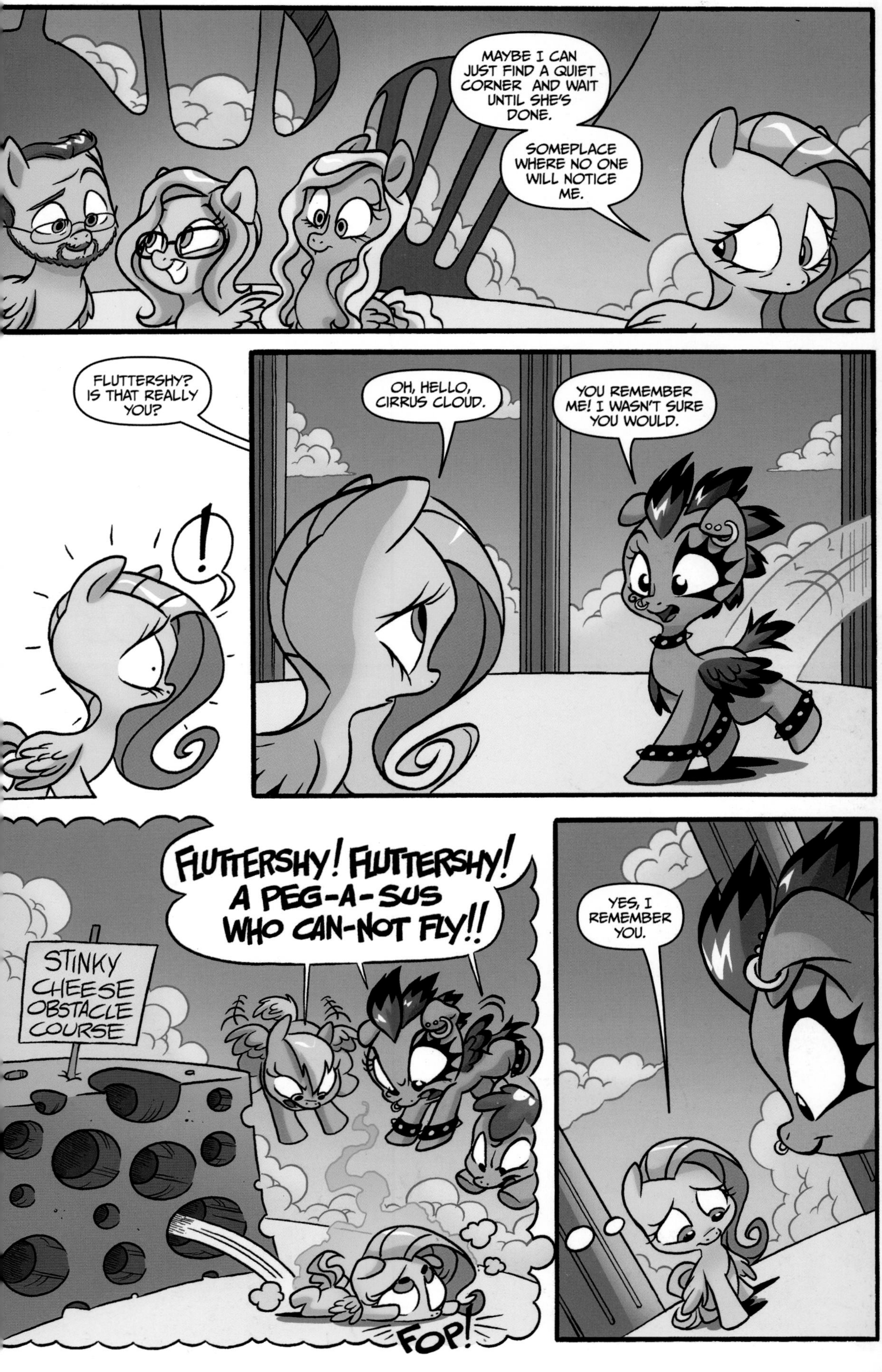
MAYBE I CAN JUST FIND A QUIET CORNER AND WAIT UNTIL SHE'S DONE.
SOMEPLACE WHERE NO ONE WILL NOTICE ME.
FLUTTERSHY? IS THAT REALLY YOU?
!
OH, HELLO, CIRRUS CLOUD.
YOU REMEMBER ME! I WASN'T SURE YOU WOULD.
FLUTTERSHY! FLUTTERSHY! A PEG-A-SUS WHO CAN-NOT FLY!!
STINKY CHEESE OBSTACLE COURSE
FOP!
YES, I REMEMBER YOU.

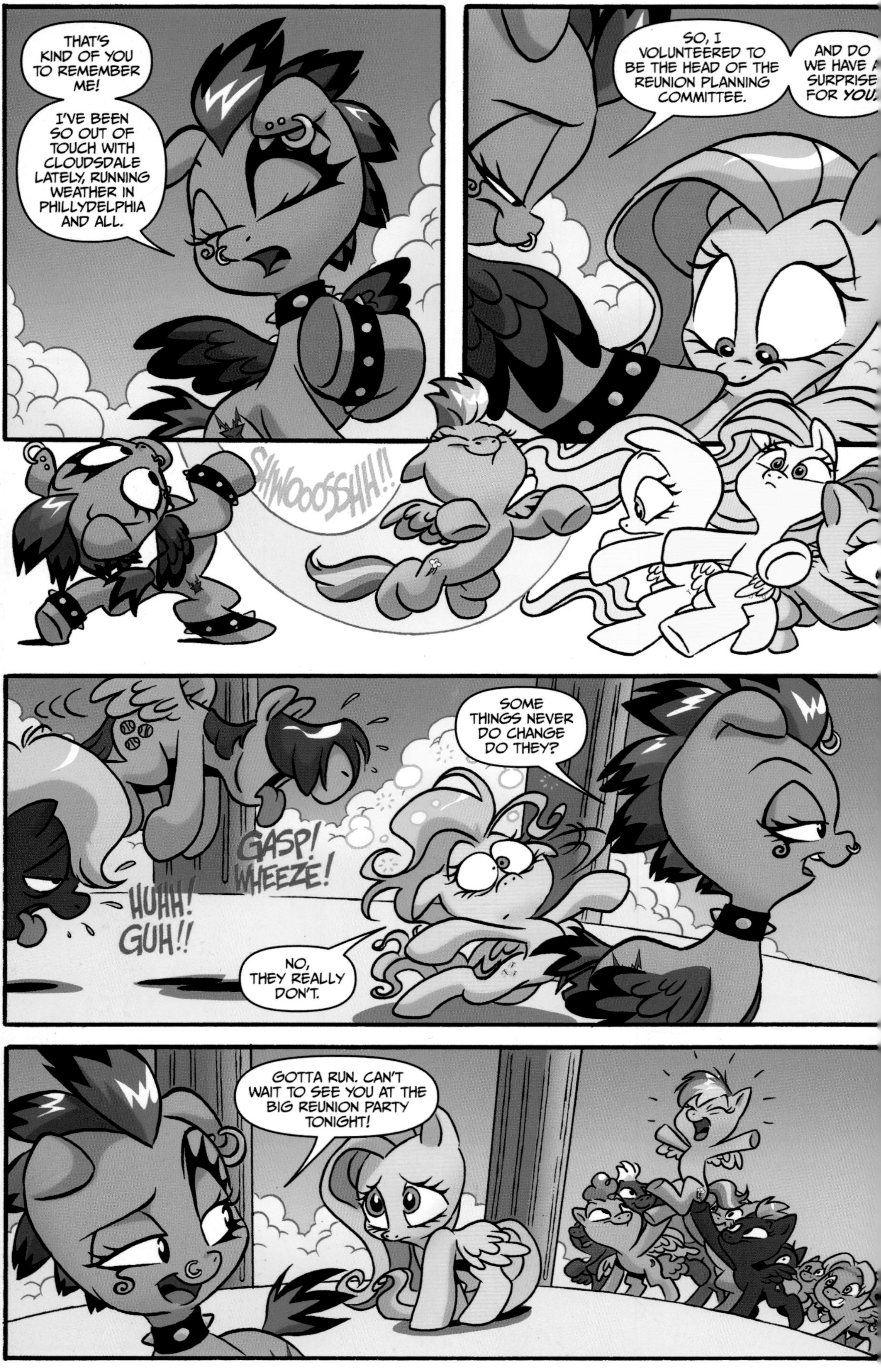
THAT'S KIND OF YOU TO REMEMBER ME!
I'VE BEEN SO OUT OF TOUCH WITH CLOUDSDALE LATELY, RUNNING WEATHER IN PHILLYDELPHIA AND ALL.
SO, I VOLUNTEERED TO BE THE HEAD OF THE REUNION PLANNING COMMITTEE.
AND DO WE HAVE A SURPRISE FOR YOU!
SHWOOOSSHH!!
SOME THINGS NEVER DO CHANGE DO THEY?
GASP! WHEEZE!
HUHH! GUH!!
NO, THEY REALLY DON'T.
GOTTA RUN. CAN'T WAIT TO SEE YOU AT THE BIG REUNION PARTY TONIGHT!

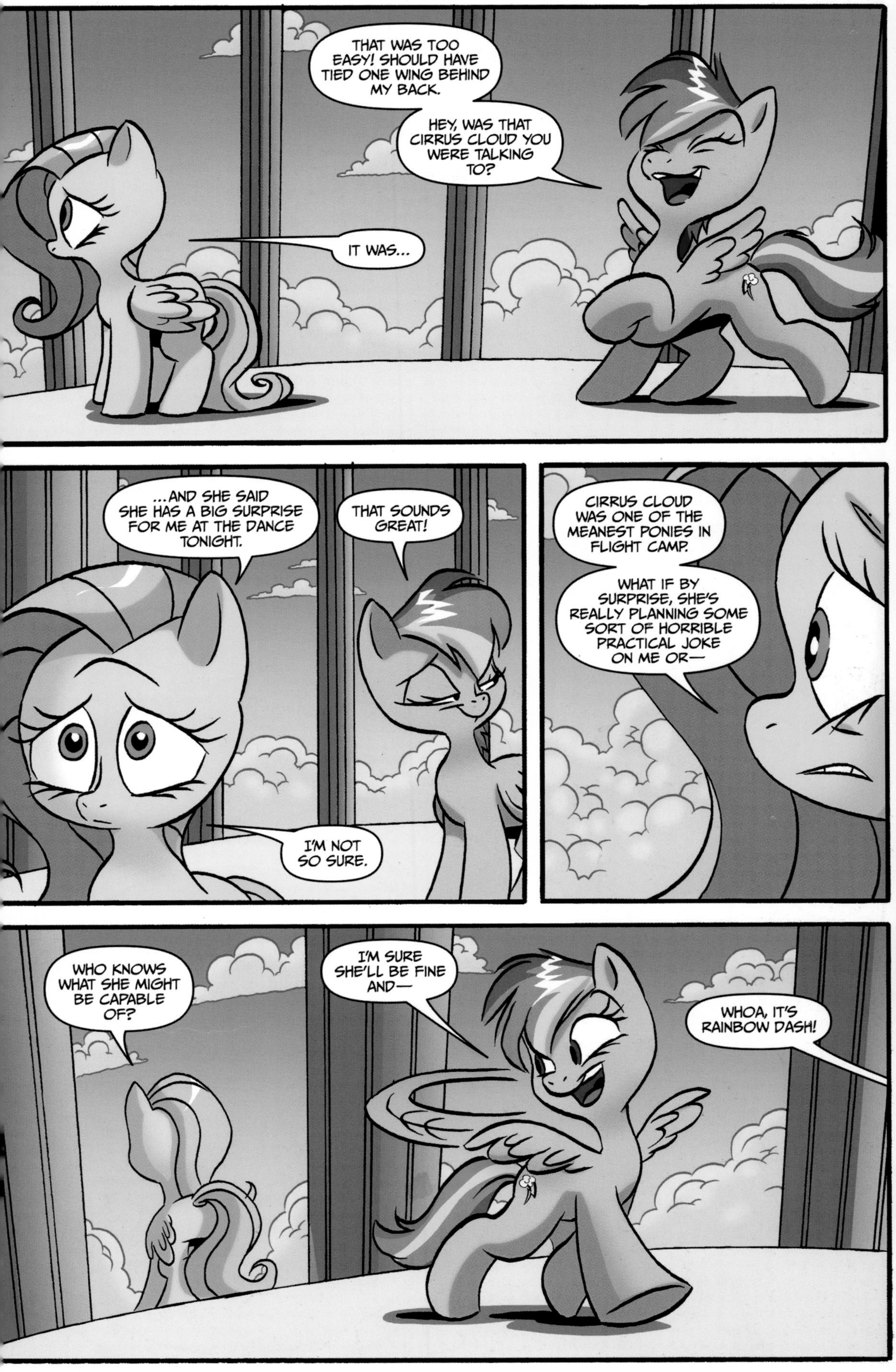
THAT WAS TOO EASY! SHOULD HAVE TIED ONE WING BEHIND MY BACK.
HEY, WAS THAT CIRRUS CLOUD YOU WERE TALKING TO?
IT WAS...
...AND SHE SAID SHE HAS A BIG SURPRISE FOR ME AT THE DANCE TONIGHT.
THAT SOUNDS GREAT!
I'M NOT SO SURE.
CIRRUS CLOUD WAS ONE OF THE MEANEST PONIES IN FLIGHT CAMP.
WHAT IF BY SURPRISE, SHE'S REALLY PLANNING SOME SORT OF HORRIBLE PRACTICAL JOKE ON ME OR—
WHO KNOWS WHAT SHE MIGHT BE CAPABLE OF?
I'M SURE SHE'LL BE FINE AND—
WHOA, IT'S RAINBOW DASH!

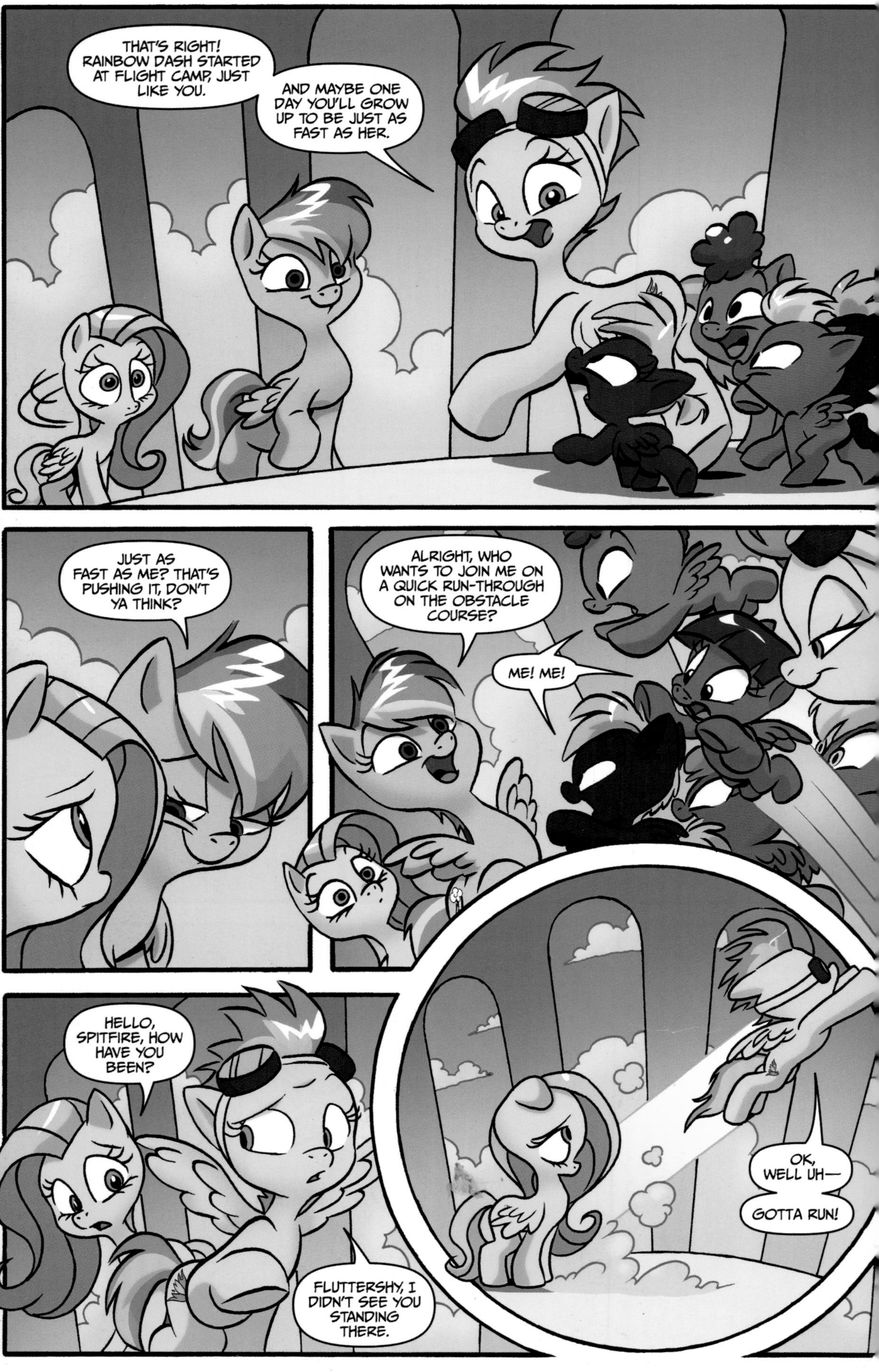
THAT'S RIGHT! RAINBOW DASH STARTED AT FLIGHT CAMP, JUST LIKE YOU.
AND MAYBE ONE DAY YOU'LL GROW UP TO BE JUST AS FAST AS HER.
JUST AS FAST AS ME? THAT'S PUSHING IT, DON'T YA THINK?
ALRIGHT, WHO WANTS TO JOIN ME ON A QUICK RUN-THROUGH ON THE OBSTACLE COURSE?
ME! ME!
HELLO, SPITFIRE, HOW HAVE YOU BEEN?
FLUTTERSHY, I DIDN'T SEE YOU STANDING THERE.
OK, WELL UH—
GOTTA RUN!

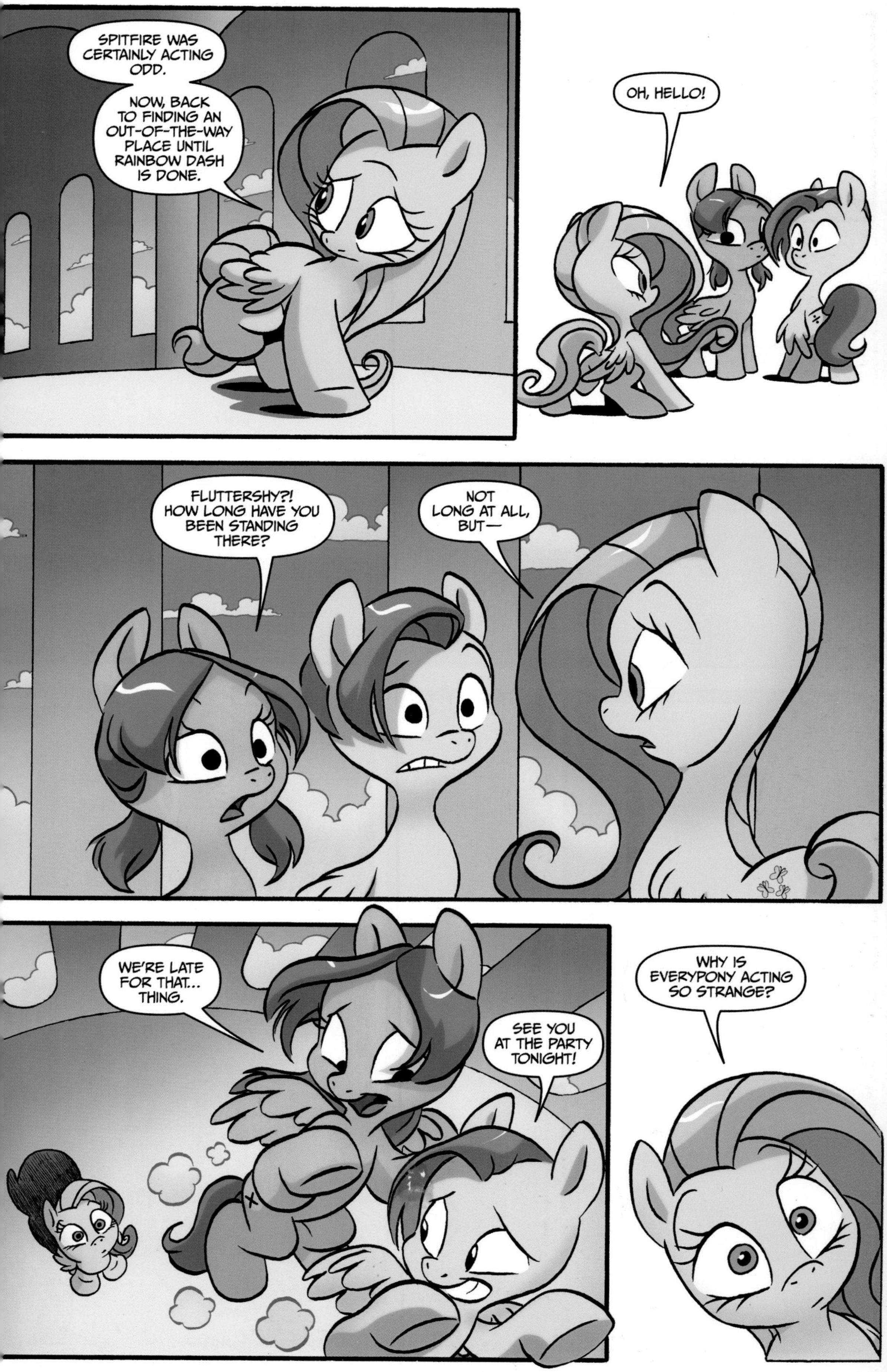

SPITFIRE WAS CERTAINLY ACTING ODD.
NOW, BACK TO FINDING AN OUT-OF-THE-WAY PLACE UNTIL RAINBOW DASH IS DONE.
OH, HELLO!
FLUTTERSHY?! HOW LONG HAVE YOU BEEN STANDING THERE?
NOT LONG AT ALL, BUT—
WE'RE LATE FOR THAT... THING.
SEE YOU AT THE PARTY TONIGHT!
WHY IS EVERYPONY ACTING SO STRANGE?

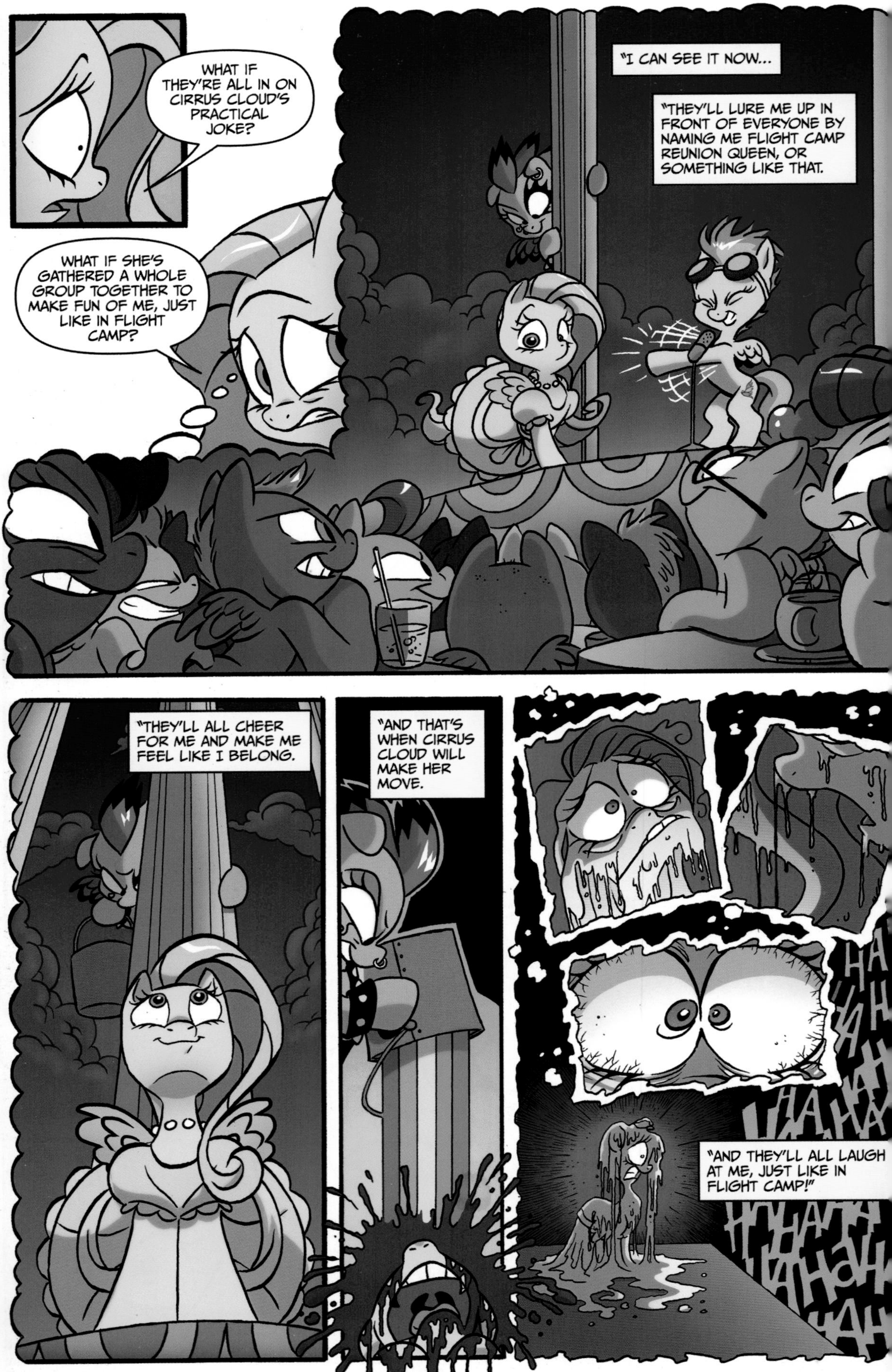
WHAT IF THEY'RE ALL IN ON CIRRUS CLOUD'S PRACTICAL JOKE?
WHAT IF SHE'S GATHERED A WHOLE GROUP TOGETHER TO MAKE FUN OF ME, JUST LIKE IN FLIGHT CAMP?
"I CAN SEE IT NOW...
"THEY'LL LURE ME UP IN FRONT OF EVERYONE BY NAMING ME FLIGHT CAMP REUNION QUEEN, OR SOMETHING LIKE THAT.
"THEY'LL ALL CHEER FOR ME AND MAKE ME FEEL LIKE I BELONG.
"AND THAT'S WHEN CIRRUS CLOUD WILL MAKE HER MOVE.
"AND THEY'LL ALL LAUGH AT ME, JUST LIKE IN FLIGHT CAMP!"

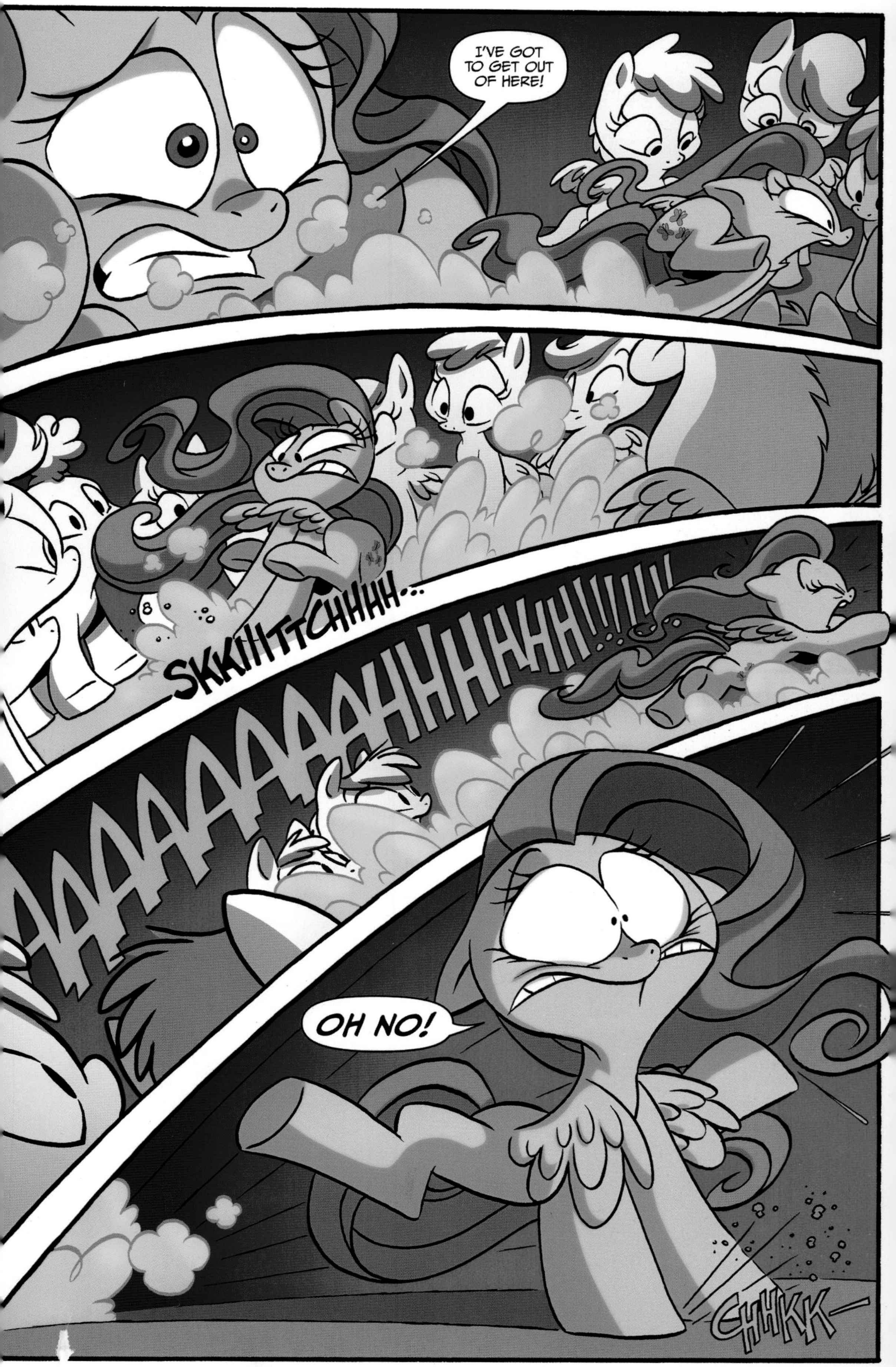
I'VE GOT TO GET OUT OF HERE!
SKKIIITTCHHHH...
AAAAAAAAAHHHHHHHH!!!!!!
OH NO!
CHHKK—

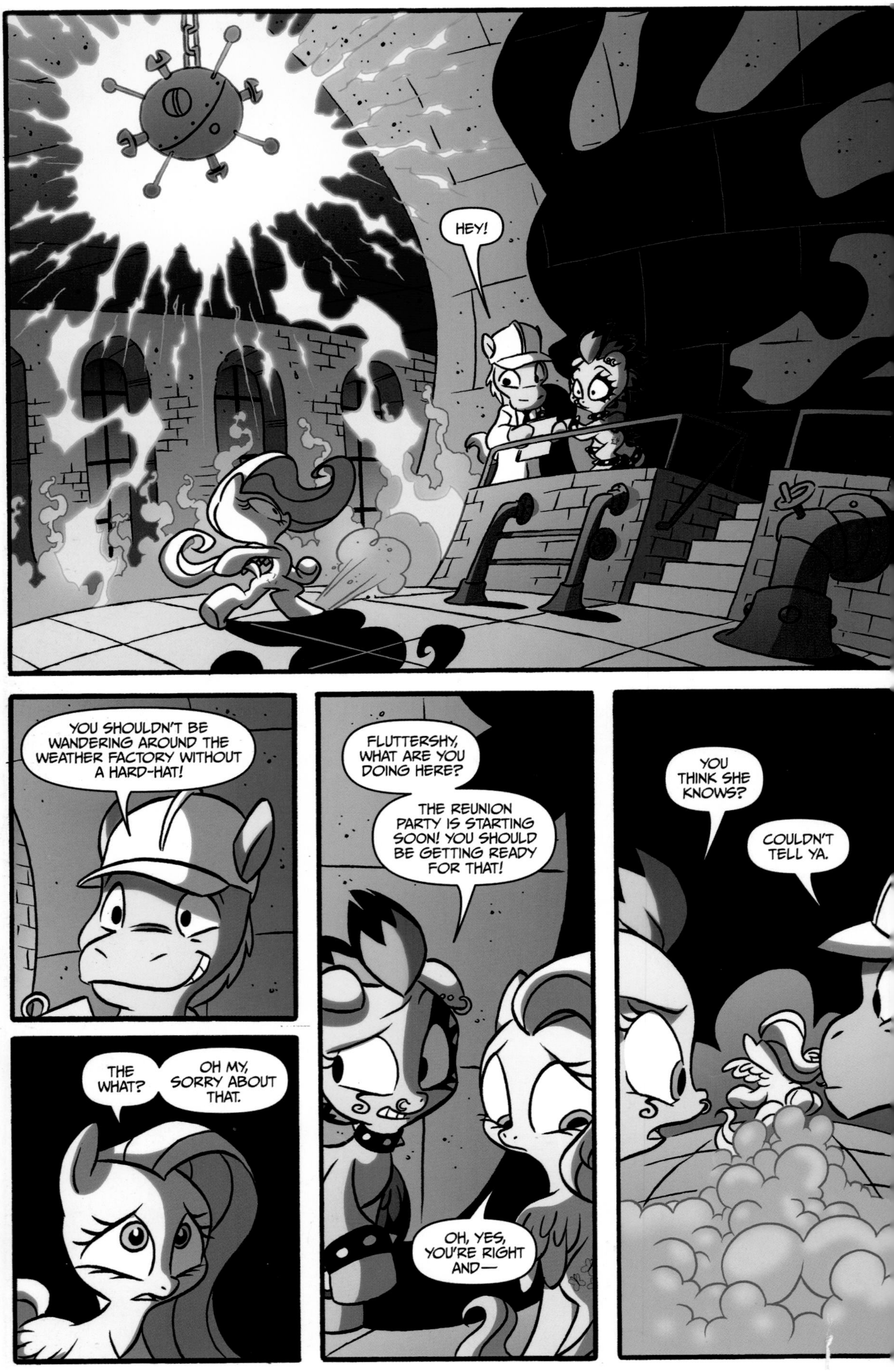
HEY!
YOU SHOULDN'T BE WANDERING AROUND THE WEATHER FACTORY WITHOUT A HARD-HAT!
THE WHAT?
OH MY, SORRY ABOUT THAT.
FLUTTERSHY, WHAT ARE YOU DOING HERE?
THE REUNION PARTY IS STARTING SOON! YOU SHOULD BE GETTING READY FOR THAT!
OH, YES, YOU'RE RIGHT AND—
YOU THINK SHE KNOWS?
COULDN'T TELL YA.

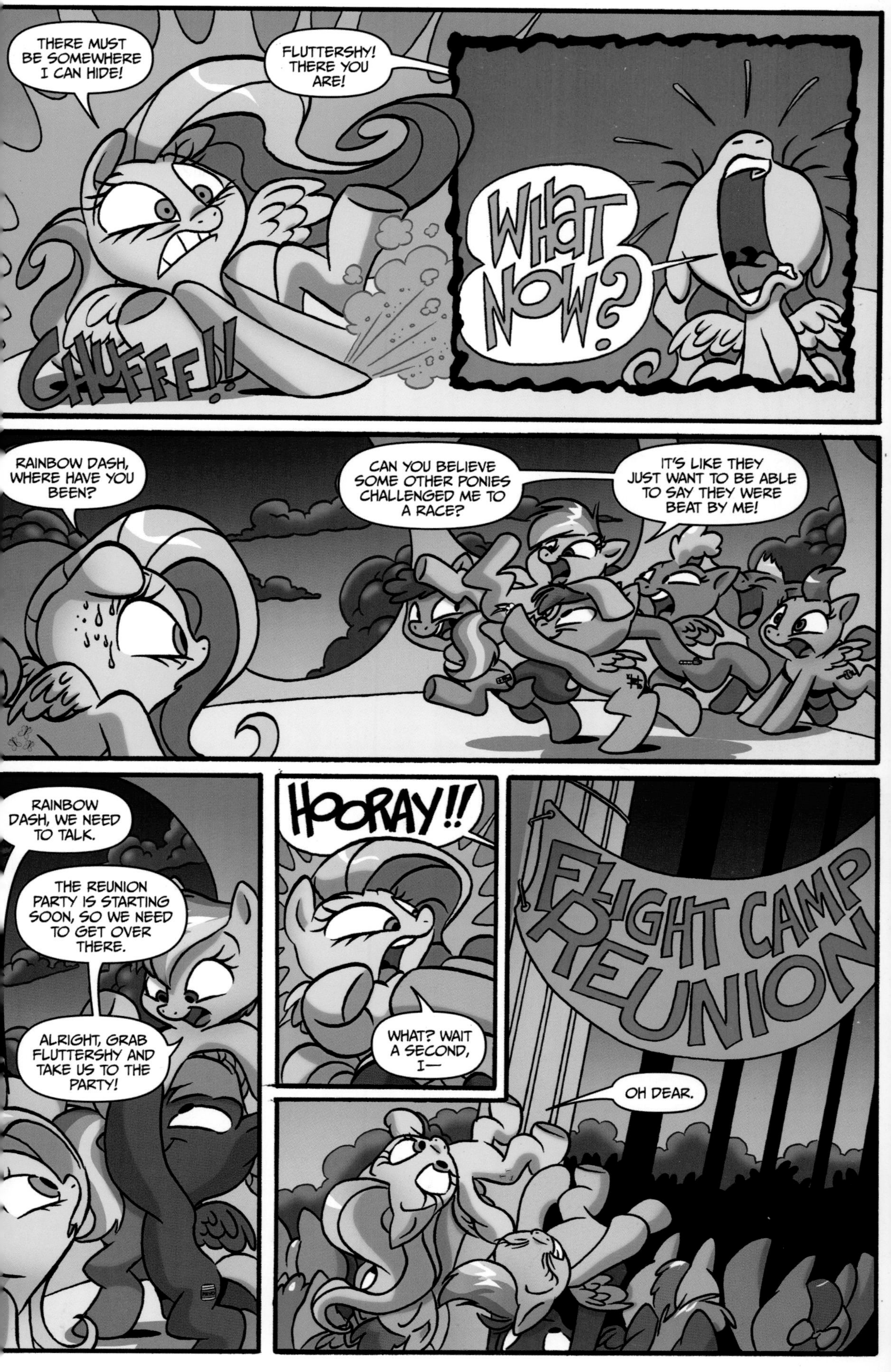
THERE MUST BE SOMEWHERE I CAN HIDE!
FLUTTERSHY! THERE YOU ARE!
CHUFFFF!!
WHAT NOW?
RAINBOW DASH, WHERE HAVE YOU BEEN?
CAN YOU BELIEVE SOME OTHER PONIES CHALLENGED ME TO A RACE?
IT'S LIKE THEY JUST WANT TO BE ABLE TO SAY THEY WERE BEAT BY ME!
RAINBOW DASH, WE NEED TO TALK.
THE REUNION PARTY IS STARTING SOON, SO WE NEED TO GET OVER THERE.
ALRIGHT, GRAB FLUTTERSHY AND TAKE US TO THE PARTY!
HOORAY!!
WHAT? WAIT A SECOND, I—
FLIGHT CAMP REUNION
OH DEAR.

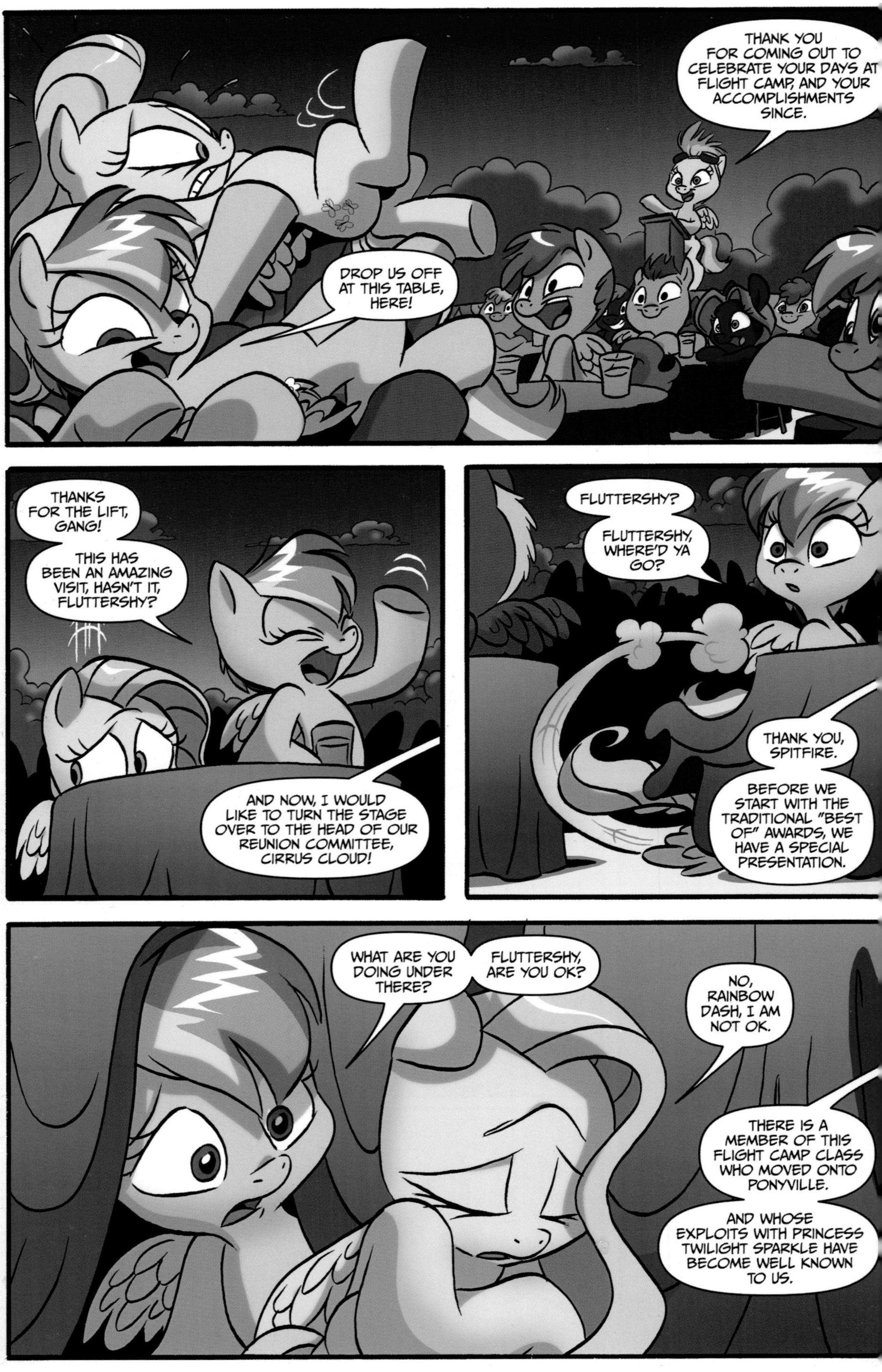
THANK YOU FOR COMING OUT TO CELEBRATE YOUR DAYS AT FLIGHT CAMP, AND YOUR ACCOMPLISHMENTS SINCE.
DROP US OFF AT THIS TABLE, HERE!
THANKS FOR THE LIFT, GANG!
THIS HAS BEEN AN AMAZING VISIT, HASN'T IT, FLUTTERSHY?
AND NOW, I WOULD LIKE TO TURN THE STAGE OVER TO THE HEAD OF OUR REUNION COMMITTEE, CIRRUS CLOUD!
FLUTTERSHY?
FLUTTERSHY, WHERE'D YA GO?
THANK YOU, SPITFIRE.
BEFORE WE START WITH THE TRADITIONAL "BEST OF" AWARDS, WE HAVE A SPECIAL PRESENTATION.
WHAT ARE YOU DOING UNDER THERE?
FLUTTERSHY, ARE YOU OK?
NO, RAINBOW DASH, I AM NOT OK.
THERE IS A MEMBER OF THIS FLIGHT CAMP CLASS WHO MOVED ONTO PONYVILLE.
AND WHOSE EXPLOITS WITH PRINCESS TWILIGHT SPARKLE HAVE BECOME WELL KNOWN TO US.

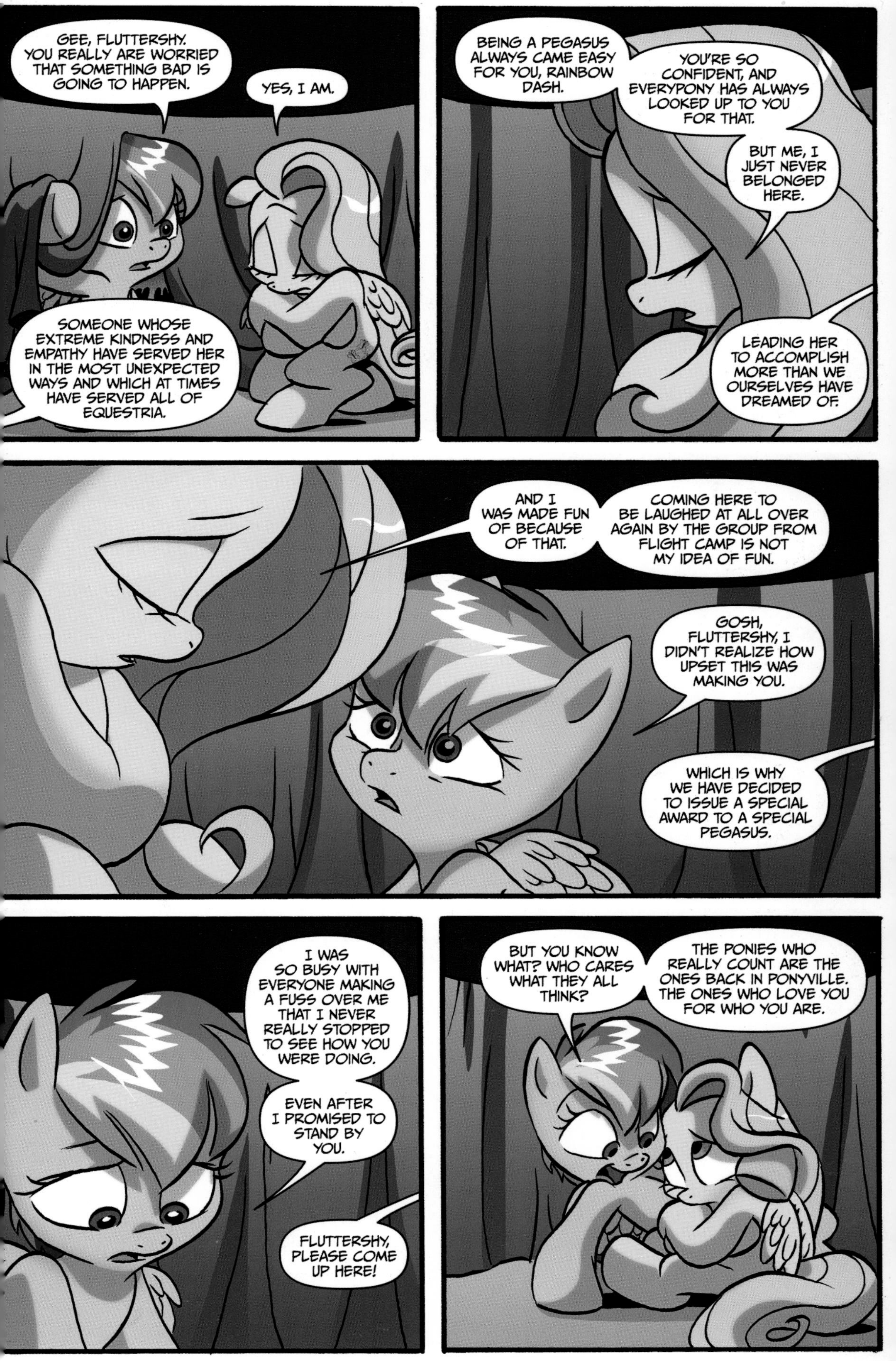
GEE, FLUTTERSHY. YOU REALLY ARE WORRIED THAT SOMETHING BAD IS GOING TO HAPPEN.
YES, I AM.
SOMEONE WHOSE EXTREME KINDNESS AND EMPATHY HAVE SERVED HER IN THE MOST UNEXPECTED WAYS AND WHICH AT TIMES HAVE SERVED ALL OF EQUESTRIA.
BEING A PEGASUS ALWAYS CAME EASY FOR YOU, RAINBOW DASH.
YOU'RE SO CONFIDENT, AND EVERYPONY HAS ALWAYS LOOKED UP TO YOU FOR THAT.
BUT ME, I JUST NEVER BELONGED HERE.
LEADING HER TO ACCOMPLISH MORE THAN WE OURSELVES HAVE DREAMED OF.
AND I WAS MADE FUN OF BECAUSE OF THAT.
COMING HERE TO BE LAUGHED AT ALL OVER AGAIN BY THE GROUP FROM FLIGHT CAMP IS NOT MY IDEA OF FUN.
GOSH, FLUTTERSHY, I DIDN'T REALIZE HOW UPSET THIS WAS MAKING YOU.
WHICH IS WHY WE HAVE DECIDED TO ISSUE A SPECIAL AWARD TO A SPECIAL PEGASUS.
I WAS SO BUSY WITH EVERYONE MAKING A FUSS OVER ME THAT I NEVER REALLY STOPPED TO SEE HOW YOU WERE DOING.
EVEN AFTER I PROMISED TO STAND BY YOU.
FLUTTERSHY, PLEASE COME UP HERE!
BUT YOU KNOW WHAT? WHO CARES WHAT THEY ALL THINK?
THE PONIES WHO REALLY COUNT ARE THE ONES BACK IN PONYVILLE. THE ONES WHO LOVE YOU FOR WHO YOU ARE.

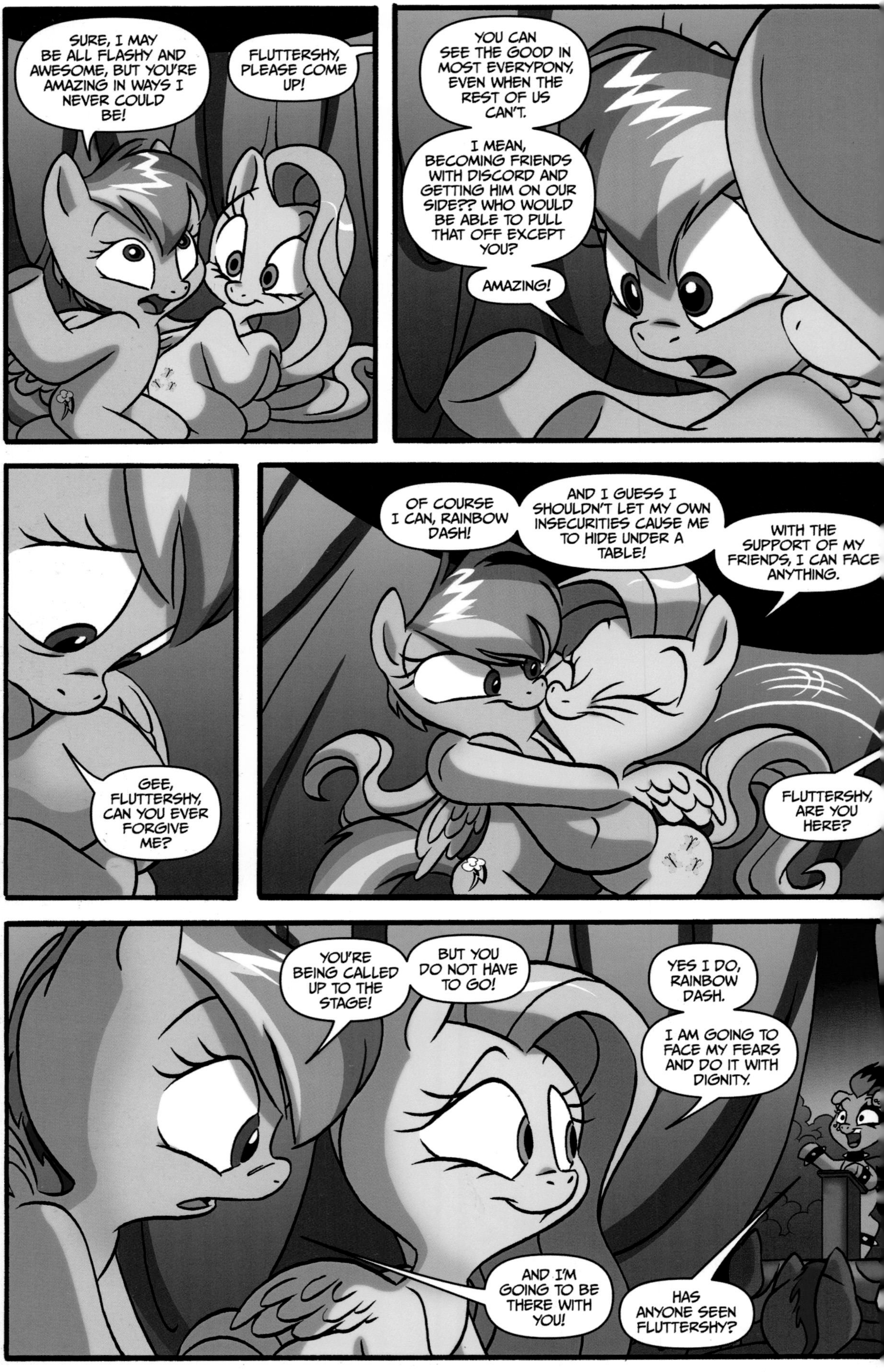
SURE, I MAY BE ALL FLASHY AND AWESOME, BUT YOU'RE AMAZING IN WAYS I NEVER COULD BE!
FLUTTERSHY, PLEASE COME UP!
YOU CAN SEE THE GOOD IN MOST EVERYPONY, EVEN WHEN THE REST OF US CAN'T.
I MEAN, BECOMING FRIENDS WITH DISCORD AND GETTING HIM ON OUR SIDE?? WHO WOULD BE ABLE TO PULL THAT OFF EXCEPT YOU?
AMAZING!
GEE, FLUTTERSHY, CAN YOU EVER FORGIVE ME?
OF COURSE I CAN, RAINBOW DASH!
AND I GUESS I SHOULDN'T LET MY OWN INSECURITIES CAUSE ME TO HIDE UNDER A TABLE!
WITH THE SUPPORT OF MY FRIENDS, I CAN FACE ANYTHING.
FLUTTERSHY, ARE YOU HERE?
YOU'RE BEING CALLED UP TO THE STAGE!
BUT YOU DO NOT HAVE TO GO!
YES I DO, RAINBOW DASH.
I AM GOING TO FACE MY FEARS AND DO IT WITH DIGNITY.
AND I'M GOING TO BE THERE WITH YOU!
HAS ANYONE SEEN FLUTTERSHY?

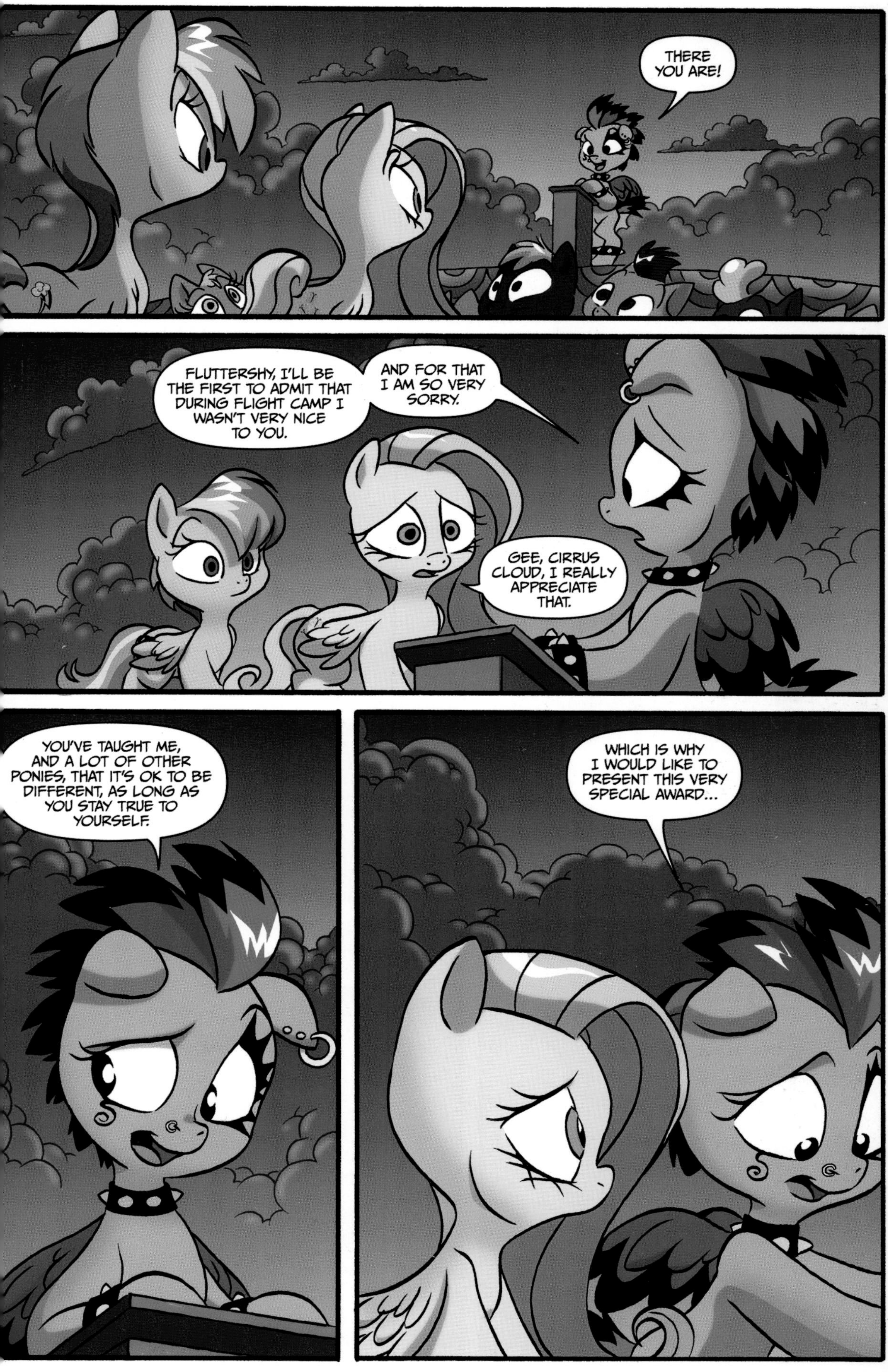
THERE YOU ARE!
FLUTTERSHY, I'LL BE THE FIRST TO ADMIT THAT DURING FLIGHT CAMP I WASN'T VERY NICE TO YOU.
AND FOR THAT I AM SO VERY SORRY.
GEE, CIRRUS CLOUD, I REALLY APPRECIATE THAT.
YOU'VE TAUGHT ME, AND A LOT OF OTHER PONIES, THAT IT'S OK TO BE DIFFERENT, AS LONG AS YOU STAY TRUE TO YOURSELF.
WHICH IS WHY I WOULD LIKE TO PRESENT THIS VERY SPECIAL AWARD...

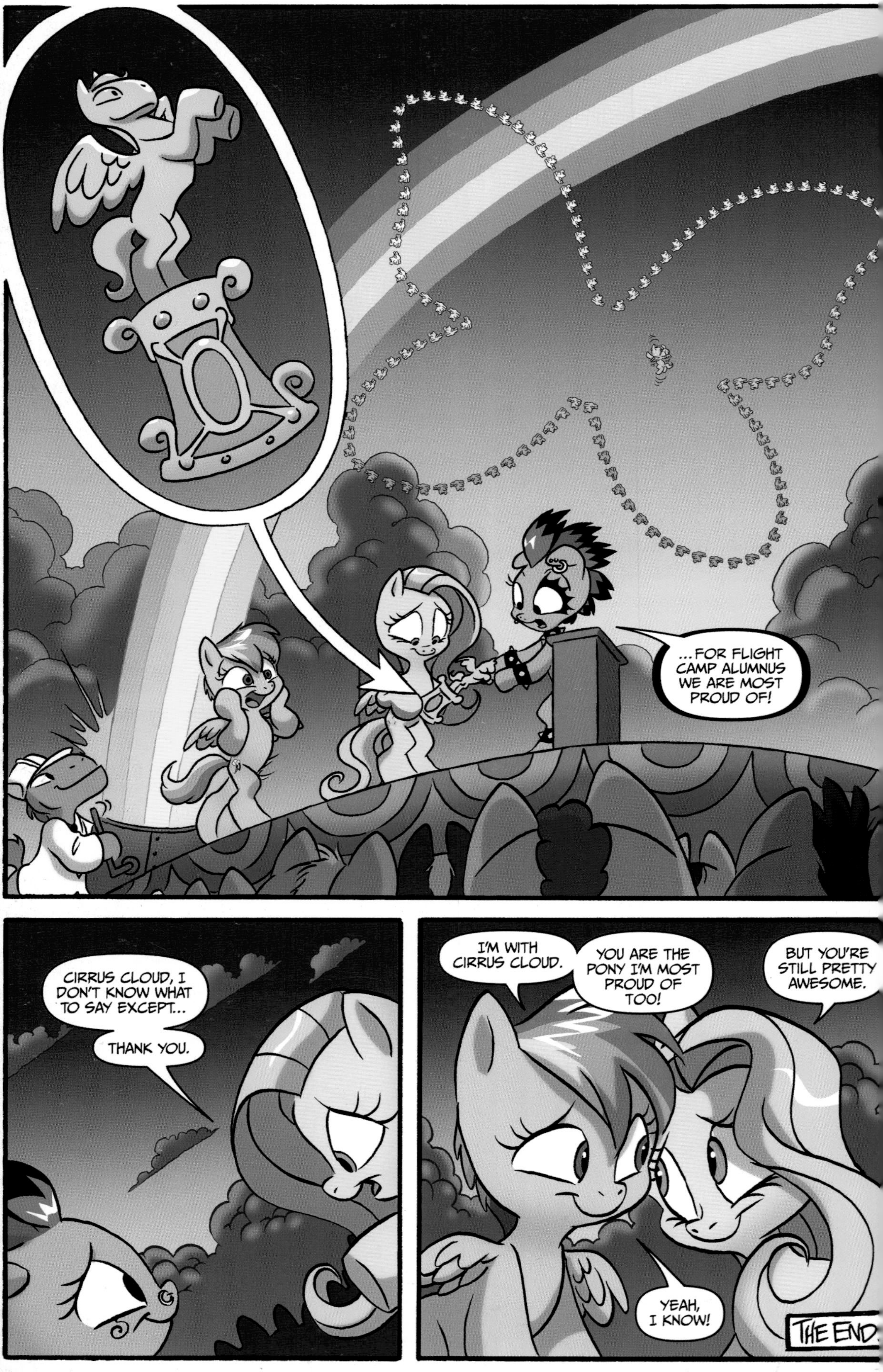
...FOR FLIGHT CAMP ALUMNUS WE ARE MOST PROUD OF!
CIRRUS CLOUD, I DON'T KNOW WHAT TO SAY EXCEPT...
THANK YOU.
I'M WITH CIRRUS CLOUD.
YOU ARE THE PONY I'M MOST PROUD OF TOO!
BUT YOU'RE STILL PRETTY AWESOME.
YEAH, I KNOW!
THE END.

My Little Pony

Friends Forever

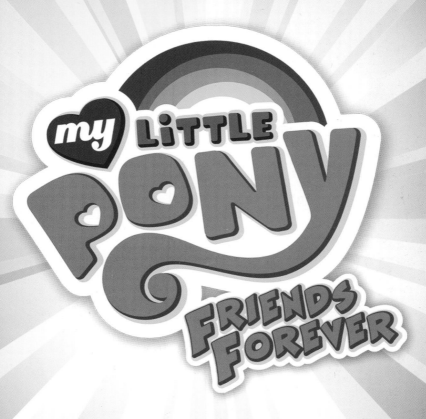

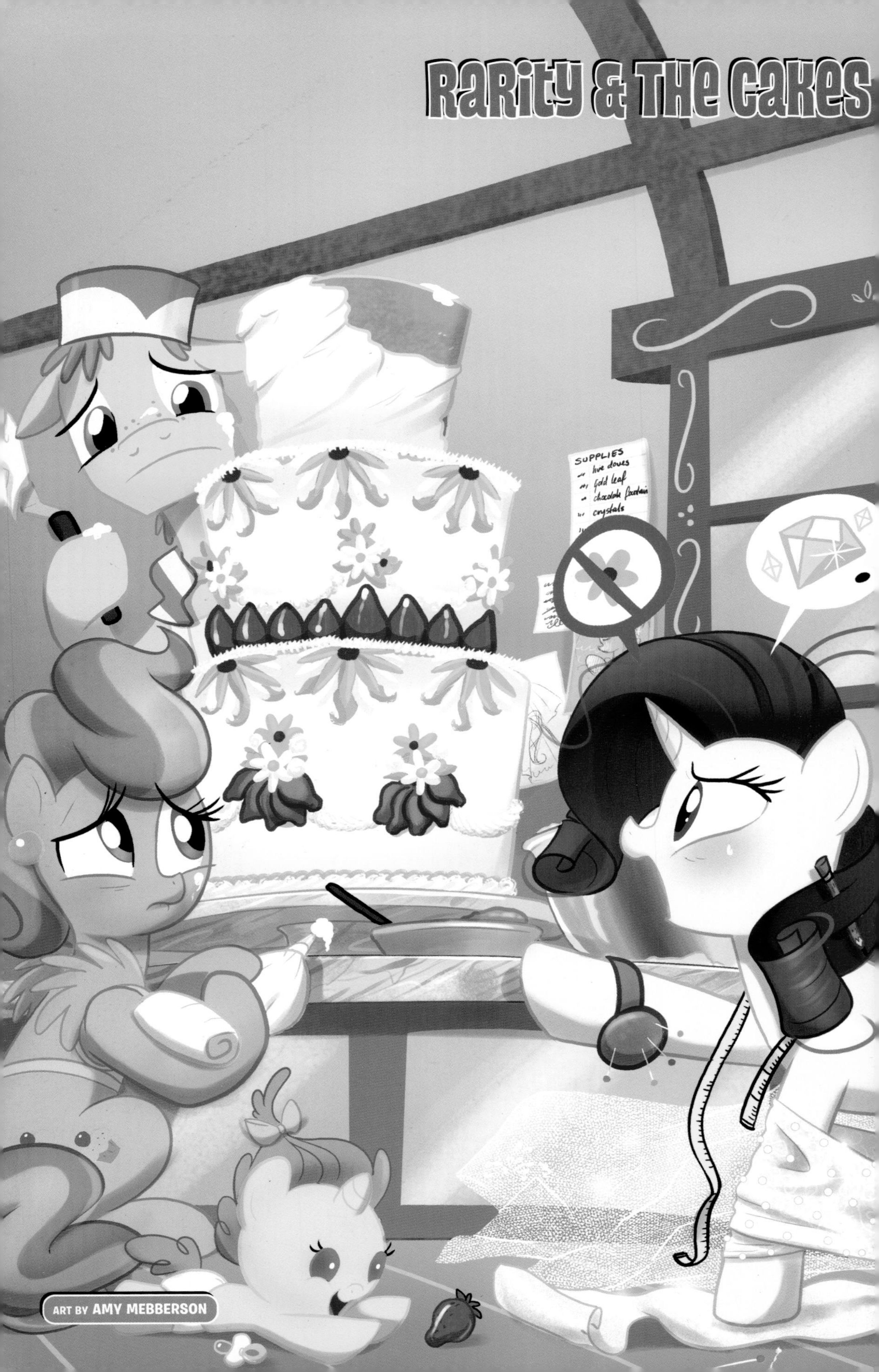
Rarity & The Cakes
SUPPLIES
live doves
gold leaf
chocolate fountain
crystals
ART BY AMY MEBBERSON

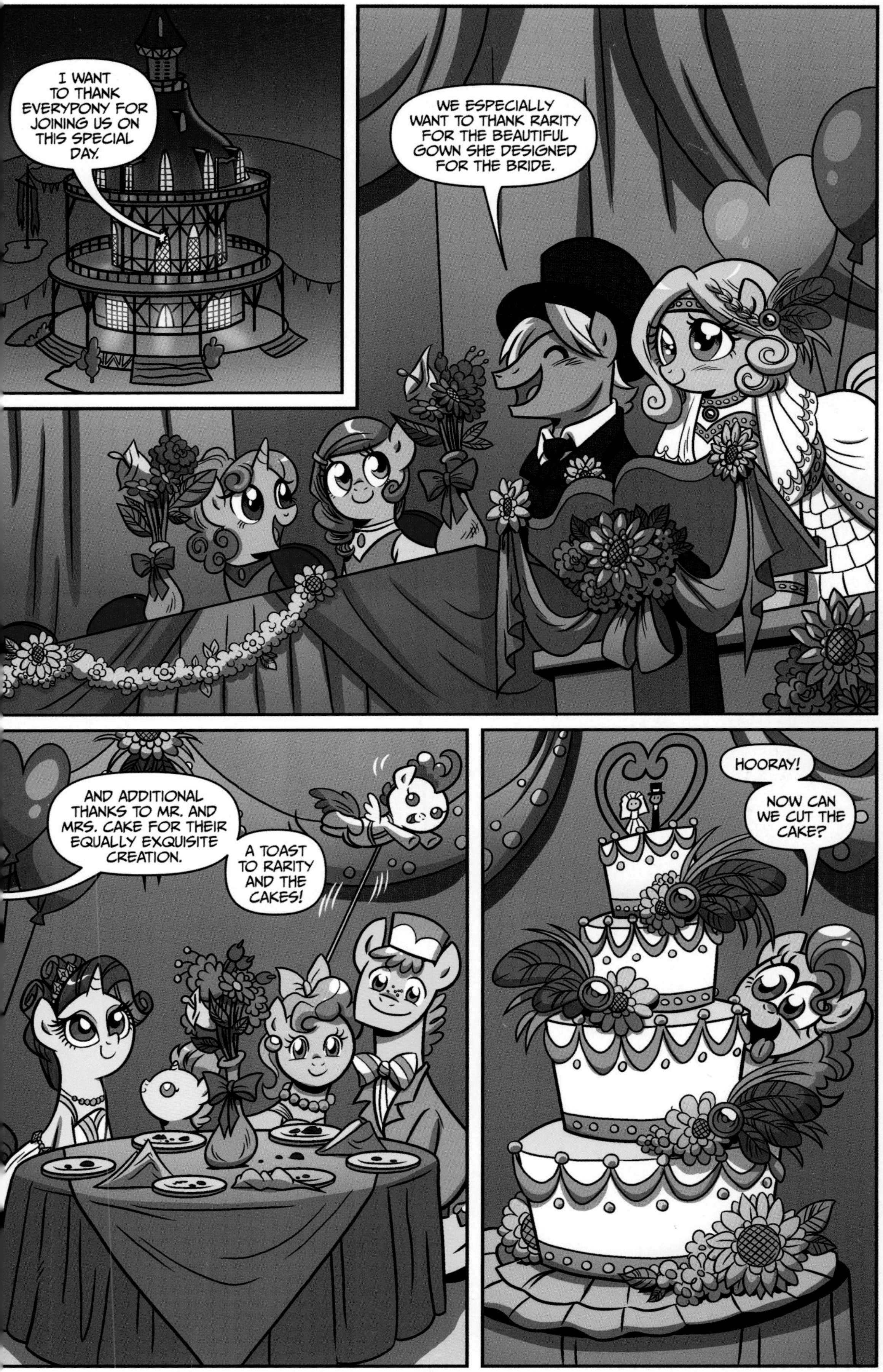
I WANT TO THANK EVERYPONY FOR JOINING US ON THIS SPECIAL DAY.
WE ESPECIALLY WANT TO THANK RARITY FOR THE BEAUTIFUL GOWN SHE DESIGNED FOR THE BRIDE.
AND ADDITIONAL THANKS TO MR. AND MRS. CAKE FOR THEIR EQUALLY EXQUISITE CREATION.
A TOAST TO RARITY AND THE CAKES!
HOORAY!
NOW CAN WE CUT THE CAKE?

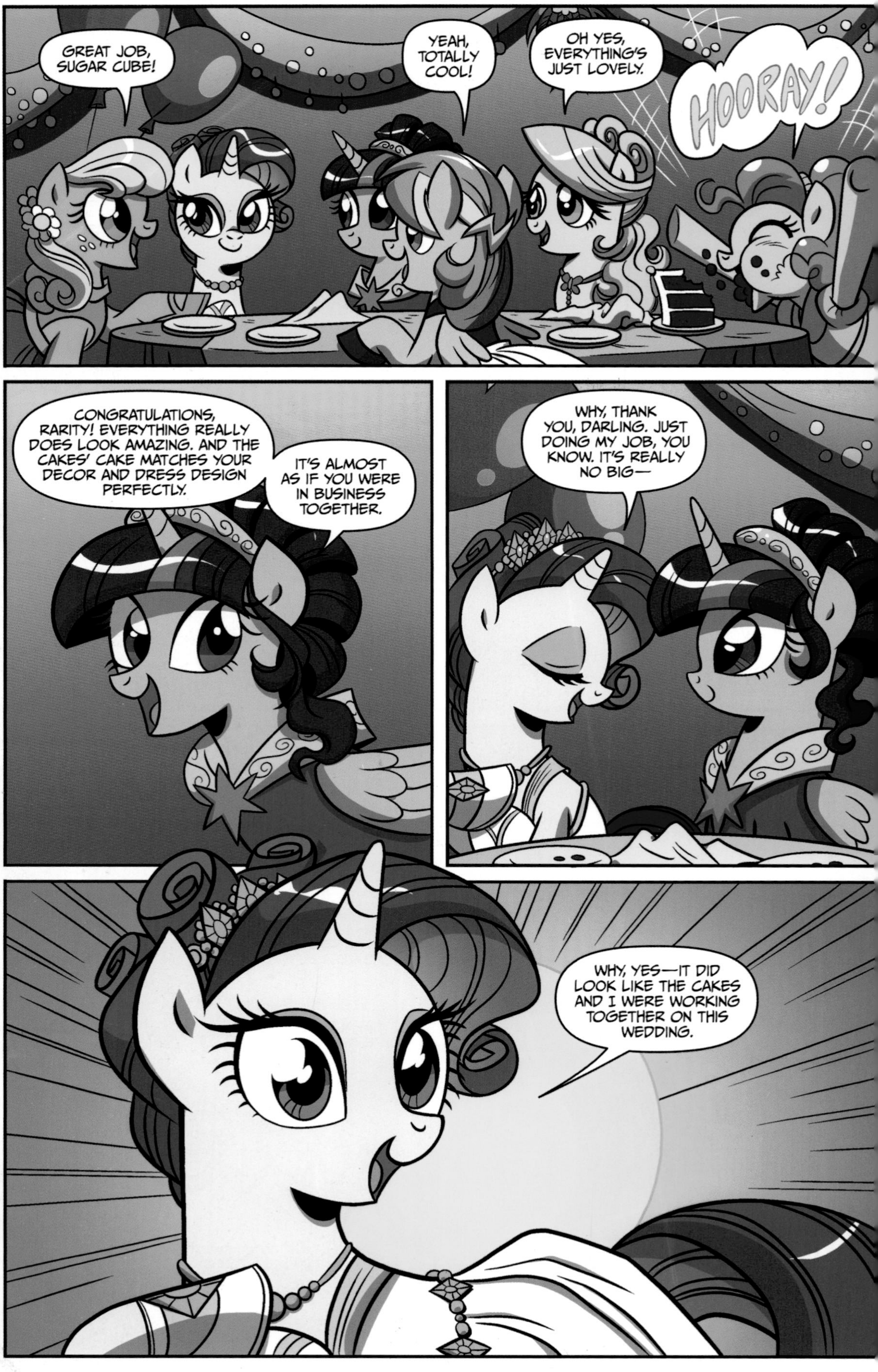
GREAT JOB, SUGAR CUBE!
YEAH, TOTALLY COOL!
OH YES, EVERYTHING'S JUST LOVELY.
HOORAY!
CONGRATULATIONS, RARITY! EVERYTHING REALLY DOES LOOK AMAZING. AND THE CAKES' CAKE MATCHES YOUR DECOR AND DRESS DESIGN PERFECTLY.
IT'S ALMOST AS IF YOU WERE IN BUSINESS TOGETHER.
WHY, THANK YOU, DARLING. JUST DOING MY JOB, YOU KNOW. IT'S REALLY NO BIG—
WHY, YES—IT DID LOOK LIKE THE CAKES AND I WERE WORKING TOGETHER ON THIS WEDDING.

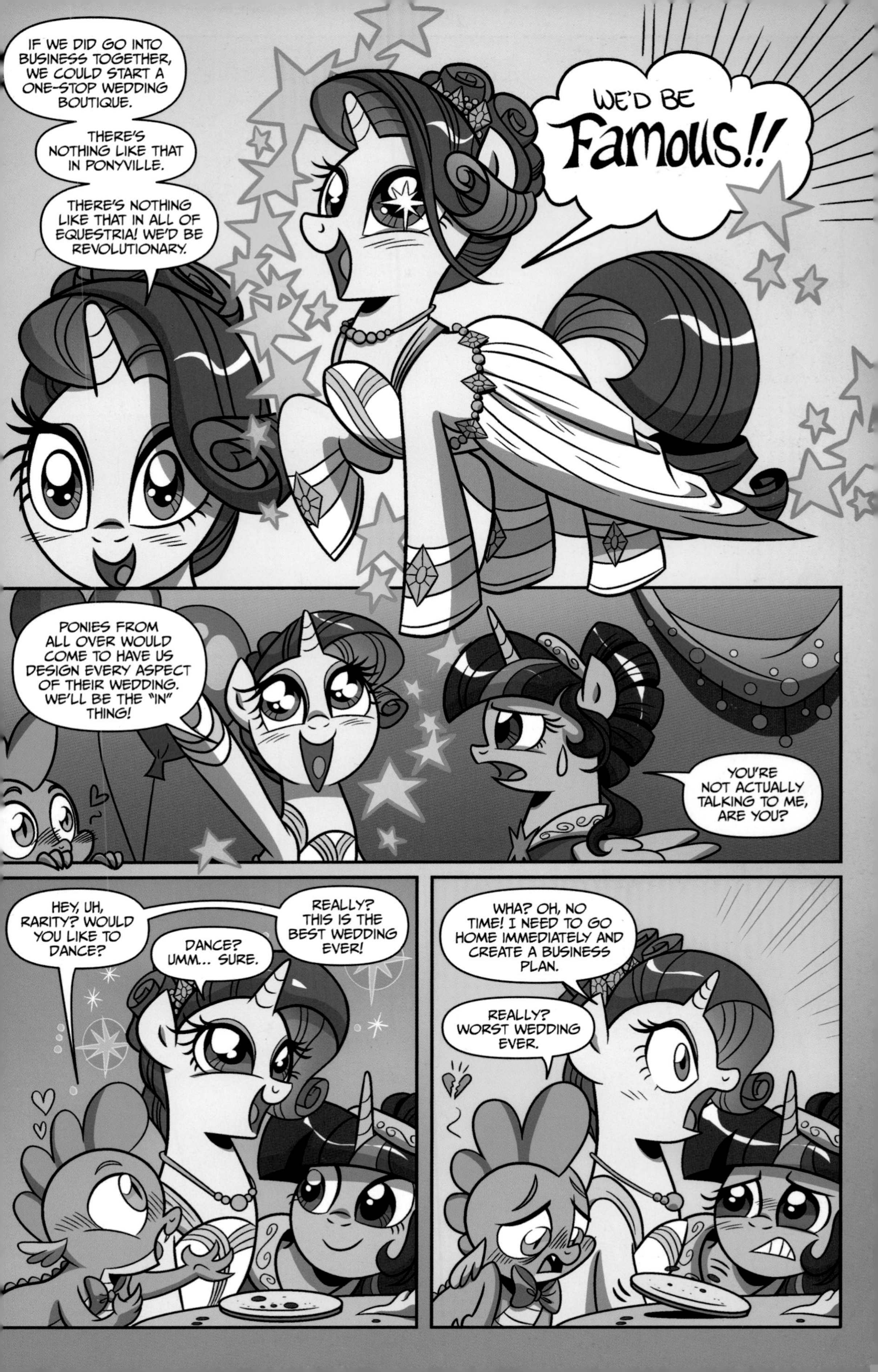
IF WE DID GO INTO BUSINESS TOGETHER, WE COULD START A ONE-STOP WEDDING BOUTIQUE.
THERE'S NOTHING LIKE THAT IN PONYVILLE.
THERE'S NOTHING LIKE THAT IN ALL OF EQUESTRIA! WE'D BE REVOLUTIONARY.
WE'D BE Famous!!
PONIES FROM ALL OVER WOULD COME TO HAVE US DESIGN EVERY ASPECT OF THEIR WEDDING. WE'LL BE THE "IN" THING!
YOU'RE NOT ACTUALLY TALKING TO ME, ARE YOU?
HEY, UH, RARITY? WOULD YOU LIKE TO DANCE?
DANCE? UMM... SURE.
REALLY? THIS IS THE BEST WEDDING EVER!
WHA? OH, NO TIME! I NEED TO GO HOME IMMEDIATELY AND CREATE A BUSINESS PLAN.
REALLY? WORST WEDDING EVER.

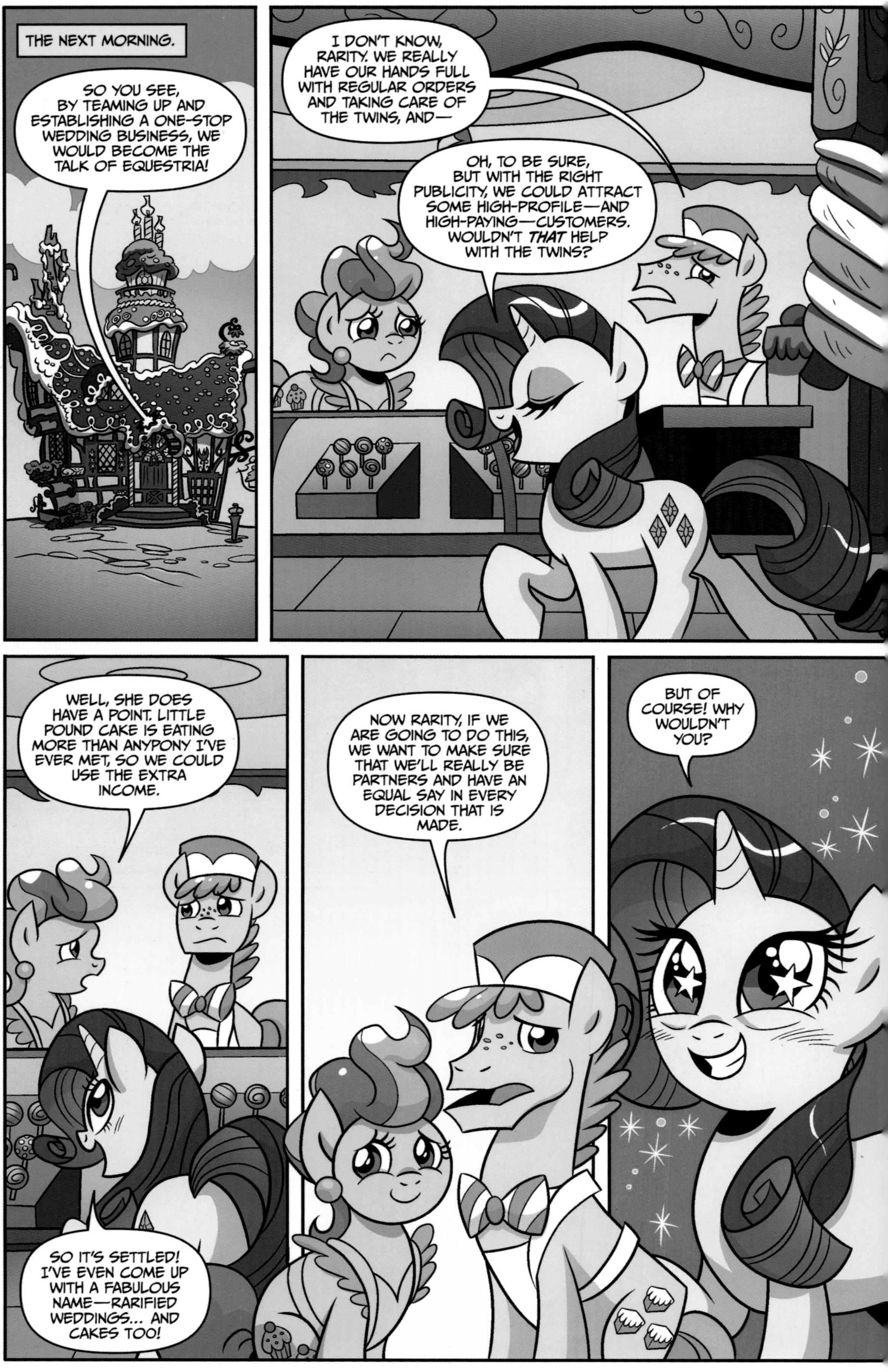
THE NEXT MORNING.
SO YOU SEE, BY TEAMING UP AND ESTABLISHING A ONE-STOP WEDDING BUSINESS, WE WOULD BECOME THE TALK OF EQUESTRIA!
I DON'T KNOW, RARITY. WE REALLY HAVE OUR HANDS FULL WITH REGULAR ORDERS AND TAKING CARE OF THE TWINS, AND—
OH, TO BE SURE, BUT WITH THE RIGHT PUBLICITY, WE COULD ATTRACT SOME HIGH-PROFILE—AND HIGH-PAYING—CUSTOMERS. WOULDN'T *THAT* HELP WITH THE TWINS?
WELL, SHE DOES HAVE A POINT. LITTLE POUND CAKE IS EATING MORE THAN ANYPONY I'VE EVER MET, SO WE COULD USE THE EXTRA INCOME.
SO IT'S SETTLED! I'VE EVEN COME UP WITH A FABULOUS NAME—RARIFIED WEDDINGS... AND CAKES TOO!
NOW RARITY, IF WE ARE GOING TO DO THIS, WE WANT TO MAKE SURE THAT WE'LL REALLY BE PARTNERS AND HAVE AN EQUAL SAY IN EVERY DECISION THAT IS MADE.
BUT OF COURSE! WHY WOULDN'T YOU?

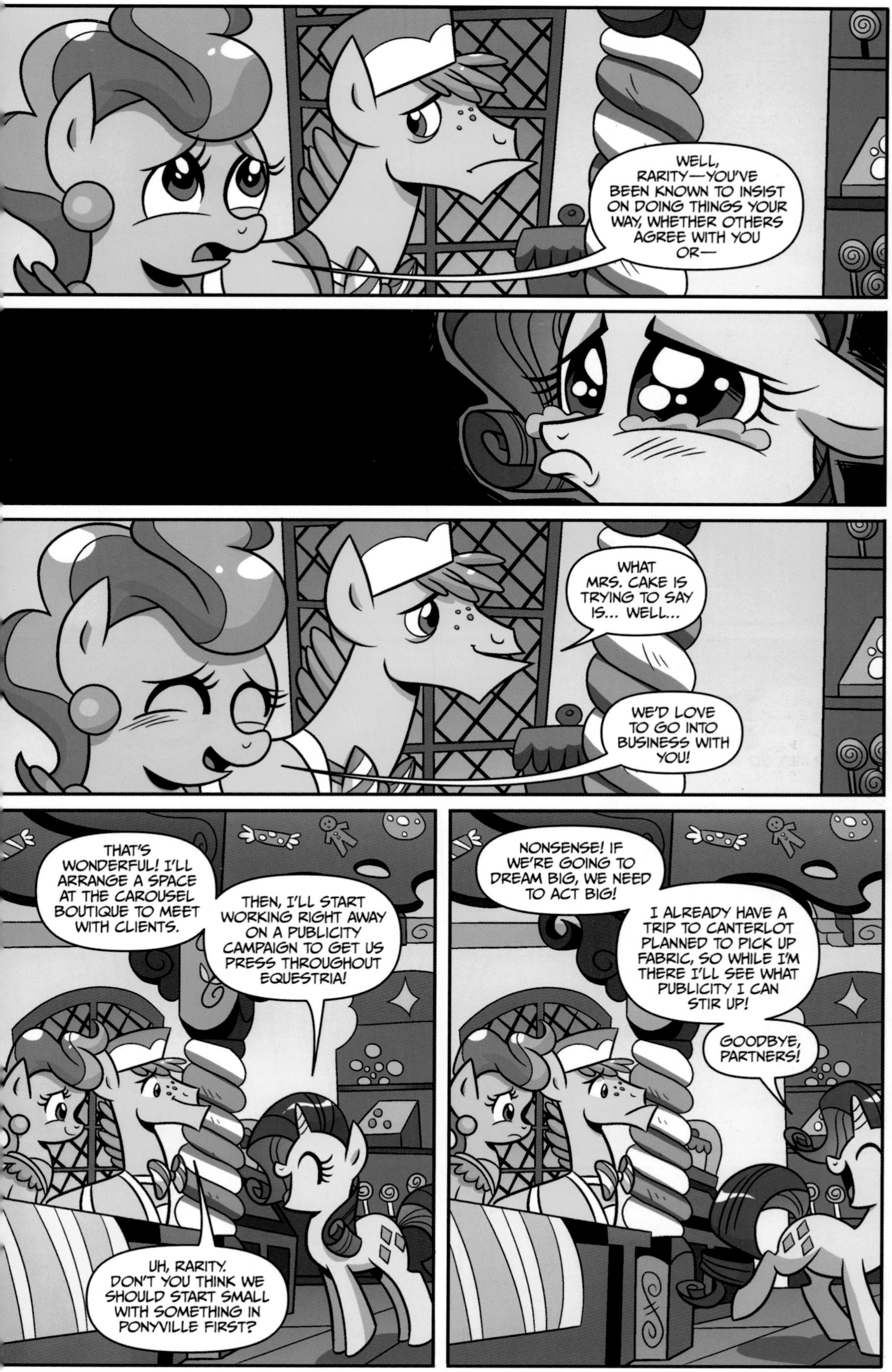
WELL, RARITY—YOU'VE BEEN KNOWN TO INSIST ON DOING THINGS YOUR WAY, WHETHER OTHERS AGREE WITH YOU OR—
WHAT MRS. CAKE IS TRYING TO SAY IS... WELL...
WE'D LOVE TO GO INTO BUSINESS WITH YOU!
THAT'S WONDERFUL! I'LL ARRANGE A SPACE AT THE CAROUSEL BOUTIQUE TO MEET WITH CLIENTS.
THEN, I'LL START WORKING RIGHT AWAY ON A PUBLICITY CAMPAIGN TO GET US PRESS THROUGHOUT EQUESTRIA!
UH, RARITY. DON'T YOU THINK WE SHOULD START SMALL WITH SOMETHING IN PONYVILLE FIRST?
NONSENSE! IF WE'RE GOING TO DREAM BIG, WE NEED TO ACT BIG!
I ALREADY HAVE A TRIP TO CANTERLOT PLANNED TO PICK UP FABRIC, SO WHILE I'M THERE I'LL SEE WHAT PUBLICITY I CAN STIR UP!
GOODBYE, PARTNERS!

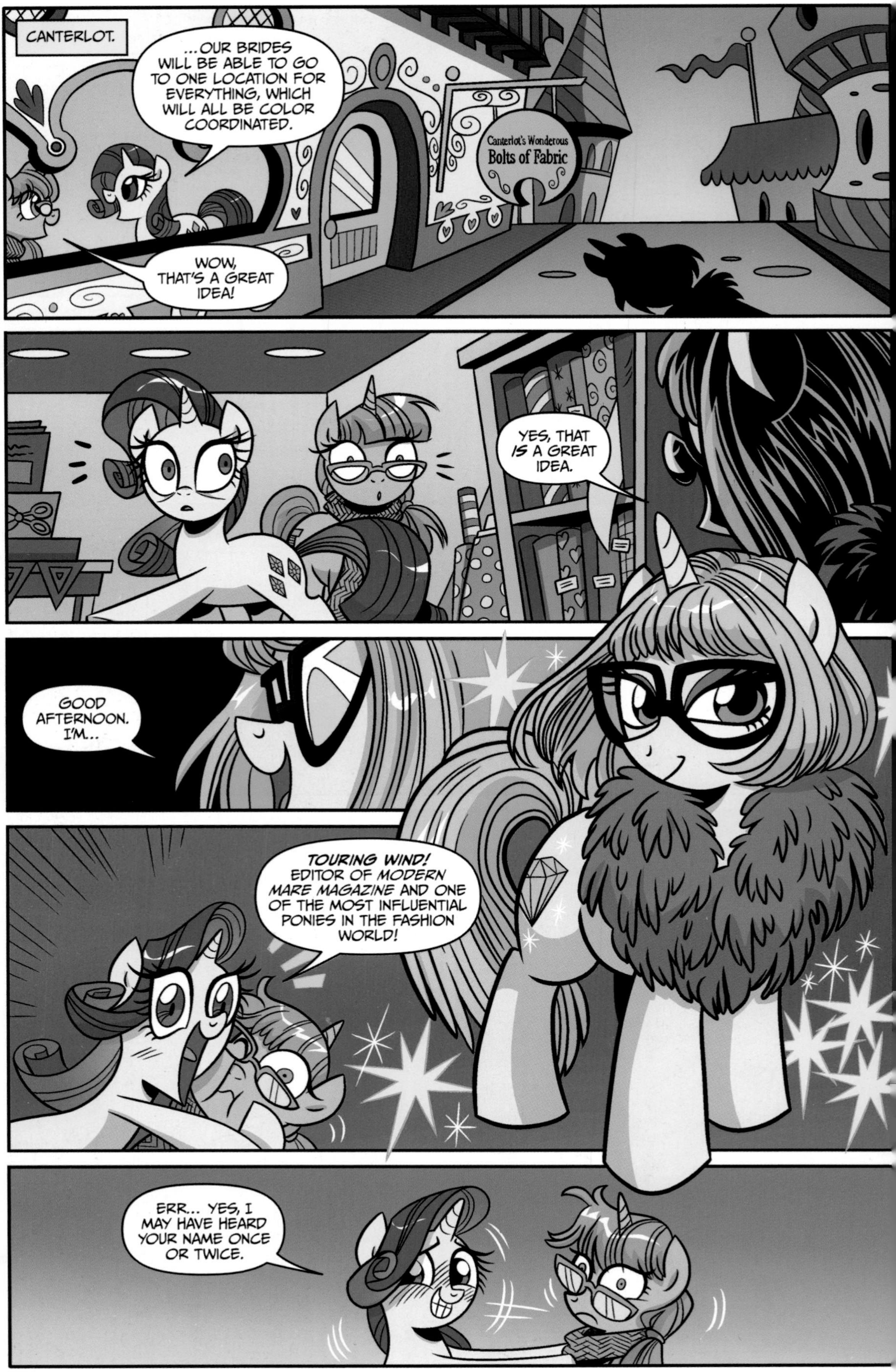
CANTERLOT.
...OUR BRIDES WILL BE ABLE TO GO TO ONE LOCATION FOR EVERYTHING, WHICH WILL ALL BE COLOR COORDINATED.
Canterlot's Wonderous Bolts of Fabric
WOW, THAT'S A GREAT IDEA!
YES, THAT *IS* A GREAT IDEA.
GOOD AFTERNOON. I'M...
TOURING WIND! EDITOR OF *MODERN MARE MAGAZINE* AND ONE OF THE MOST INFLUENTIAL PONIES IN THE FASHION WORLD!
ERR... YES, I MAY HAVE HEARD YOUR NAME ONCE OR TWICE.

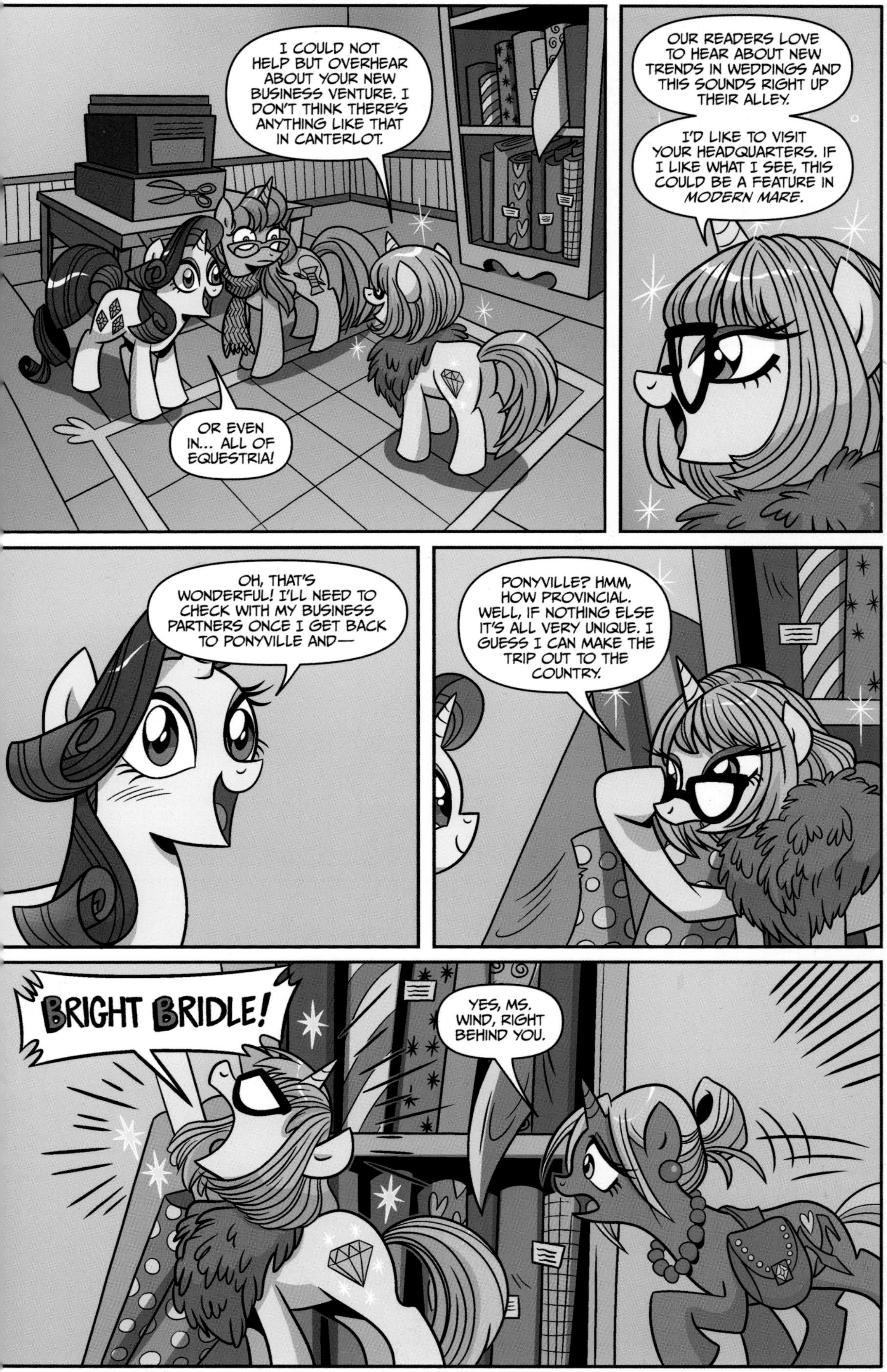
I COULD NOT HELP BUT OVERHEAR ABOUT YOUR NEW BUSINESS VENTURE. I DON'T THINK THERE'S ANYTHING LIKE THAT IN CANTERLOT.
OR EVEN IN... ALL OF EQUESTRIA!
OUR READERS LOVE TO HEAR ABOUT NEW TRENDS IN WEDDINGS AND THIS SOUNDS RIGHT UP THEIR ALLEY.
I'D LIKE TO VISIT YOUR HEADQUARTERS. IF I LIKE WHAT I SEE, THIS COULD BE A FEATURE IN *MODERN MARE*.
OH, THAT'S WONDERFUL! I'LL NEED TO CHECK WITH MY BUSINESS PARTNERS ONCE I GET BACK TO PONYVILLE AND—
PONYVILLE? HMM, HOW PROVINCIAL. WELL, IF NOTHING ELSE IT'S ALL VERY UNIQUE. I GUESS I CAN MAKE THE TRIP OUT TO THE COUNTRY.
BRIGHT BRIDLE!
YES, MS. WIND, RIGHT BEHIND YOU.

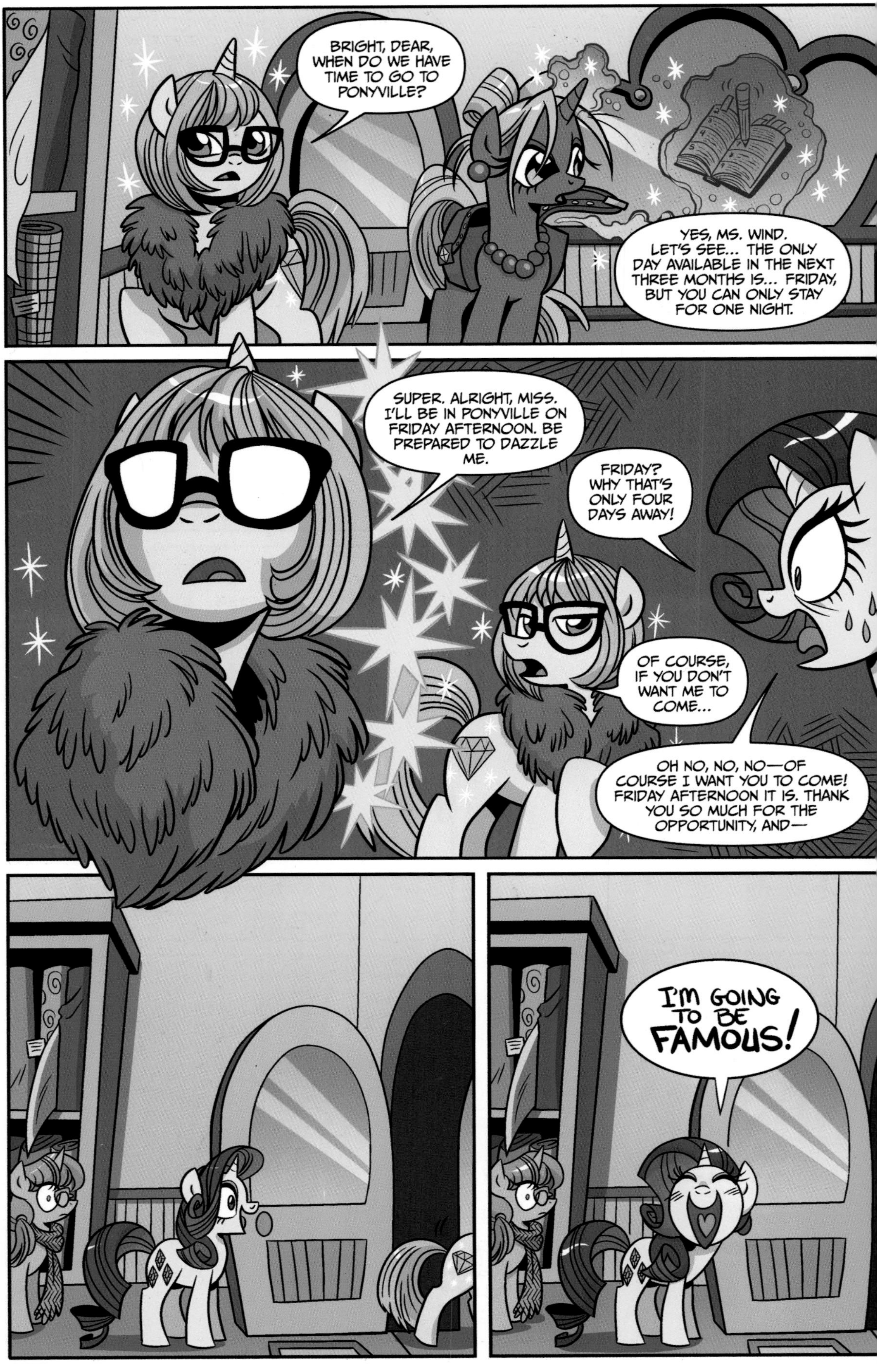
BRIGHT, DEAR, WHEN DO WE HAVE TIME TO GO TO PONYVILLE?
YES, MS. WIND. LET'S SEE... THE ONLY DAY AVAILABLE IN THE NEXT THREE MONTHS IS... FRIDAY, BUT YOU CAN ONLY STAY FOR ONE NIGHT.
SUPER. ALRIGHT, MISS. I'LL BE IN PONYVILLE ON FRIDAY AFTERNOON. BE PREPARED TO DAZZLE ME.
FRIDAY? WHY THAT'S ONLY FOUR DAYS AWAY!
OF COURSE, IF YOU DON'T WANT ME TO COME...
OH NO, NO, NO—OF COURSE I WANT YOU TO COME! FRIDAY AFTERNOON IT IS. THANK YOU SO MUCH FOR THE OPPORTUNITY, AND—
I'M GOING TO BE FAMOUS!

OH, SPIKE, IT WAS REALLY DARLING OF YOU TO MEET ME AT THE TRAIN STATION AND GATHER MY FEW PARCELS.

NOT A PROBLEM. ALWAYS. HAPPY. TO. HELP.

THERE'S SO MUCH TO DO TO PREPARE FOR TOURING WIND'S VISIT. DON'T FORGET YOU'LL NEED TO MEET HER AT THE STATION. I'LL JUST DROP OFF THE LUGGAGE AND THEN HEAD OVER TO THE—

CAKES!

HOWDY, SUGARCUBE!

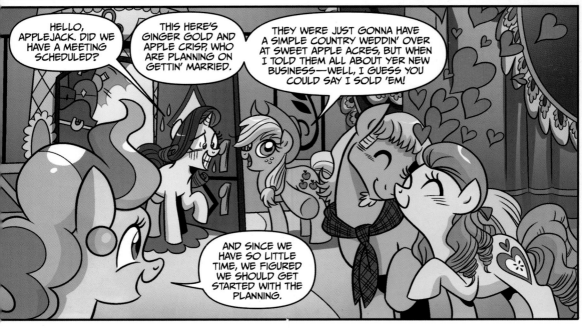

HELLO, APPLEJACK. DID WE HAVE A MEETING SCHEDULED?

THIS HERE'S GINGER GOLD AND APPLE CRISP, WHO ARE PLANNING ON GETTIN' MARRIED.

THEY WERE JUST GONNA HAVE A SIMPLE COUNTRY WEDDIN' OVER AT SWEET APPLE ACRES, BUT WHEN I TOLD THEM ALL ABOUT YER NEW BUSINESS—WELL, I GUESS YOU COULD SAY I SOLD 'EM!

AND SINCE WE HAVE SO LITTLE TIME, WE FIGURED WE SHOULD GET STARTED WITH THE PLANNING.

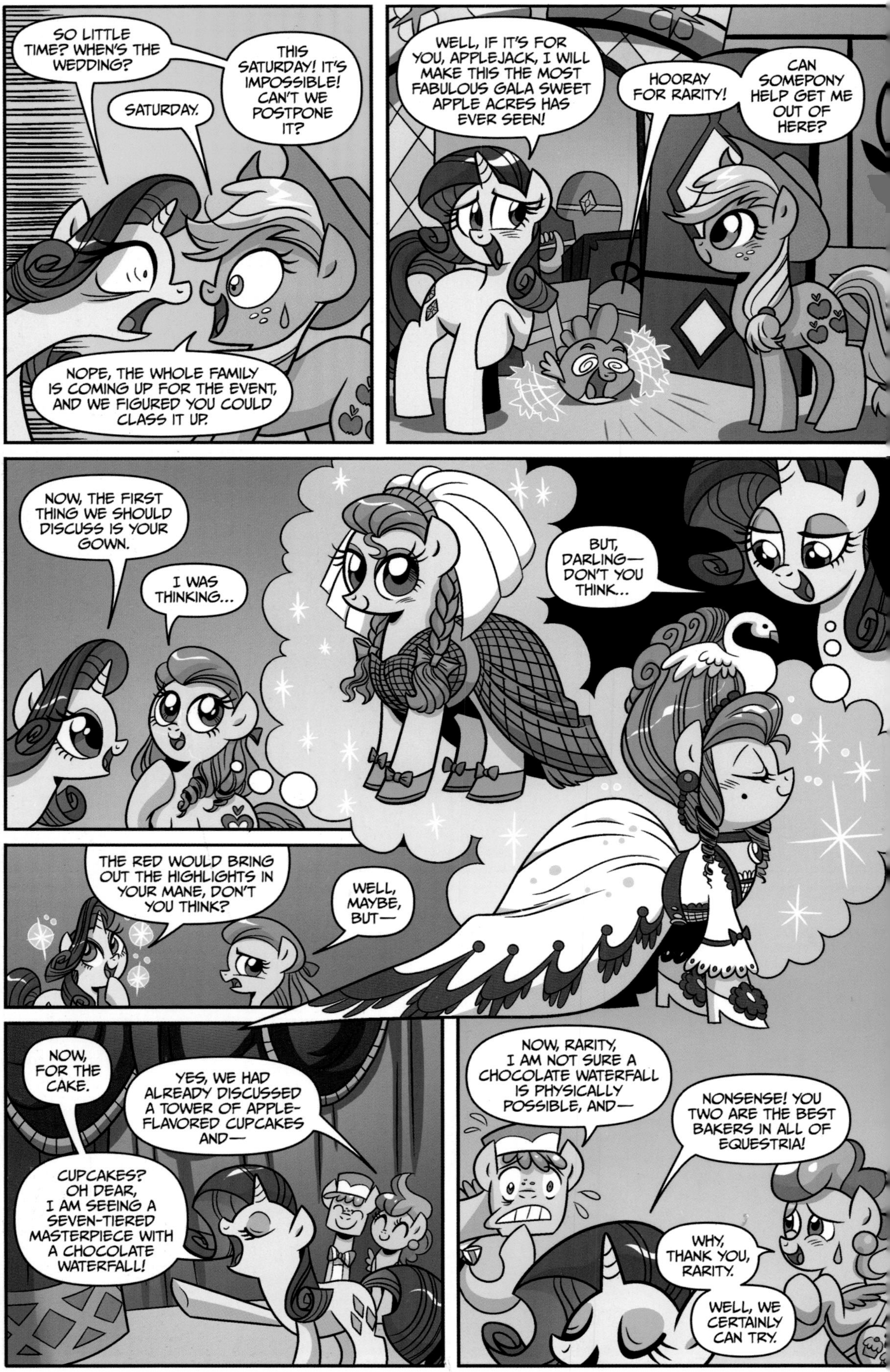
SO LITTLE TIME? WHEN'S THE WEDDING?
SATURDAY.
THIS SATURDAY! IT'S IMPOSSIBLE! CAN'T WE POSTPONE IT?
NOPE, THE WHOLE FAMILY IS COMING UP FOR THE EVENT, AND WE FIGURED YOU COULD CLASS IT UP.
WELL, IF IT'S FOR YOU, APPLEJACK, I WILL MAKE THIS THE MOST FABULOUS GALA SWEET APPLE ACRES HAS EVER SEEN!
HOORAY FOR RARITY!
CAN SOMEPONY HELP GET ME OUT OF HERE?
NOW, THE FIRST THING WE SHOULD DISCUSS IS YOUR GOWN.
I WAS THINKING...
BUT, DARLING— DON'T YOU THINK...
THE RED WOULD BRING OUT THE HIGHLIGHTS IN YOUR MANE, DON'T YOU THINK?
WELL, MAYBE, BUT—
NOW, FOR THE CAKE.
YES, WE HAD ALREADY DISCUSSED A TOWER OF APPLE-FLAVORED CUPCAKES AND—
CUPCAKES? OH DEAR, I AM SEEING A SEVEN-TIERED MASTERPIECE WITH A CHOCOLATE WATERFALL!
NOW, RARITY, I AM NOT SURE A CHOCOLATE WATERFALL IS PHYSICALLY POSSIBLE, AND—
NONSENSE! YOU TWO ARE THE BEST BAKERS IN ALL OF EQUESTRIA!
WHY, THANK YOU, RARITY.
WELL, WE CERTAINLY CAN TRY.

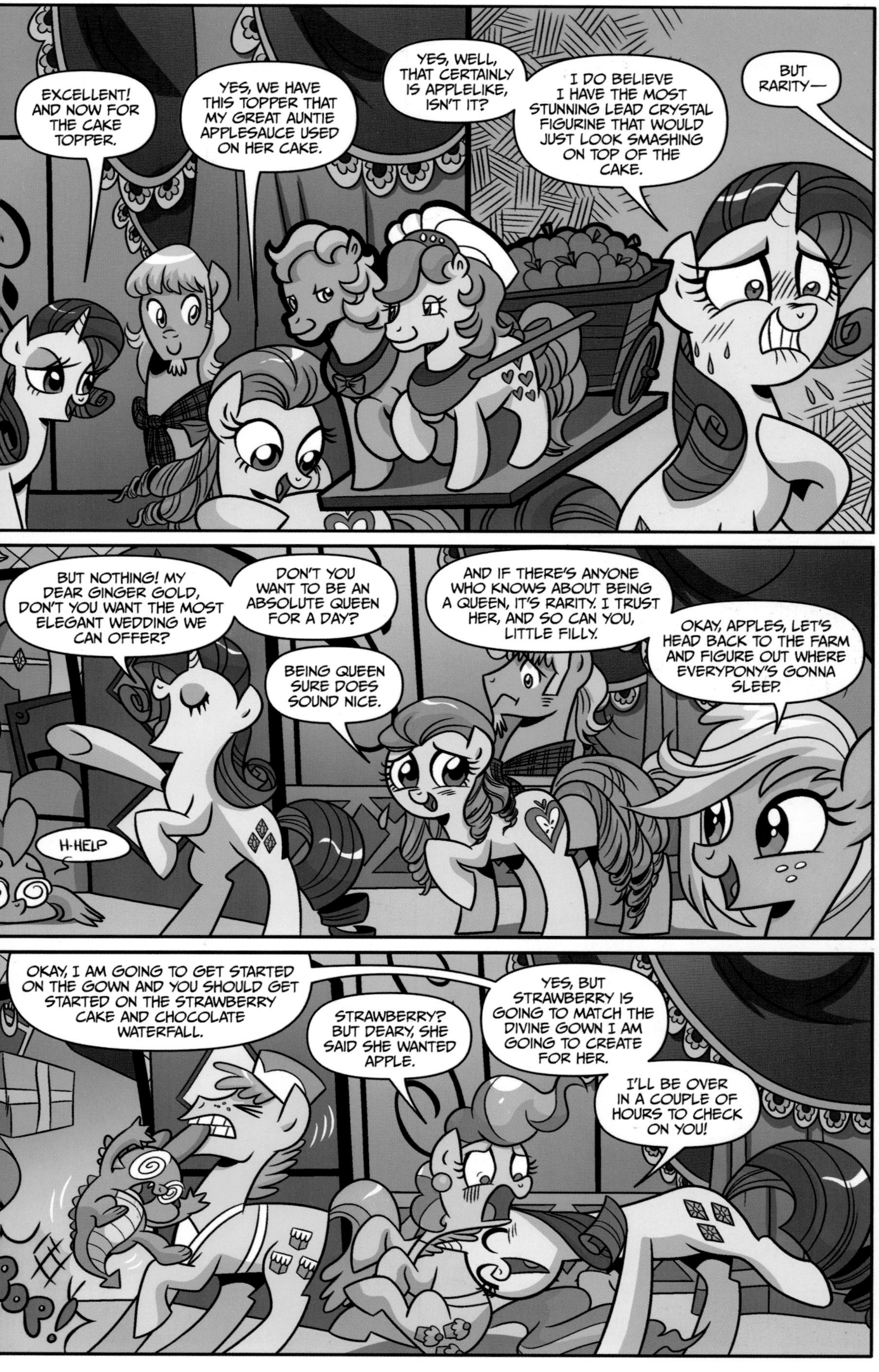
EXCELLENT! AND NOW FOR THE CAKE TOPPER.
YES, WE HAVE THIS TOPPER THAT MY GREAT AUNTIE APPLESAUCE USED ON HER CAKE.
YES, WELL, THAT CERTAINLY IS APPLELIKE, ISN'T IT?
I DO BELIEVE I HAVE THE MOST STUNNING LEAD CRYSTAL FIGURINE THAT WOULD JUST LOOK SMASHING ON TOP OF THE CAKE.
BUT RARITY—
BUT NOTHING! MY DEAR GINGER GOLD, DON'T YOU WANT THE MOST ELEGANT WEDDING WE CAN OFFER?
DON'T YOU WANT TO BE AN ABSOLUTE QUEEN FOR A DAY?
BEING QUEEN SURE DOES SOUND NICE.
H-HELP
AND IF THERE'S ANYONE WHO KNOWS ABOUT BEING A QUEEN, IT'S RARITY. I TRUST HER, AND SO CAN YOU, LITTLE FILLY.
OKAY, APPLES, LET'S HEAD BACK TO THE FARM AND FIGURE OUT WHERE EVERYPONY'S GONNA SLEEP.
OKAY, I AM GOING TO GET STARTED ON THE GOWN AND YOU SHOULD GET STARTED ON THE STRAWBERRY CAKE AND CHOCOLATE WATERFALL.
STRAWBERRY? BUT DEARY, SHE SAID SHE WANTED APPLE.
YES, BUT STRAWBERRY IS GOING TO MATCH THE DIVINE GOWN I AM GOING TO CREATE FOR HER.
I'LL BE OVER IN A COUPLE OF HOURS TO CHECK ON YOU!
BOP!

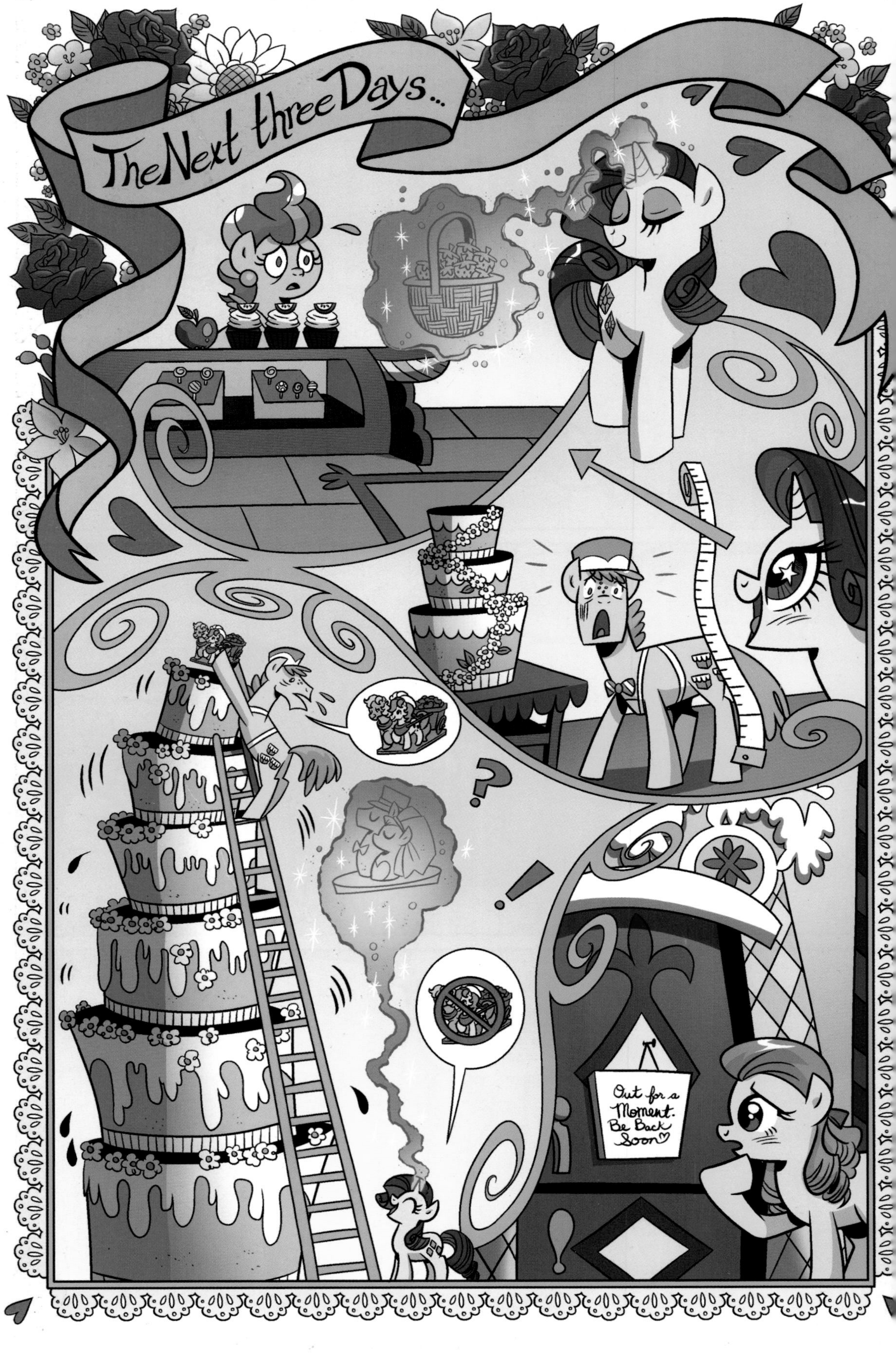
The Next three Days...
?
!
Out for a Moment. Be Back Soon♡

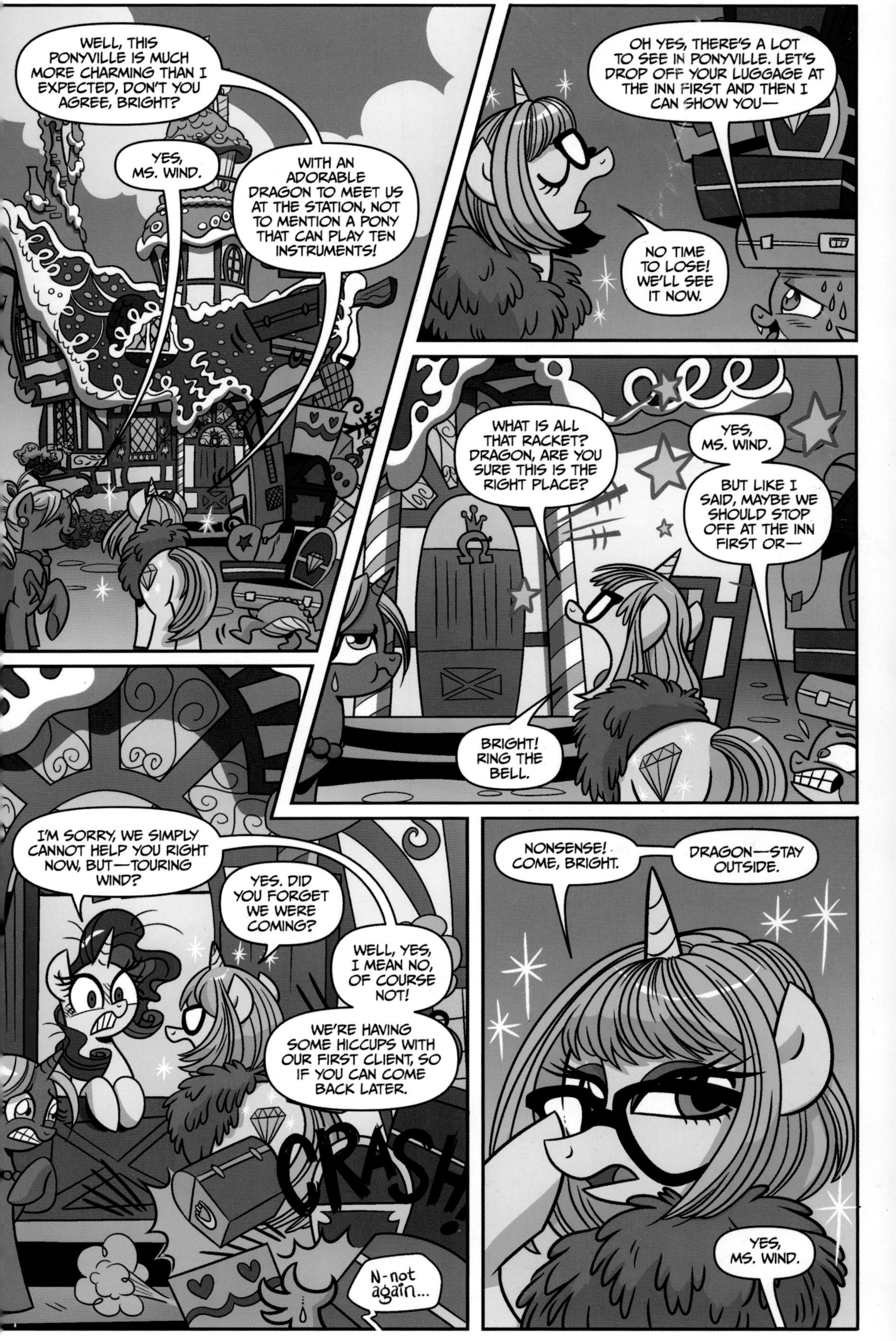
WELL, THIS PONYVILLE IS MUCH MORE CHARMING THAN I EXPECTED, DON'T YOU AGREE, BRIGHT?
YES, MS. WIND.
WITH AN ADORABLE DRAGON TO MEET US AT THE STATION, NOT TO MENTION A PONY THAT CAN PLAY TEN INSTRUMENTS!
OH YES, THERE'S A LOT TO SEE IN PONYVILLE. LET'S DROP OFF YOUR LUGGAGE AT THE INN FIRST AND THEN I CAN SHOW YOU—
NO TIME TO LOSE! WE'LL SEE IT NOW.
WHAT IS ALL THAT RACKET? DRAGON, ARE YOU SURE THIS IS THE RIGHT PLACE?
YES, MS. WIND.
BUT LIKE I SAID, MAYBE WE SHOULD STOP OFF AT THE INN FIRST OR—
BRIGHT! RING THE BELL.
I'M SORRY, WE SIMPLY CANNOT HELP YOU RIGHT NOW, BUT—TOURING WIND?
YES. DID YOU FORGET WE WERE COMING?
WELL, YES, I MEAN NO, OF COURSE NOT!
WE'RE HAVING SOME HICCUPS WITH OUR FIRST CLIENT, SO IF YOU CAN COME BACK LATER.
CRASH!
N-not again...
NONSENSE! COME, BRIGHT.
DRAGON—STAY OUTSIDE.
YES, MS. WIND.

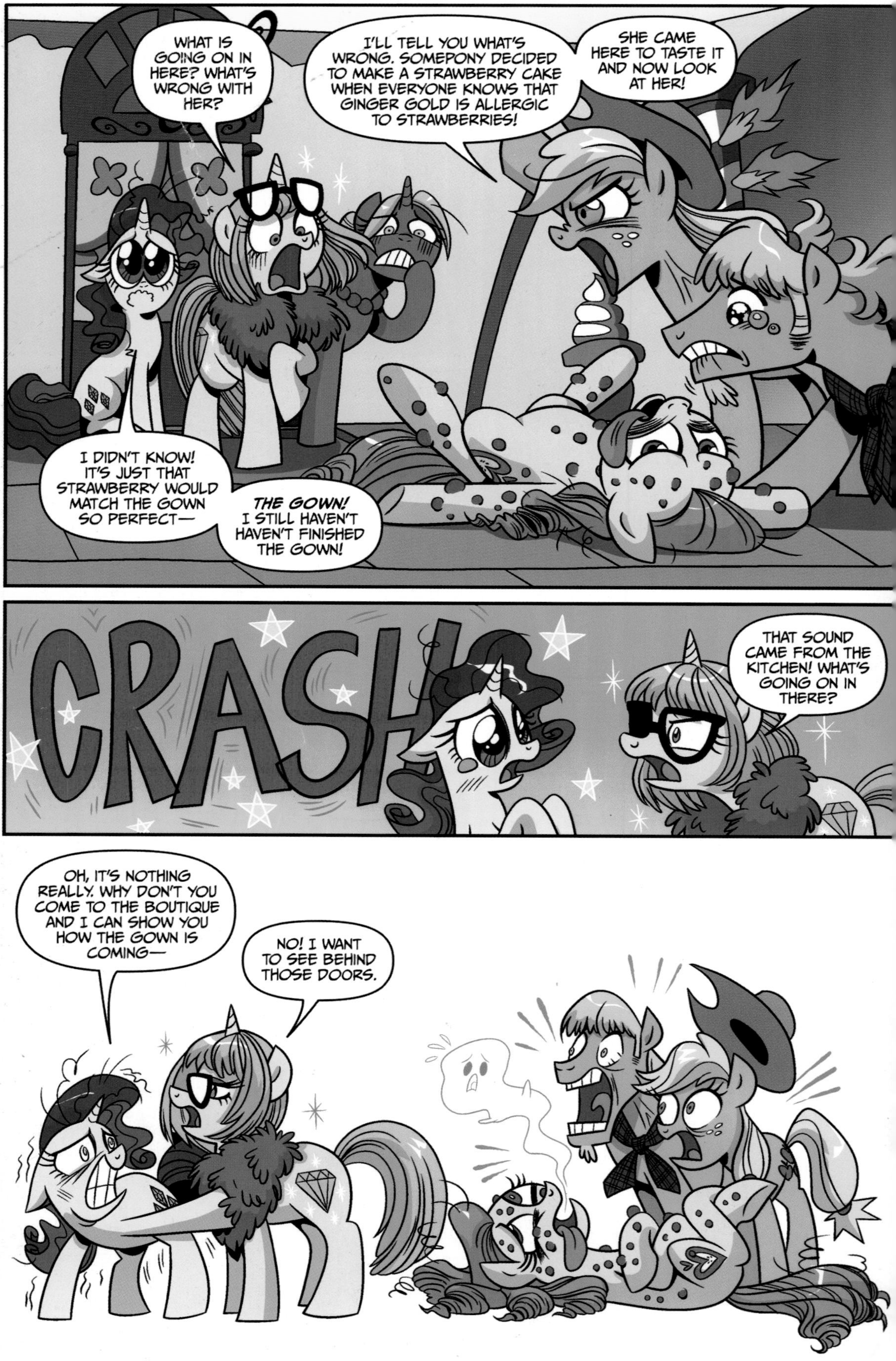

WHAT IS GOING ON IN HERE? WHAT'S WRONG WITH HER?
I'LL TELL YOU WHAT'S WRONG. SOMEPONY DECIDED TO MAKE A STRAWBERRY CAKE WHEN EVERYONE KNOWS THAT GINGER GOLD IS ALLERGIC TO STRAWBERRIES!
SHE CAME HERE TO TASTE IT AND NOW LOOK AT HER!
I DIDN'T KNOW! IT'S JUST THAT STRAWBERRY WOULD MATCH THE GOWN SO PERFECT—
THE GOWN! I STILL HAVEN'T HAVEN'T FINISHED THE GOWN!
CRASH!
THAT SOUND CAME FROM THE KITCHEN! WHAT'S GOING ON IN THERE?
OH, IT'S NOTHING REALLY. WHY DON'T YOU COME TO THE BOUTIQUE AND I CAN SHOW YOU HOW THE GOWN IS COMING—
NO! I WANT TO SEE BEHIND THOSE DOORS.

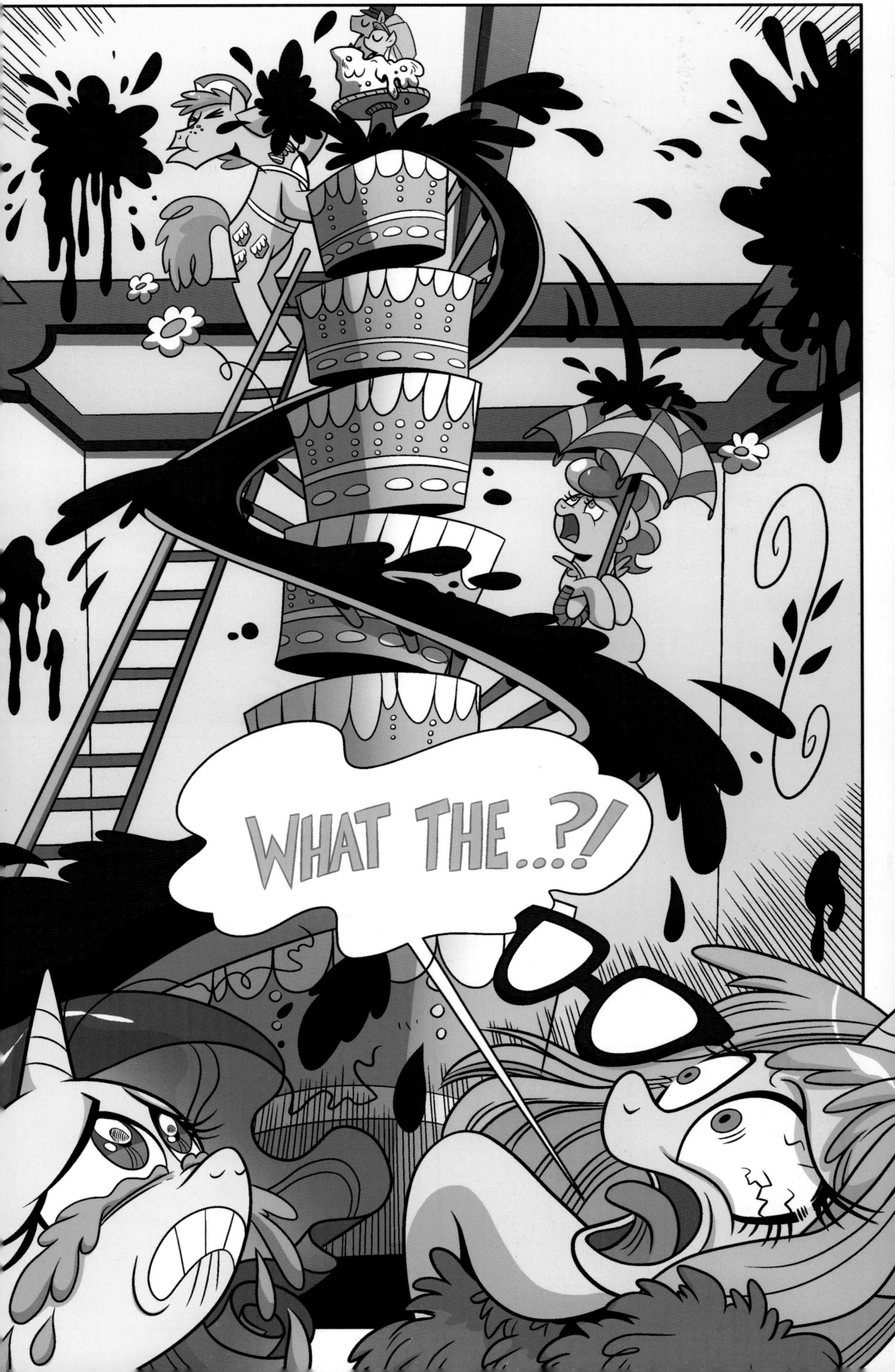
WHAT THE...?!

I HAVE NEVER SEEN SUCH RANK AMATEURS IN ALL MY LIFE!

WELL, CERTAINLY EVERY BUSINESS HAS A FEW BUMPS IN THE ROAD AT FIRST.

COMING THROUGH, DEARIES!

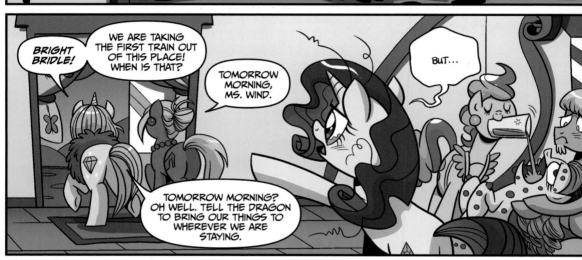

BRIGHT BRIDLE!

WE ARE TAKING THE FIRST TRAIN OUT OF THIS PLACE! WHEN IS THAT?

TOMORROW MORNING, MS. WIND.

BUT...

TOMORROW MORNING? OH WELL. TELL THE DRAGON TO BRING OUR THINGS TO WHEREVER WE ARE STAYING.

THAT'S IT. WE'LL NEVER GET WRITTEN UP IN *MODERN MARE*. WE'LL NEVER BE FAMOUS THROUGHOUT EQUESTRIA.

EVEN WORSE, I ABSOLUTELY RUINED THE WEDDING! I LET APPLEJACK DOWN!

I'M A TERRIBLE PONY!

IT'S NOT ALL THAT BAD, DEARY.

IT'S NOT? WHY, GINGER GOLD—YOU'RE CURED? MRS. CAKE, I DIDN'T THINK YOU KNEW MAGIC!

IT'S NOT MAGIC. JUST AN OLD FASHIONED HOME REMEDY.

LITTLE PUMPKIN IS ALSO ALLERGIC TO STRAWBERRIES, BUT STILL MANAGES TO FIND AND EAT THEM. WE KEEP A JAR OF THIS READY AT ALL TIMES.

BUT THE WEDDING IS STILL RUINED!

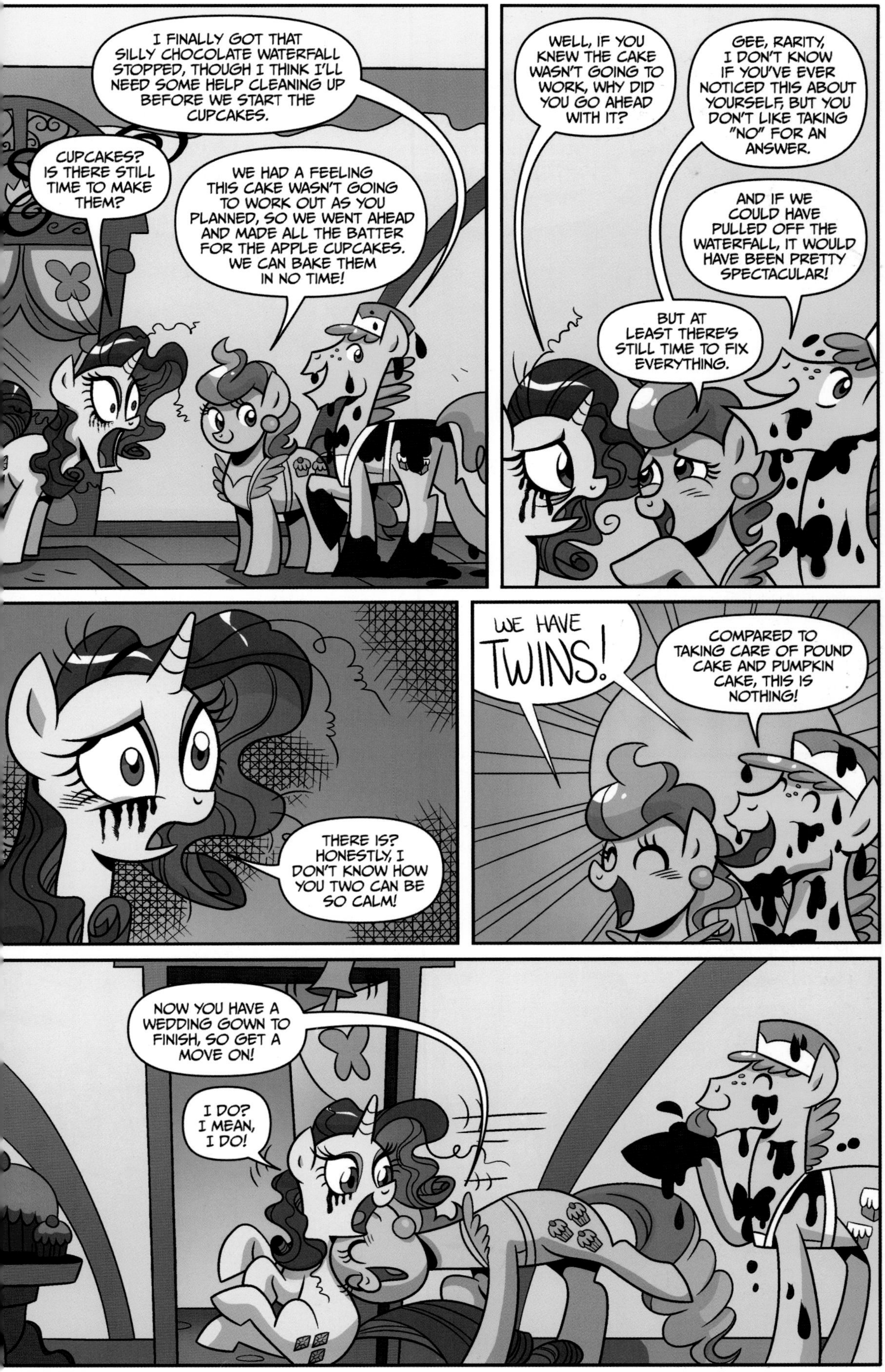
I FINALLY GOT THAT SILLY CHOCOLATE WATERFALL STOPPED, THOUGH I THINK I'LL NEED SOME HELP CLEANING UP BEFORE WE START THE CUPCAKES.
CUPCAKES? IS THERE STILL TIME TO MAKE THEM?
WE HAD A FEELING THIS CAKE WASN'T GOING TO WORK OUT AS YOU PLANNED, SO WE WENT AHEAD AND MADE ALL THE BATTER FOR THE APPLE CUPCAKES. WE CAN BAKE THEM IN NO TIME!
WELL, IF YOU KNEW THE CAKE WASN'T GOING TO WORK, WHY DID YOU GO AHEAD WITH IT?
GEE, RARITY, I DON'T KNOW IF YOU'VE EVER NOTICED THIS ABOUT YOURSELF, BUT YOU DON'T LIKE TAKING "NO" FOR AN ANSWER.
AND IF WE COULD HAVE PULLED OFF THE WATERFALL, IT WOULD HAVE BEEN PRETTY SPECTACULAR!
BUT AT LEAST THERE'S STILL TIME TO FIX EVERYTHING.
THERE IS? HONESTLY, I DON'T KNOW HOW YOU TWO CAN BE SO CALM!
WE HAVE TWINS!
COMPARED TO TAKING CARE OF POUND CAKE AND PUMPKIN CAKE, THIS IS NOTHING!
NOW YOU HAVE A WEDDING GOWN TO FINISH, SO GET A MOVE ON!
I DO? I MEAN, I DO!

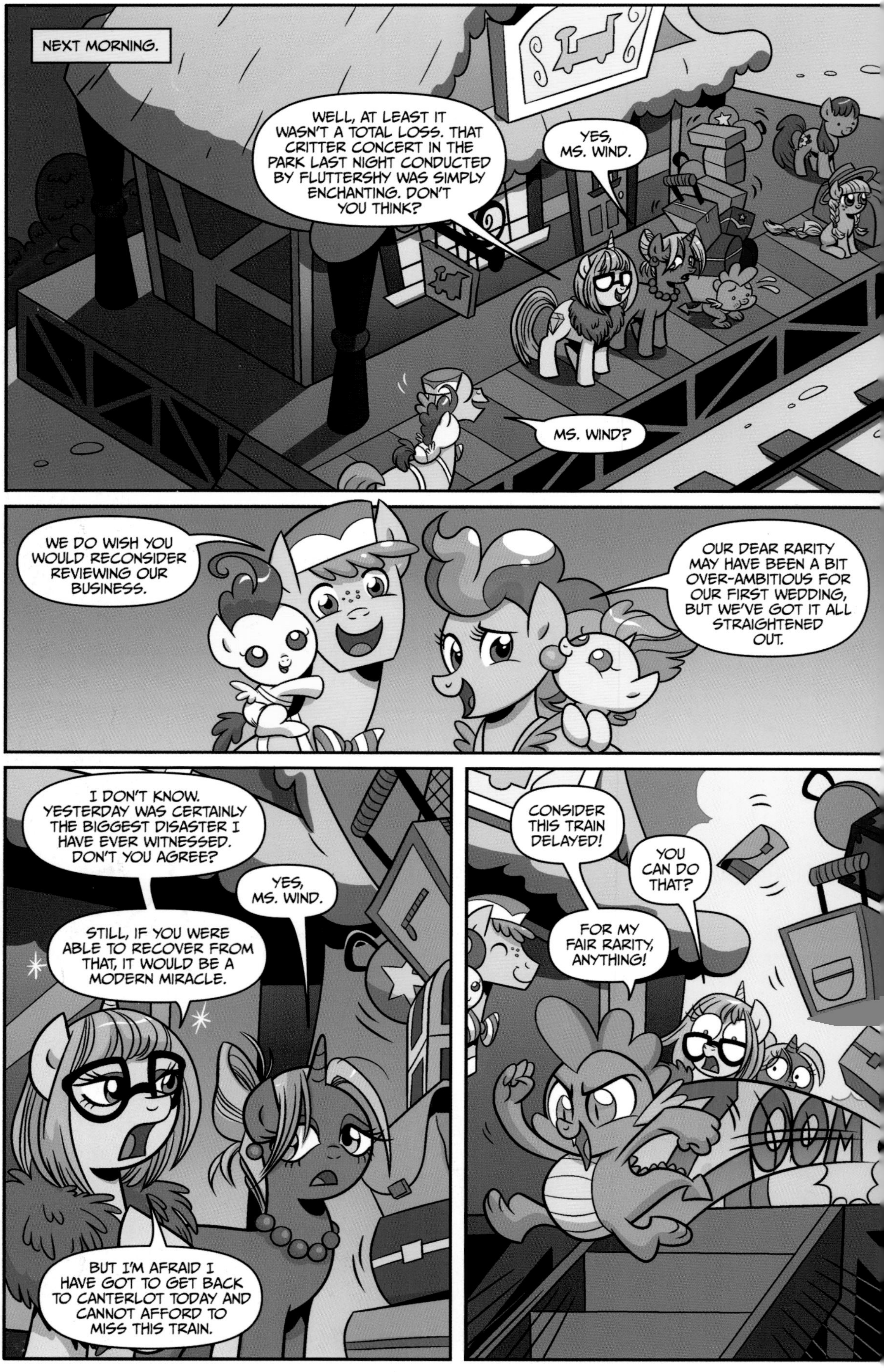
NEXT MORNING.
WELL, AT LEAST IT WASN'T A TOTAL LOSS. THAT CRITTER CONCERT IN THE PARK LAST NIGHT CONDUCTED BY FLUTTERSHY WAS SIMPLY ENCHANTING. DON'T YOU THINK?
YES, MS. WIND.
MS. WIND?
WE DO WISH YOU WOULD RECONSIDER REVIEWING OUR BUSINESS.
OUR DEAR RARITY MAY HAVE BEEN A BIT OVER-AMBITIOUS FOR OUR FIRST WEDDING, BUT WE'VE GOT IT ALL STRAIGHTENED OUT.
I DON'T KNOW. YESTERDAY WAS CERTAINLY THE BIGGEST DISASTER I HAVE EVER WITNESSED. DON'T YOU AGREE?
YES, MS. WIND.
STILL, IF YOU WERE ABLE TO RECOVER FROM THAT, IT WOULD BE A MODERN MIRACLE.
BUT I'M AFRAID I HAVE GOT TO GET BACK TO CANTERLOT TODAY AND CANNOT AFFORD TO MISS THIS TRAIN.
CONSIDER THIS TRAIN DELAYED!
YOU CAN DO THAT?
FOR MY FAIR RARITY, ANYTHING!
OOM

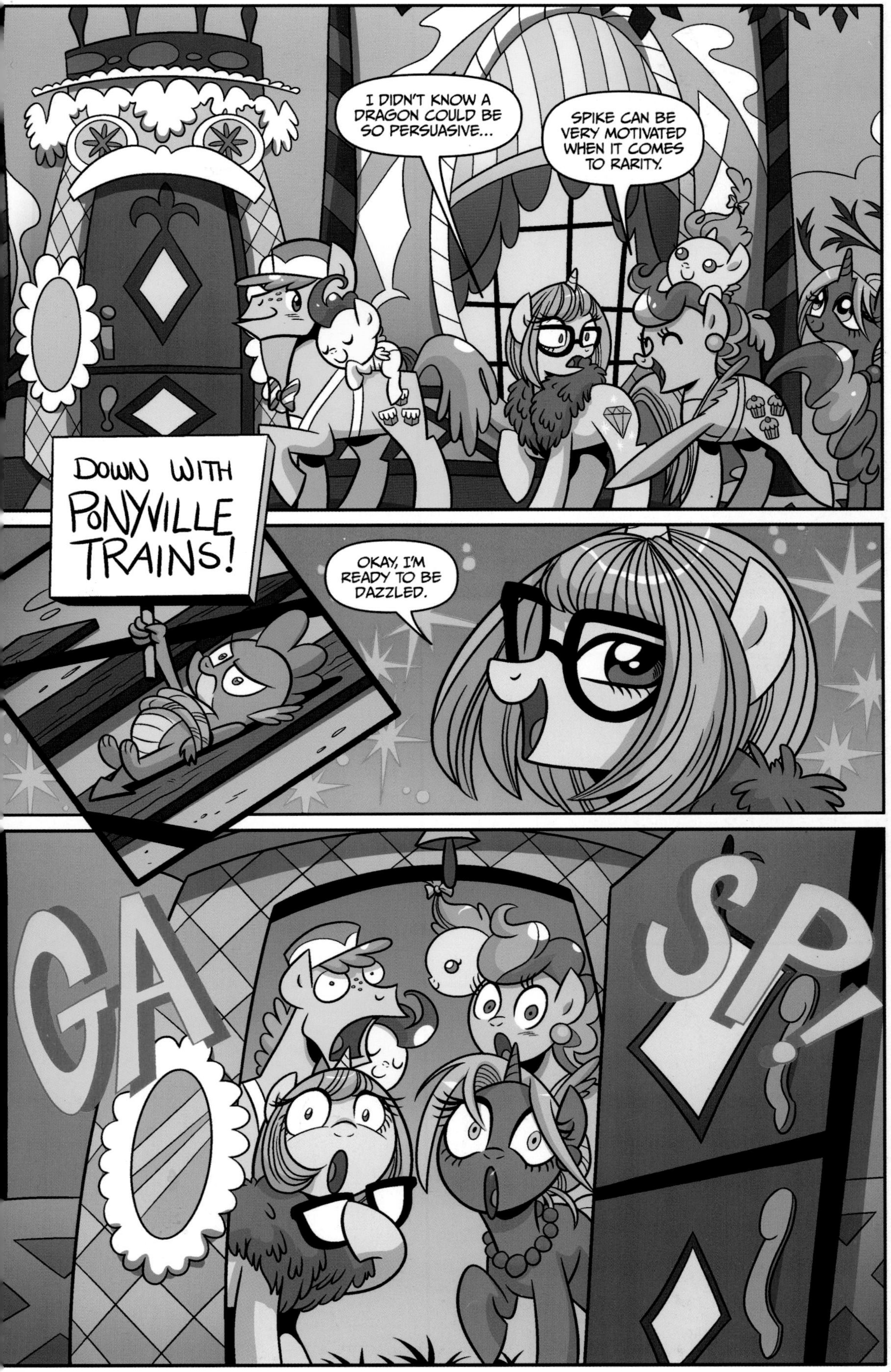

I DIDN'T KNOW A DRAGON COULD BE SO PERSUASIVE...
SPIKE CAN BE VERY MOTIVATED WHEN IT COMES TO RARITY.
DOWN WITH PONYVILLE TRAINS!
OKAY, I'M READY TO BE DAZZLED.
GASP!

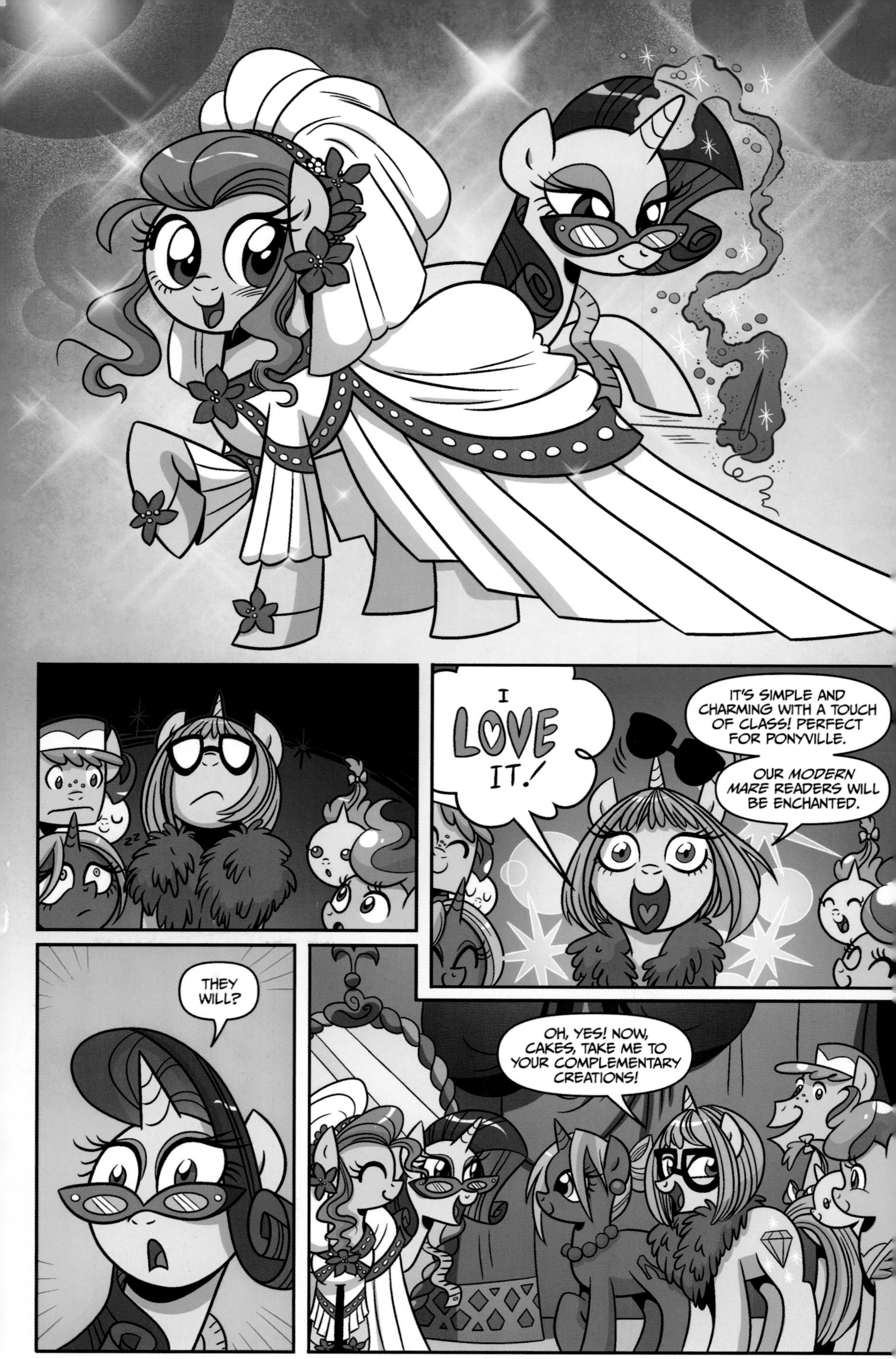
I LOVE IT!
IT'S SIMPLE AND CHARMING WITH A TOUCH OF CLASS! PERFECT FOR PONYVILLE.
OUR MODERN MARE READERS WILL BE ENCHANTED.
THEY WILL?
OH, YES! NOW, CAKES, TAKE ME TO YOUR COMPLEMENTARY CREATIONS!

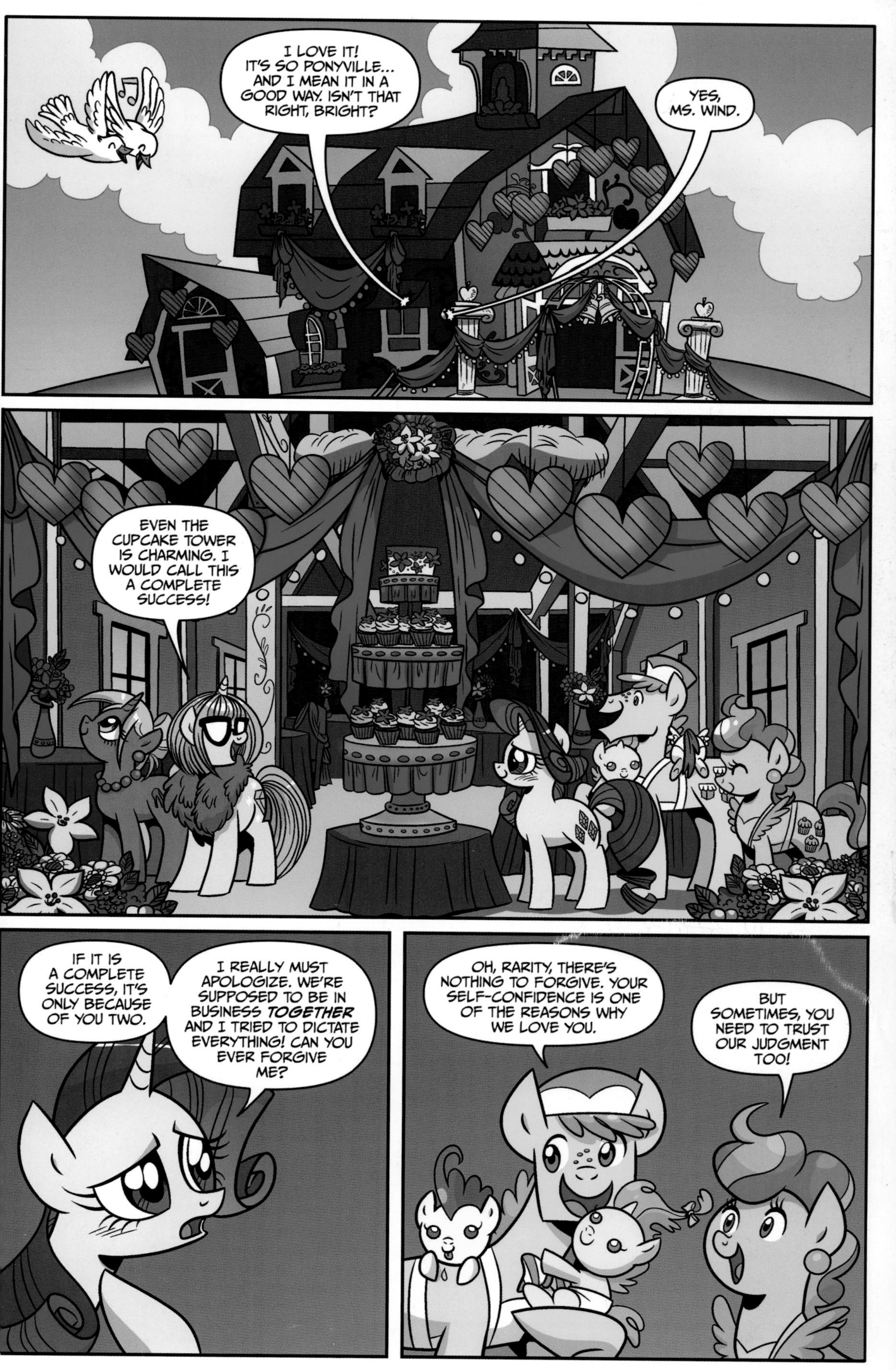
I LOVE IT! IT'S SO PONYVILLE... AND I MEAN IT IN A GOOD WAY. ISN'T THAT RIGHT, BRIGHT?
YES, MS. WIND.
EVEN THE CUPCAKE TOWER IS CHARMING. I WOULD CALL THIS A COMPLETE SUCCESS!
IF IT IS A COMPLETE SUCCESS, IT'S ONLY BECAUSE OF YOU TWO.
I REALLY MUST APOLOGIZE. WE'RE SUPPOSED TO BE IN BUSINESS *TOGETHER* AND I TRIED TO DICTATE EVERYTHING! CAN YOU EVER FORGIVE ME?
OH, RARITY, THERE'S NOTHING TO FORGIVE. YOUR SELF-CONFIDENCE IS ONE OF THE REASONS WHY WE LOVE YOU.
BUT SOMETIMES, YOU NEED TO TRUST OUR JUDGMENT TOO!

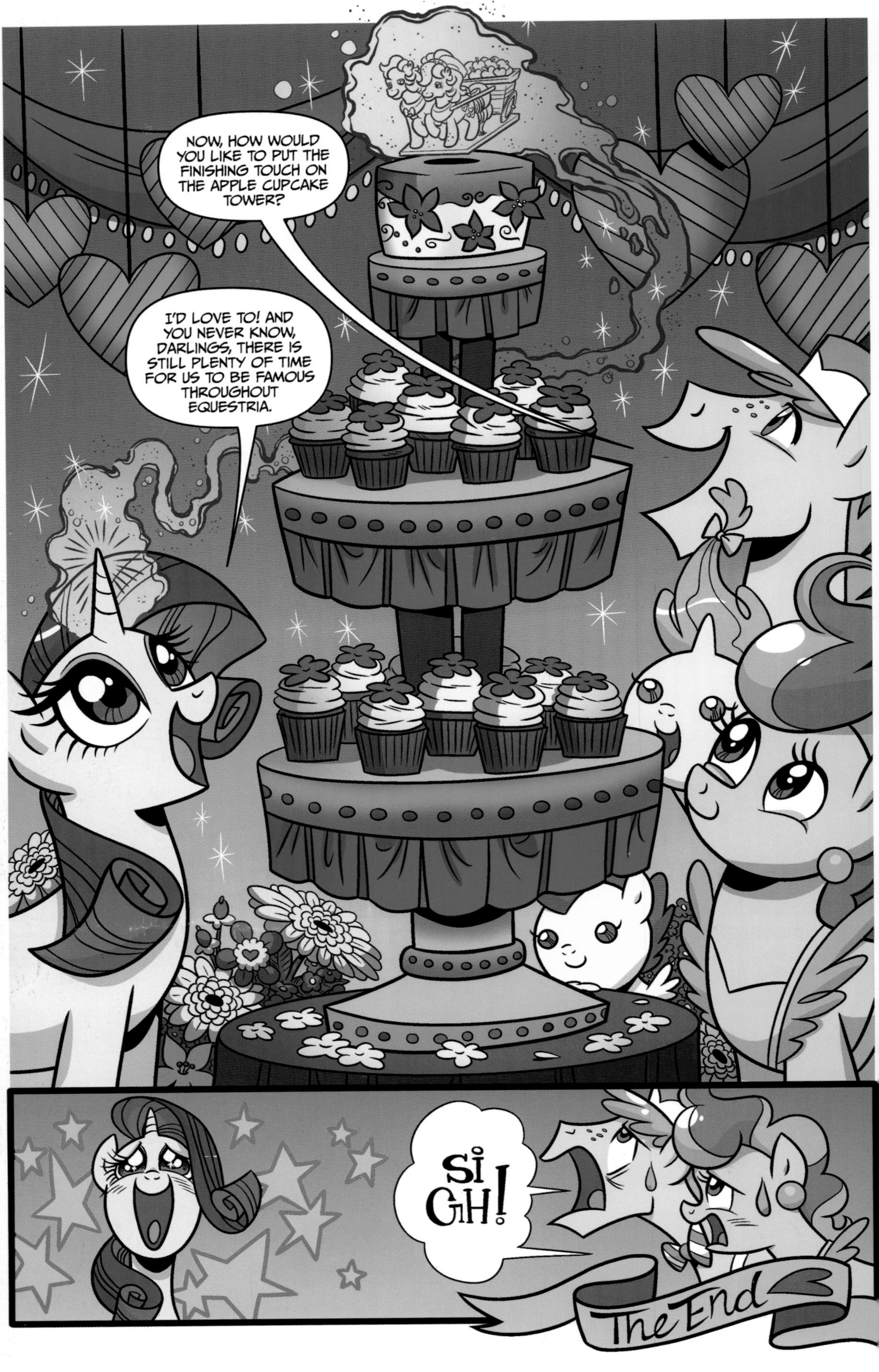
NOW, HOW WOULD YOU LIKE TO PUT THE FINISHING TOUCH ON THE APPLE CUPCAKE TOWER?
I'D LOVE TO! AND YOU NEVER KNOW, DARLINGS, THERE IS STILL PLENTY OF TIME FOR US TO BE FAMOUS THROUGHOUT EQUESTRIA.
SIGH!
The End

My Little Pony
Friends Forever

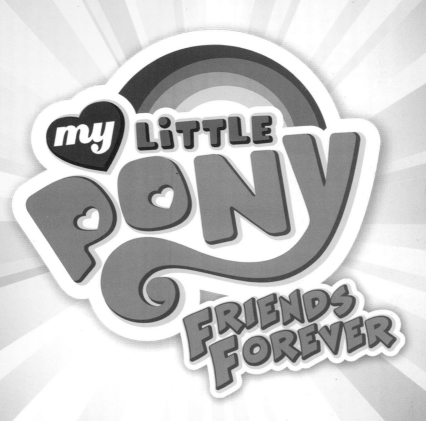

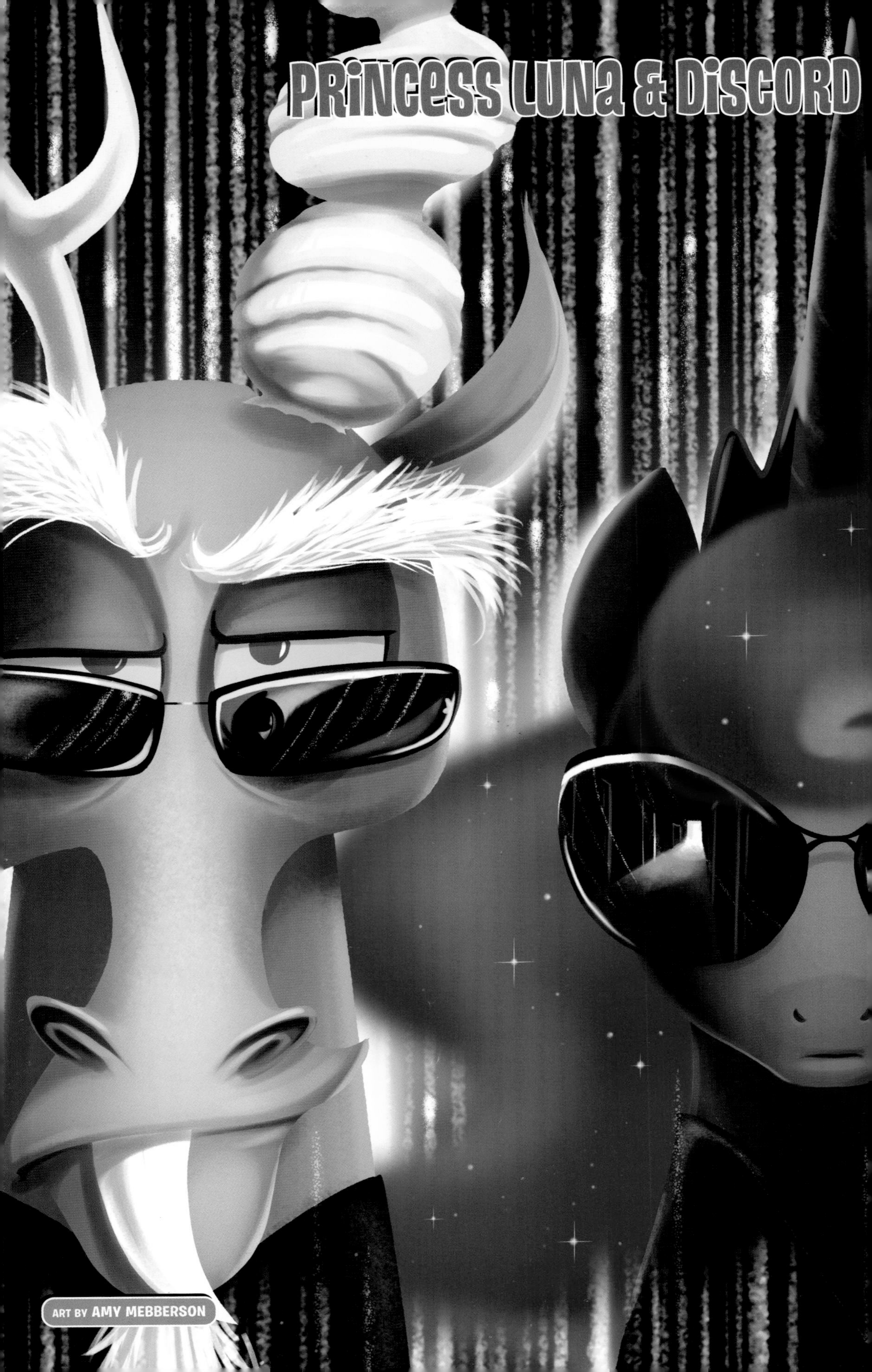
PRINCESS LUNA & DISCORD
ART BY AMY MEBBERSON

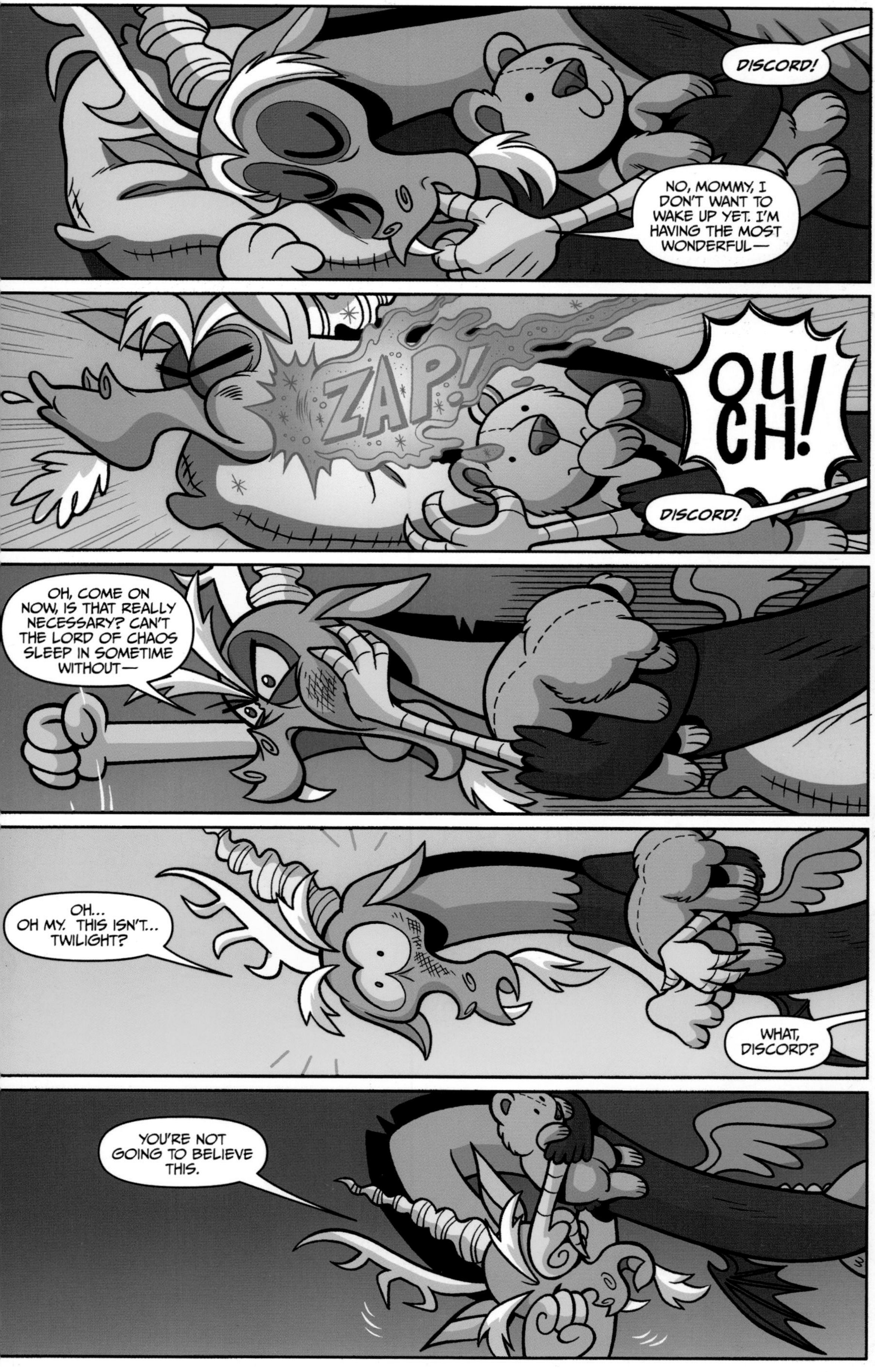
DISCORD!
NO, MOMMY, I DON'T WANT TO WAKE UP YET. I'M HAVING THE MOST WONDERFUL—
ZAP!
OUCH!
DISCORD!
OH, COME ON NOW, IS THAT REALLY NECESSARY? CAN'T THE LORD OF CHAOS SLEEP IN SOMETIME WITHOUT—
OH... OH MY. THIS ISN'T... TWILIGHT?
WHAT, DISCORD?
YOU'RE NOT GOING TO BELIEVE THIS.

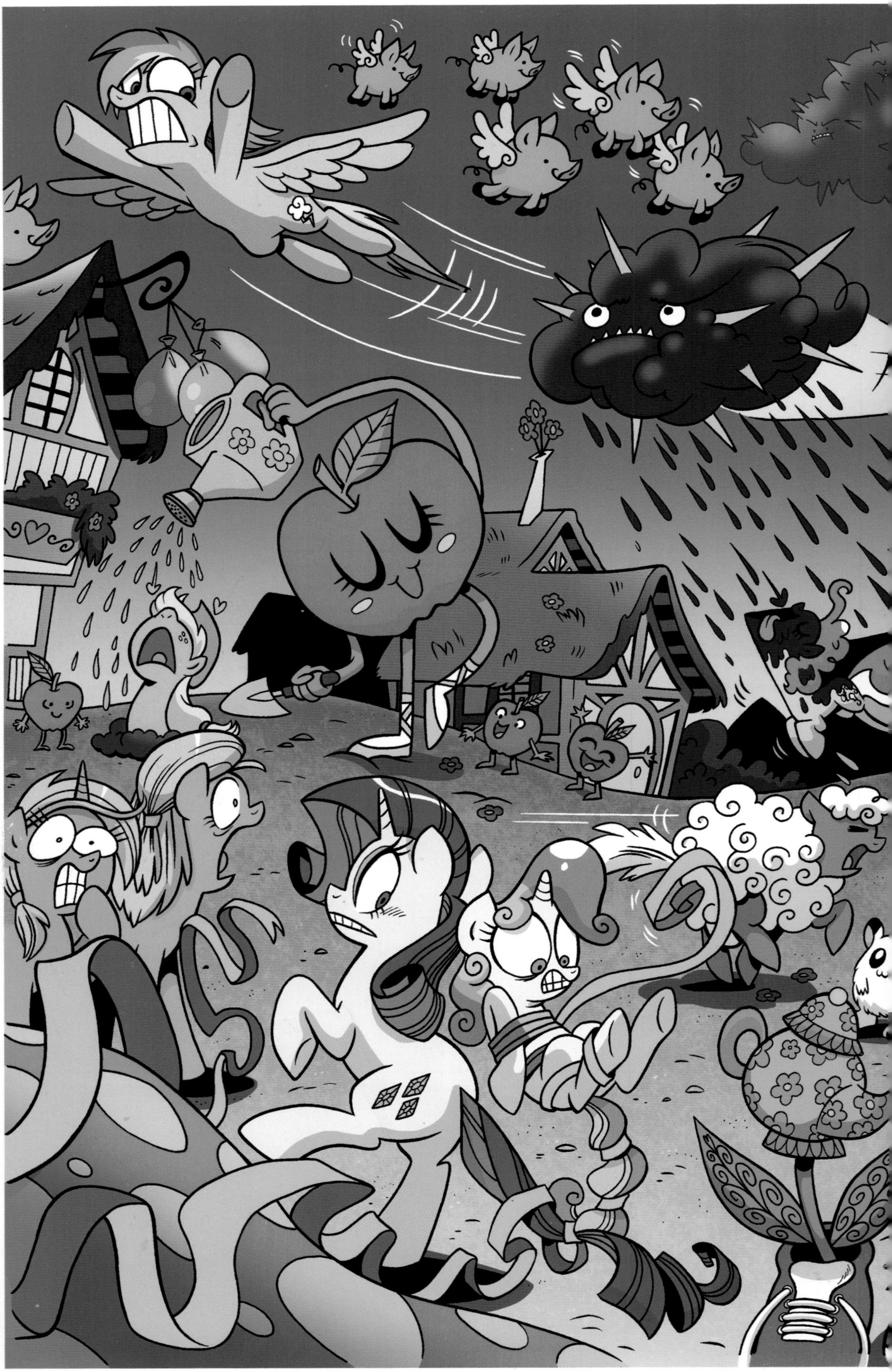

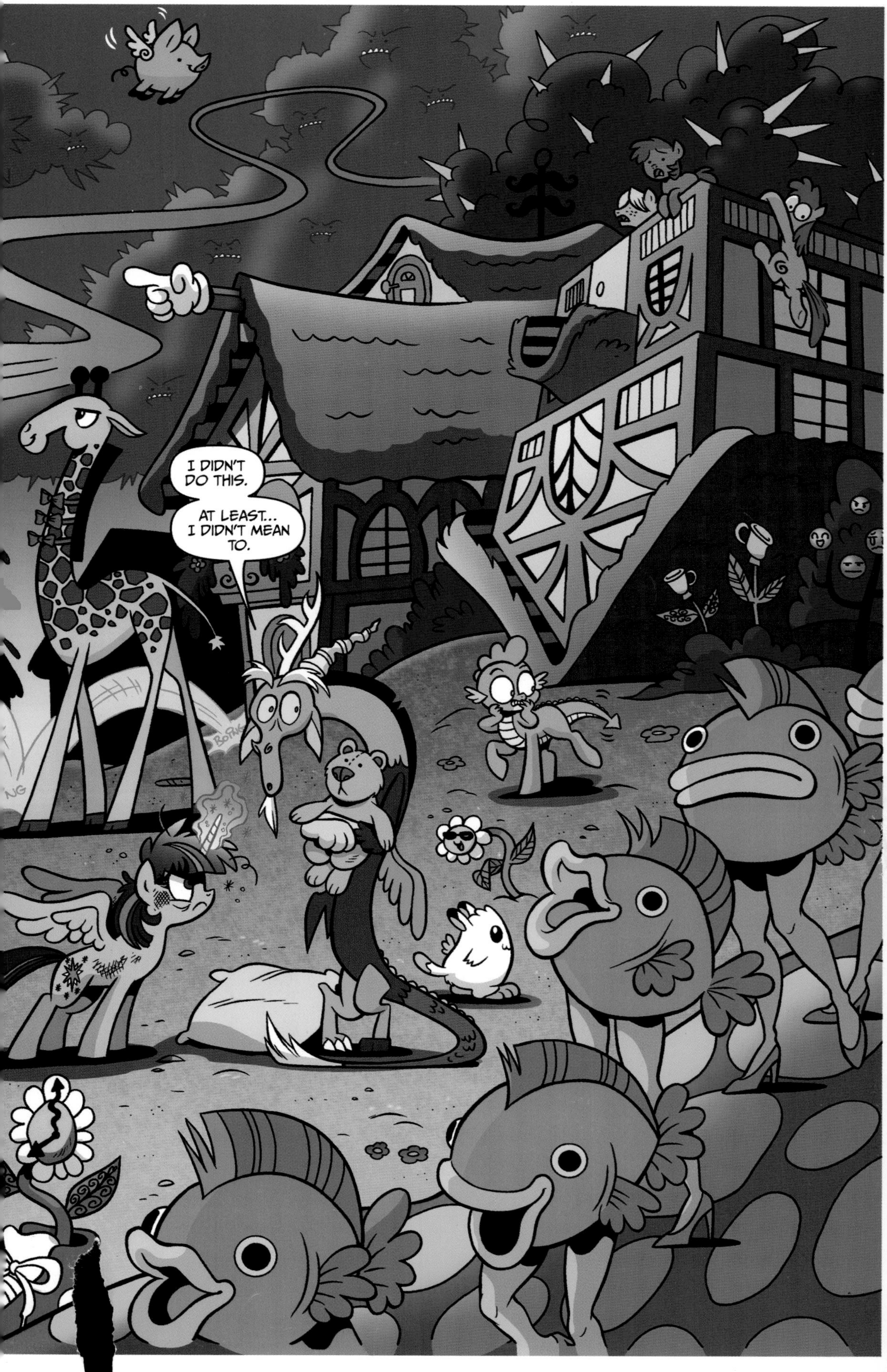

I DIDN'T DO THIS.
AT LEAST... I DIDN'T MEAN TO.

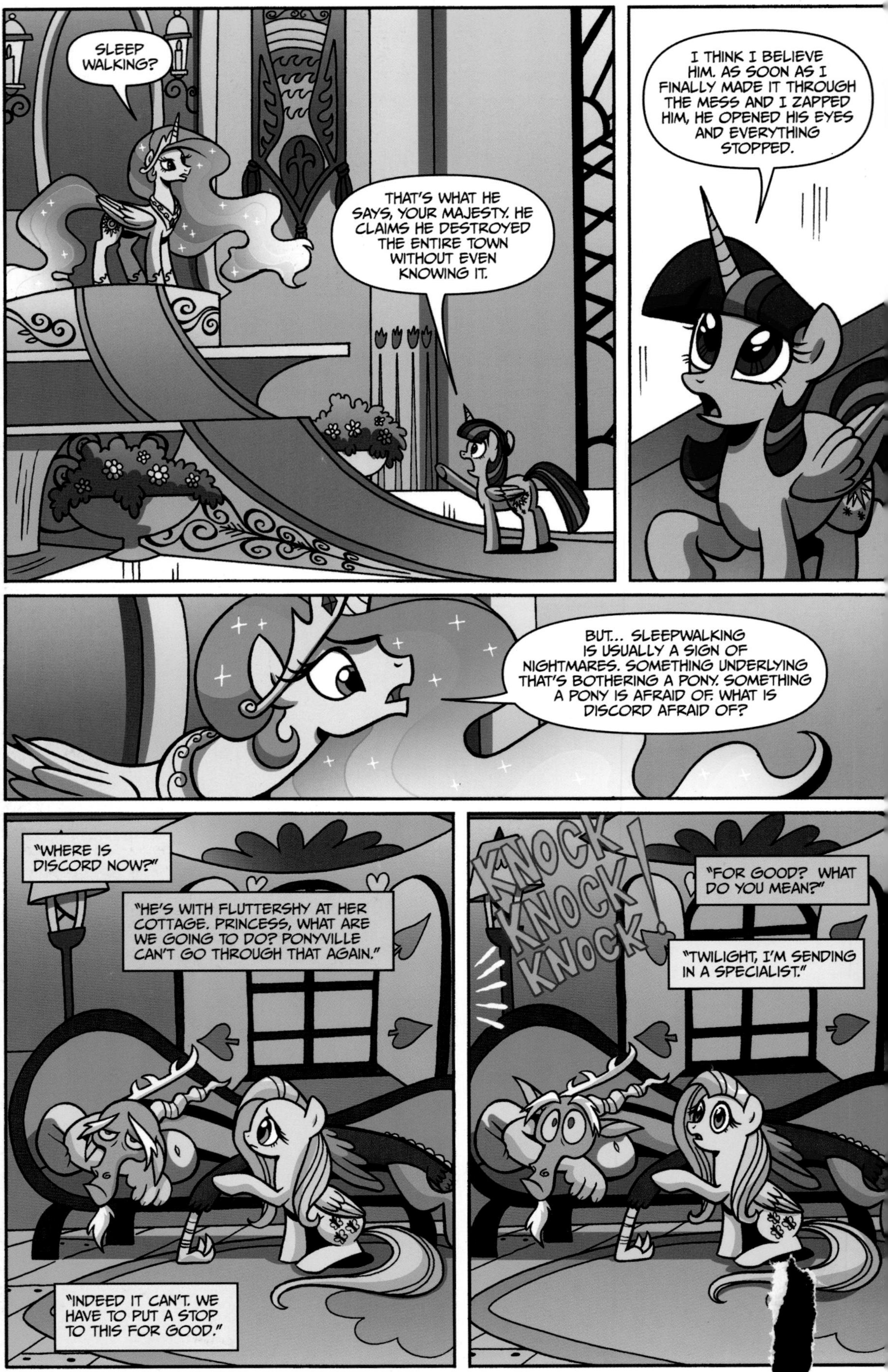
SLEEP WALKING?
THAT'S WHAT HE SAYS, YOUR MAJESTY. HE CLAIMS HE DESTROYED THE ENTIRE TOWN WITHOUT EVEN KNOWING IT.
I THINK I BELIEVE HIM. AS SOON AS I FINALLY MADE IT THROUGH THE MESS AND I ZAPPED HIM, HE OPENED HIS EYES AND EVERYTHING STOPPED.
BUT... SLEEPWALKING IS USUALLY A SIGN OF NIGHTMARES. SOMETHING UNDERLYING THAT'S BOTHERING A PONY. SOMETHING A PONY IS AFRAID OF. WHAT IS DISCORD AFRAID OF?
"WHERE IS DISCORD NOW?"
"HE'S WITH FLUTTERSHY AT HER COTTAGE. PRINCESS, WHAT ARE WE GOING TO DO? PONYVILLE CAN'T GO THROUGH THAT AGAIN."
"INDEED IT CAN'T. WE HAVE TO PUT A STOP TO THIS FOR GOOD."
KNOCK! KNOCK KNOCK
"FOR GOOD? WHAT DO YOU MEAN?"
"TWILIGHT, I'M SENDING IN A SPECIALIST."

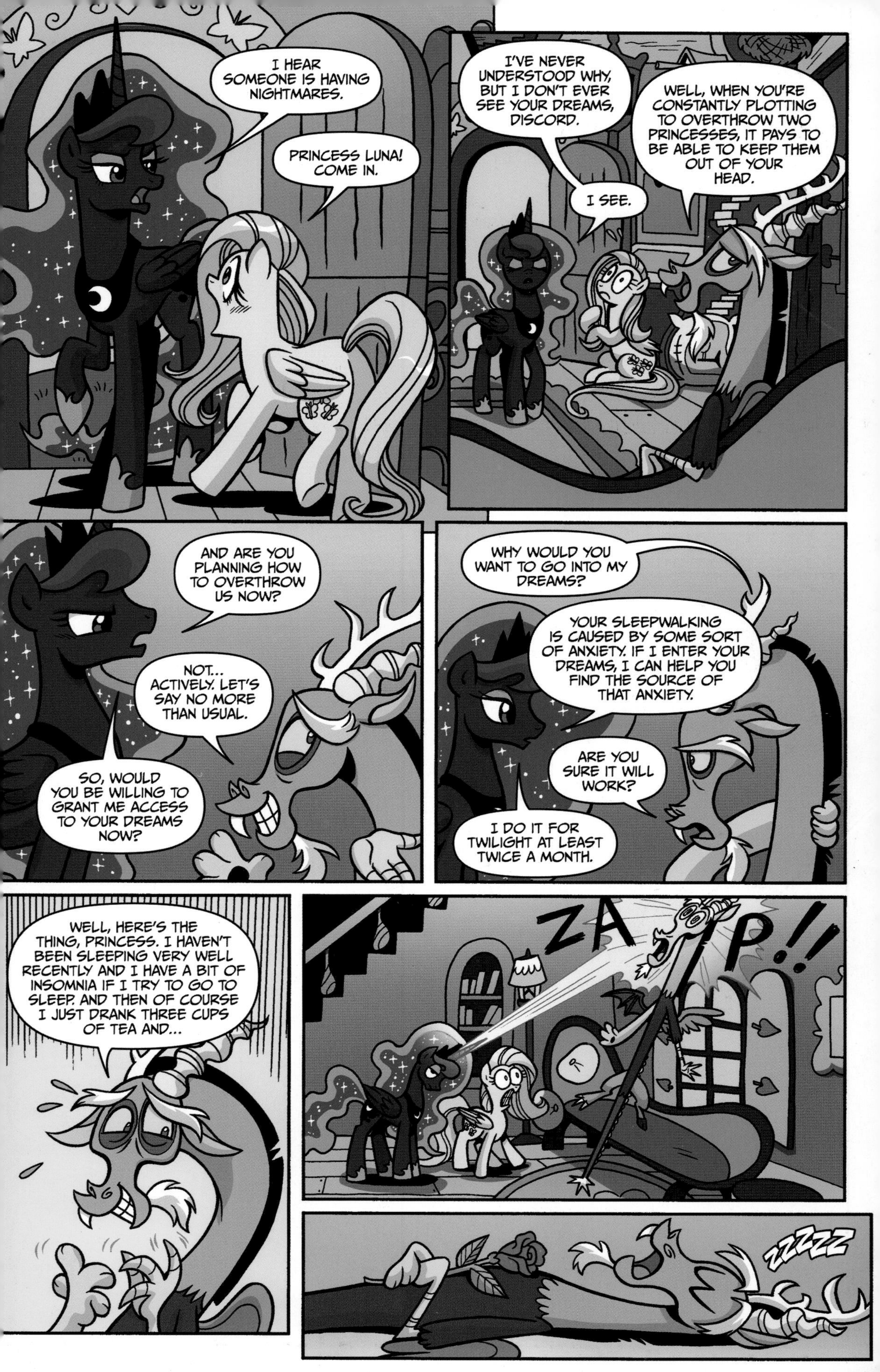
I HEAR SOMEONE IS HAVING NIGHTMARES.
PRINCESS LUNA! COME IN.
I'VE NEVER UNDERSTOOD WHY, BUT I DON'T EVER SEE YOUR DREAMS, DISCORD.
WELL, WHEN YOU'RE CONSTANTLY PLOTTING TO OVERTHROW TWO PRINCESSES, IT PAYS TO BE ABLE TO KEEP THEM OUT OF YOUR HEAD.
I SEE.
AND ARE YOU PLANNING HOW TO OVERTHROW US NOW?
NOT... ACTIVELY. LET'S SAY NO MORE THAN USUAL.
SO, WOULD YOU BE WILLING TO GRANT ME ACCESS TO YOUR DREAMS NOW?
WHY WOULD YOU WANT TO GO INTO MY DREAMS?
YOUR SLEEPWALKING IS CAUSED BY SOME SORT OF ANXIETY. IF I ENTER YOUR DREAMS, I CAN HELP YOU FIND THE SOURCE OF THAT ANXIETY.
ARE YOU SURE IT WILL WORK?
I DO IT FOR TWILIGHT AT LEAST TWICE A MONTH.
WELL, HERE'S THE THING, PRINCESS. I HAVEN'T BEEN SLEEPING VERY WELL RECENTLY AND I HAVE A BIT OF INSOMNIA IF I TRY TO GO TO SLEEP. AND THEN OF COURSE I JUST DRANK THREE CUPS OF TEA AND...
ZAP!!
ZZZZZ

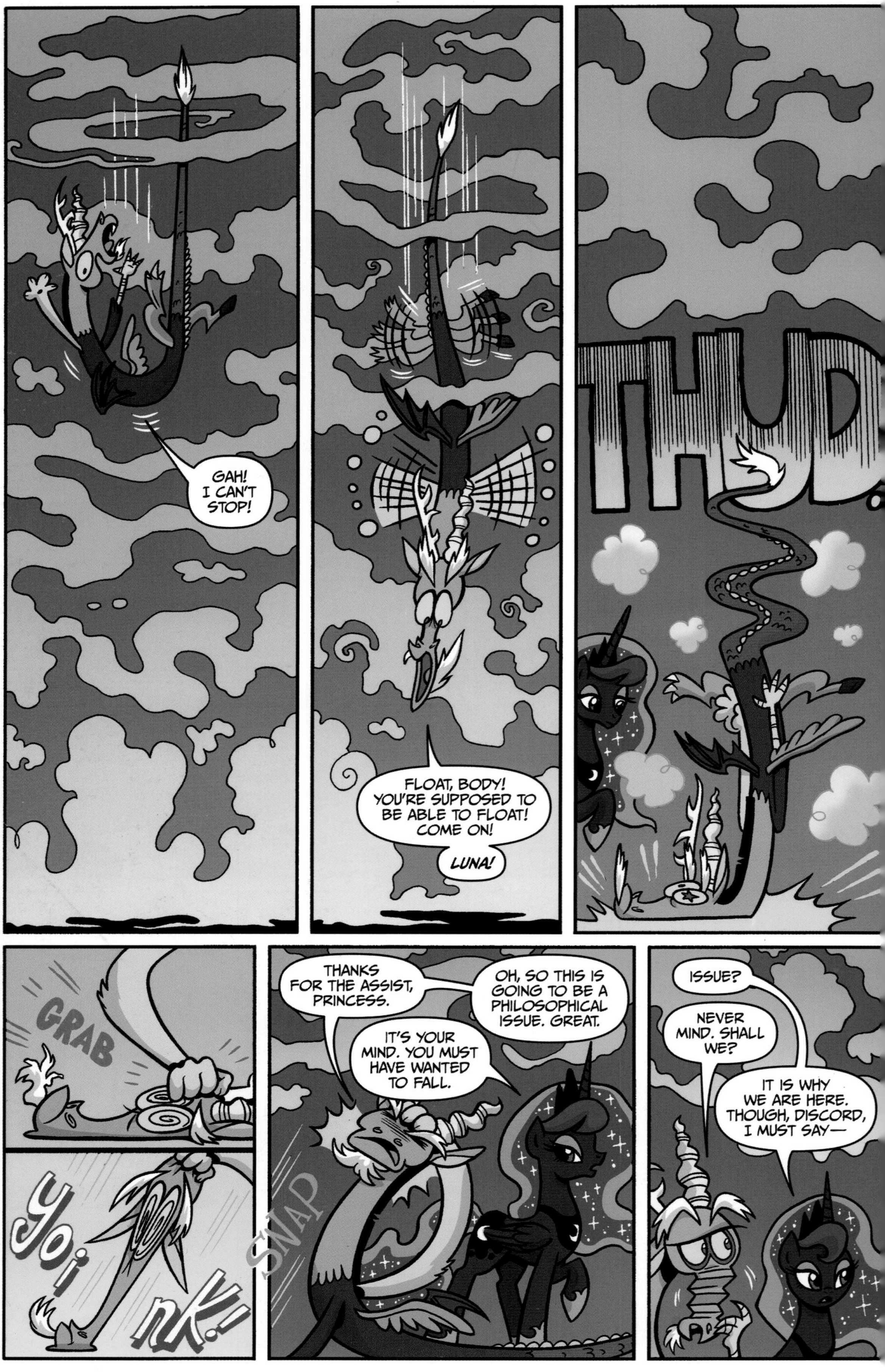
GAH! I CAN'T STOP!
FLOAT, BODY! YOU'RE SUPPOSED TO BE ABLE TO FLOAT! COME ON!
LUNA!
THUD.
GRAB
YOINK!
THANKS FOR THE ASSIST, PRINCESS.
IT'S YOUR MIND. YOU MUST HAVE WANTED TO FALL.
OH, SO THIS IS GOING TO BE A PHILOSOPHICAL ISSUE. GREAT.
SNAP
ISSUE?
NEVER MIND. SHALL WE?
IT IS WHY WE ARE HERE. THOUGH, DISCORD, I MUST SAY—

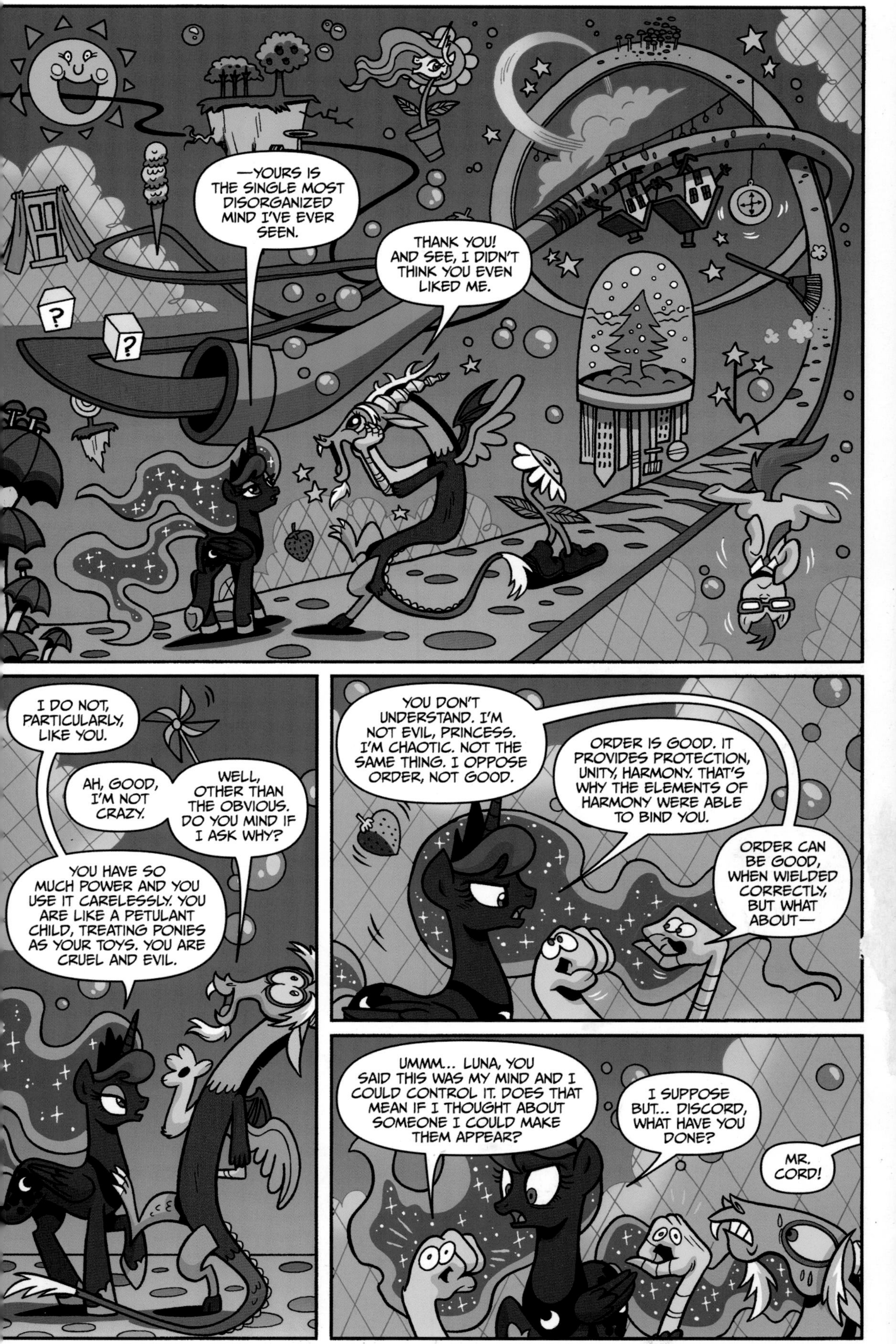
—YOURS IS THE SINGLE MOST DISORGANIZED MIND I'VE EVER SEEN.
THANK YOU! AND SEE, I DIDN'T THINK YOU EVEN LIKED ME.
I DO NOT, PARTICULARLY, LIKE YOU.
AH, GOOD, I'M NOT CRAZY.
WELL, OTHER THAN THE OBVIOUS. DO YOU MIND IF I ASK WHY?
YOU HAVE SO MUCH POWER AND YOU USE IT CARELESSLY. YOU ARE LIKE A PETULANT CHILD, TREATING PONIES AS YOUR TOYS. YOU ARE CRUEL AND EVIL.
YOU DON'T UNDERSTAND. I'M NOT EVIL, PRINCESS. I'M CHAOTIC. NOT THE SAME THING. I OPPOSE ORDER, NOT GOOD.
ORDER IS GOOD. IT PROVIDES PROTECTION, UNITY, HARMONY. THAT'S WHY THE ELEMENTS OF HARMONY WERE ABLE TO BIND YOU.
ORDER CAN BE GOOD, WHEN WIELDED CORRECTLY, BUT WHAT ABOUT—
UMMM... LUNA, YOU SAID THIS WAS MY MIND AND I COULD CONTROL IT. DOES THAT MEAN IF I THOUGHT ABOUT SOMEONE I COULD MAKE THEM APPEAR?
I SUPPOSE BUT... DISCORD, WHAT HAVE YOU DONE?
MR. CORD!

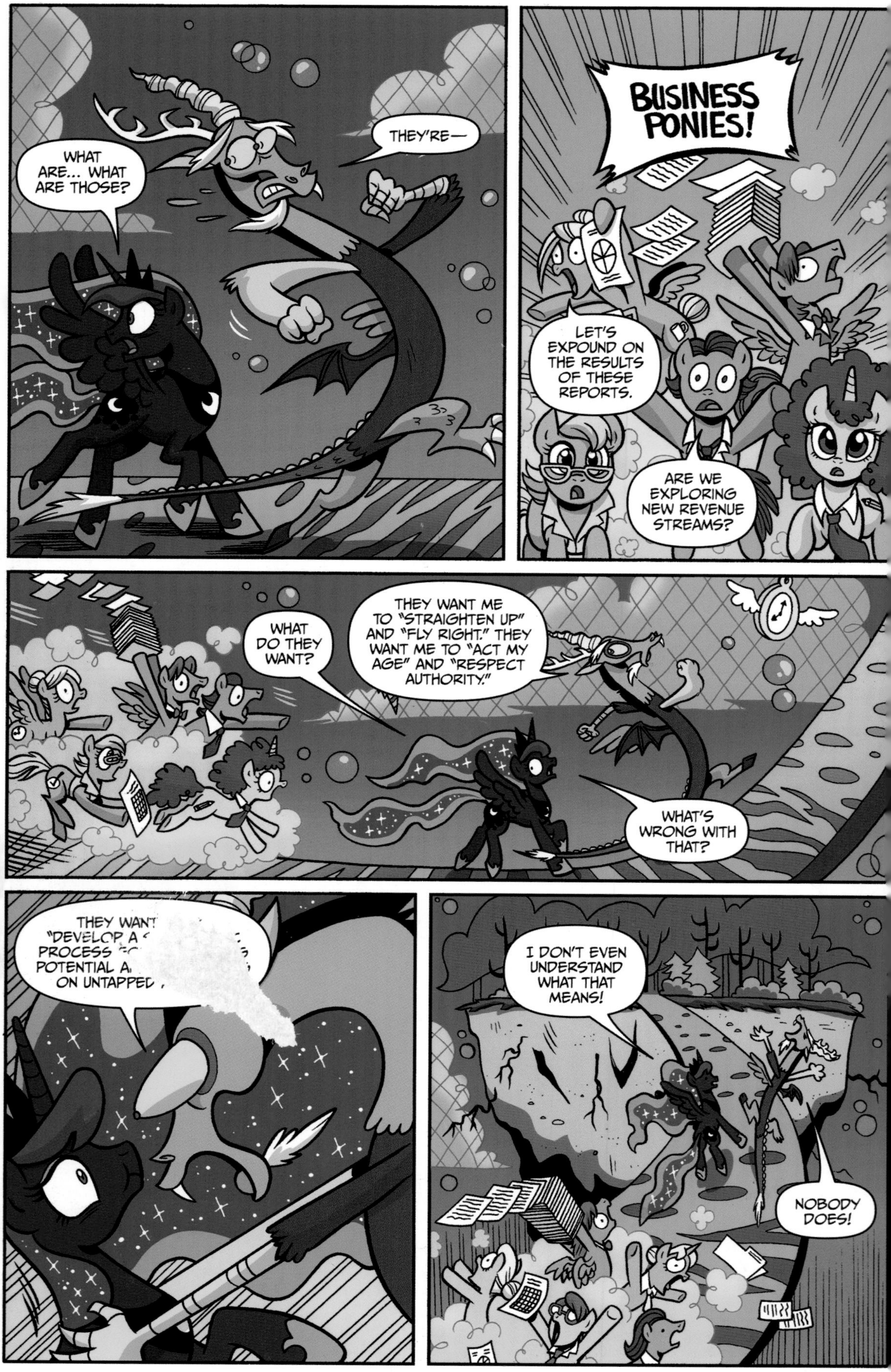
WHAT ARE... WHAT ARE THOSE?
THEY'RE—
BUSINESS PONIES!
LET'S EXPOUND ON THE RESULTS OF THESE REPORTS.
ARE WE EXPLORING NEW REVENUE STREAMS?
WHAT DO THEY WANT?
THEY WANT ME TO "STRAIGHTEN UP" AND "FLY RIGHT." THEY WANT ME TO "ACT MY AGE" AND "RESPECT AUTHORITY."
WHAT'S WRONG WITH THAT?
THEY WANT
"DEVELOP A
PROCESS
POTENTIAL A
ON UNTAPPED
I DON'T EVEN UNDERSTAND WHAT THAT MEANS!
NOBODY DOES!

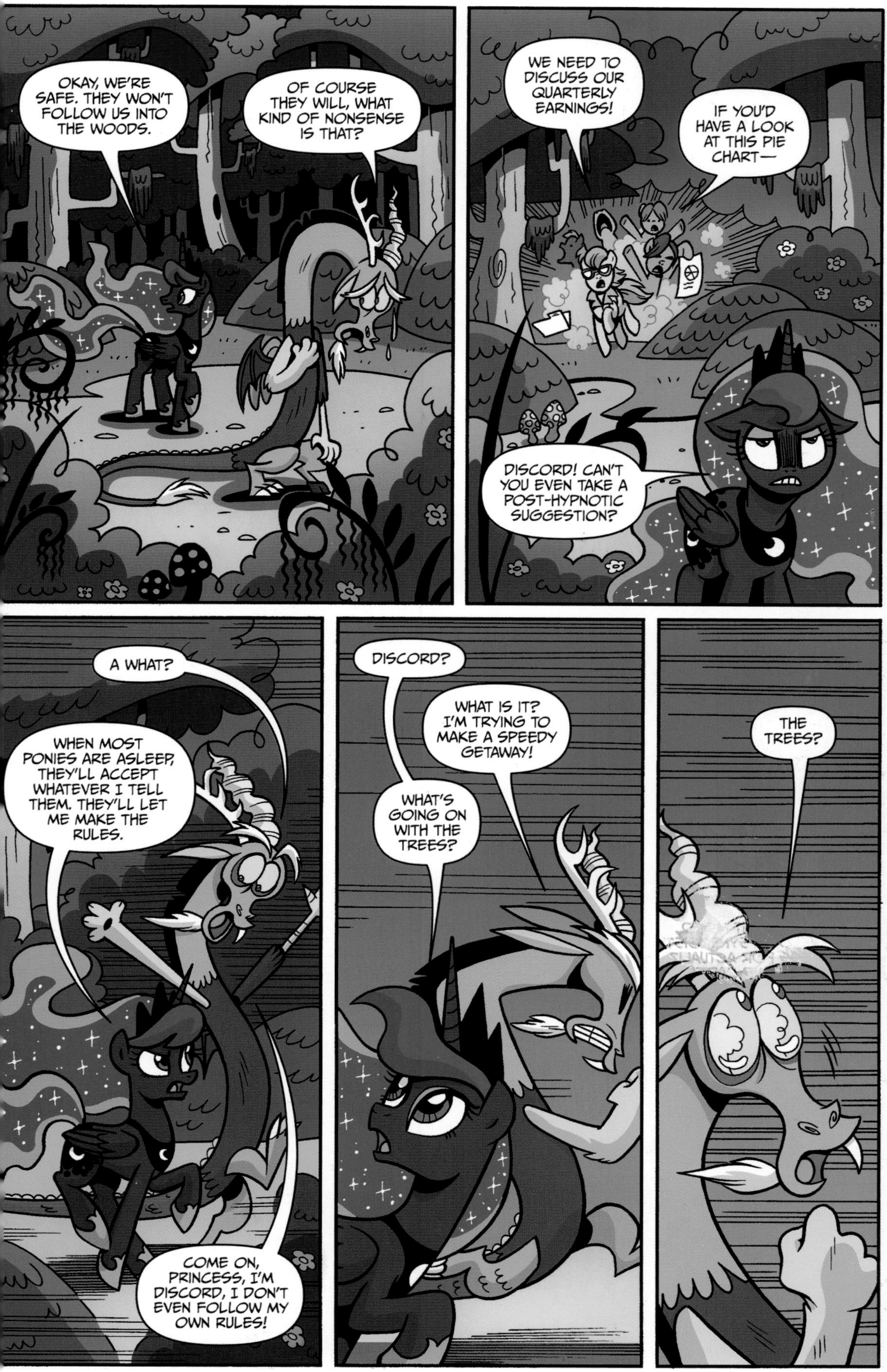
OKAY, WE'RE SAFE. THEY WON'T FOLLOW US INTO THE WOODS.
OF COURSE THEY WILL, WHAT KIND OF NONSENSE IS THAT?
WE NEED TO DISCUSS OUR QUARTERLY EARNINGS!
IF YOU'D HAVE A LOOK AT THIS PIE CHART—
DISCORD! CAN'T YOU EVEN TAKE A POST-HYPNOTIC SUGGESTION?
A WHAT?
WHEN MOST PONIES ARE ASLEEP, THEY'LL ACCEPT WHATEVER I TELL THEM. THEY'LL LET ME MAKE THE RULES.
COME ON, PRINCESS, I'M DISCORD, I DON'T EVEN FOLLOW MY OWN RULES!
DISCORD?
WHAT IS IT? I'M TRYING TO MAKE A SPEEDY GETAWAY!
WHAT'S GOING ON WITH THE TREES?
THE TREES?

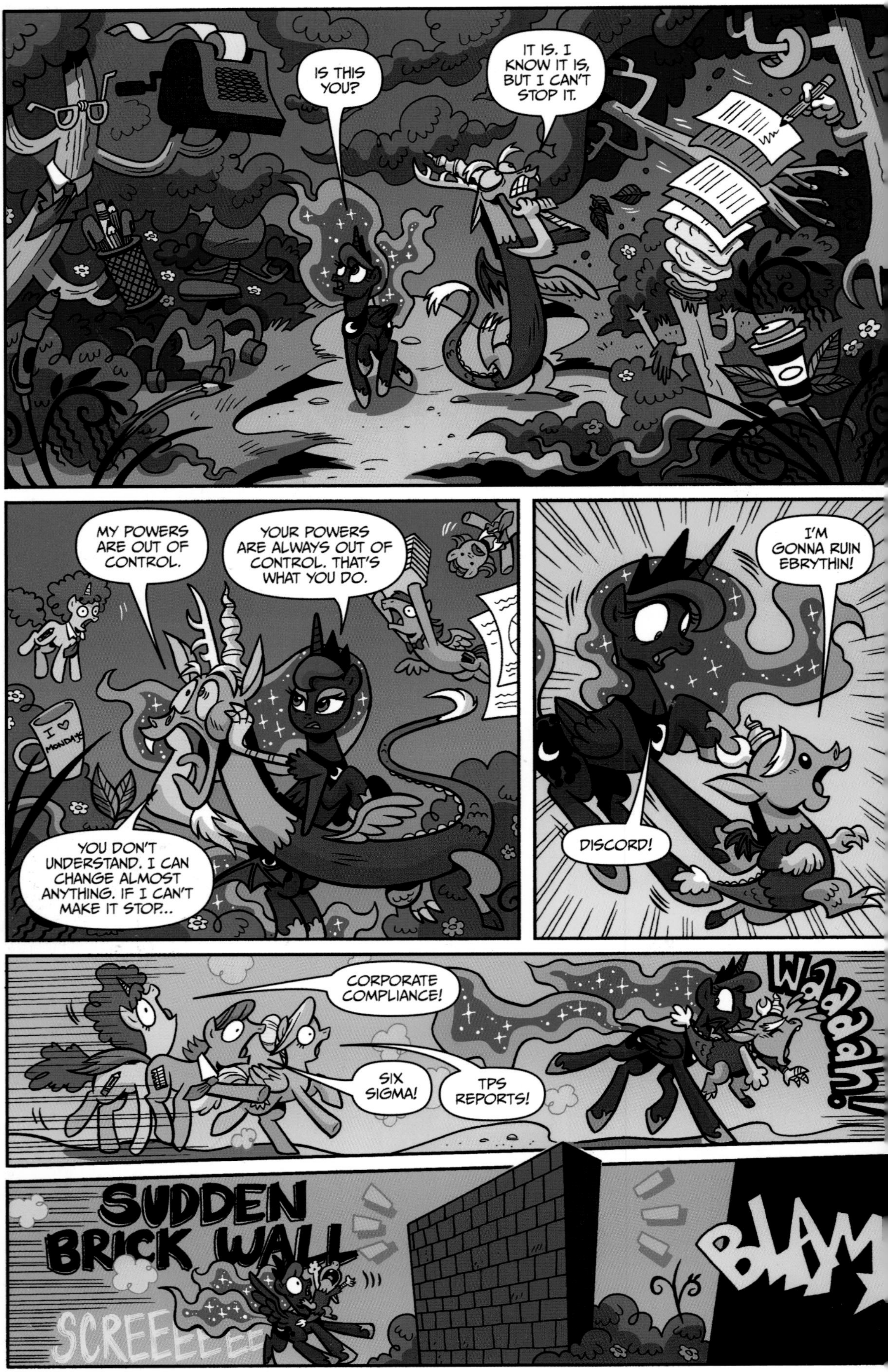
IS THIS YOU?
IT IS. I KNOW IT IS, BUT I CAN'T STOP IT.
MY POWERS ARE OUT OF CONTROL.
YOUR POWERS ARE ALWAYS OUT OF CONTROL. THAT'S WHAT YOU DO.
YOU DON'T UNDERSTAND. I CAN CHANGE ALMOST ANYTHING. IF I CAN'T MAKE IT STOP...
I ♥ MONDAYS
I'M GONNA RUIN EBRYTHIN!
DISCORD!
CORPORATE COMPLIANCE!
SIX SIGMA!
TPS REPORTS!
Waaaah!
SUDDEN BRICK WALL
SCREEEEEEE
BLAM

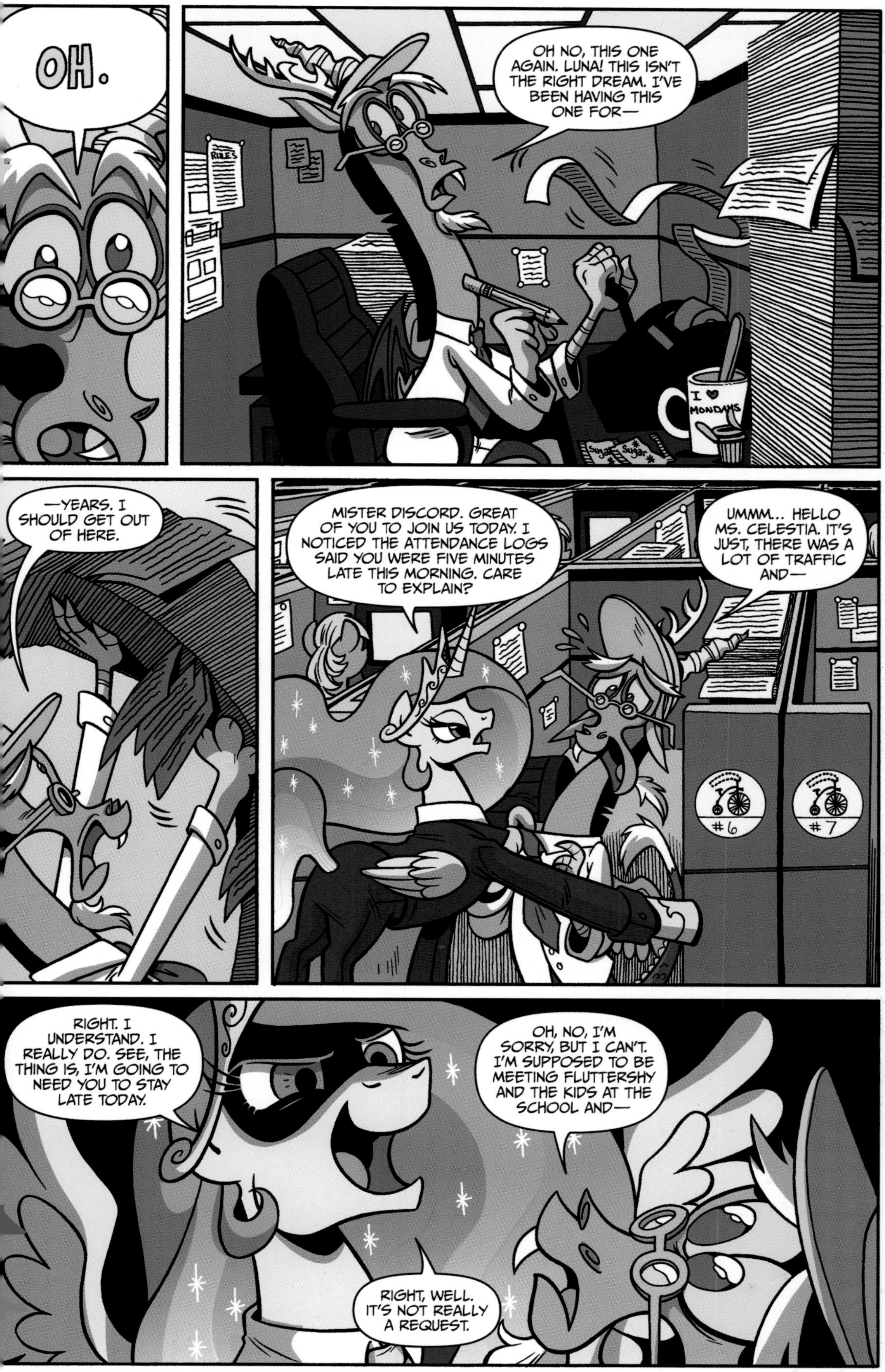
OH.
OH NO, THIS ONE AGAIN. LUNA! THIS ISN'T THE RIGHT DREAM. I'VE BEEN HAVING THIS ONE FOR—
RULES
I ♥ MONDAYS
Sugar
Sugar
—YEARS. I SHOULD GET OUT OF HERE.
MISTER DISCORD. GREAT OF YOU TO JOIN US TODAY. I NOTICED THE ATTENDANCE LOGS SAID YOU WERE FIVE MINUTES LATE THIS MORNING. CARE TO EXPLAIN?
UMMM... HELLO MS. CELESTIA. IT'S JUST, THERE WAS A LOT OF TRAFFIC AND—
#6
#7
RIGHT. I UNDERSTAND. I REALLY DO. SEE, THE THING IS, I'M GOING TO NEED YOU TO STAY LATE TODAY.
OH, NO, I'M SORRY, BUT I CAN'T. I'M SUPPOSED TO BE MEETING FLUTTERSHY AND THE KIDS AT THE SCHOOL AND—
RIGHT, WELL. IT'S NOT REALLY A REQUEST.

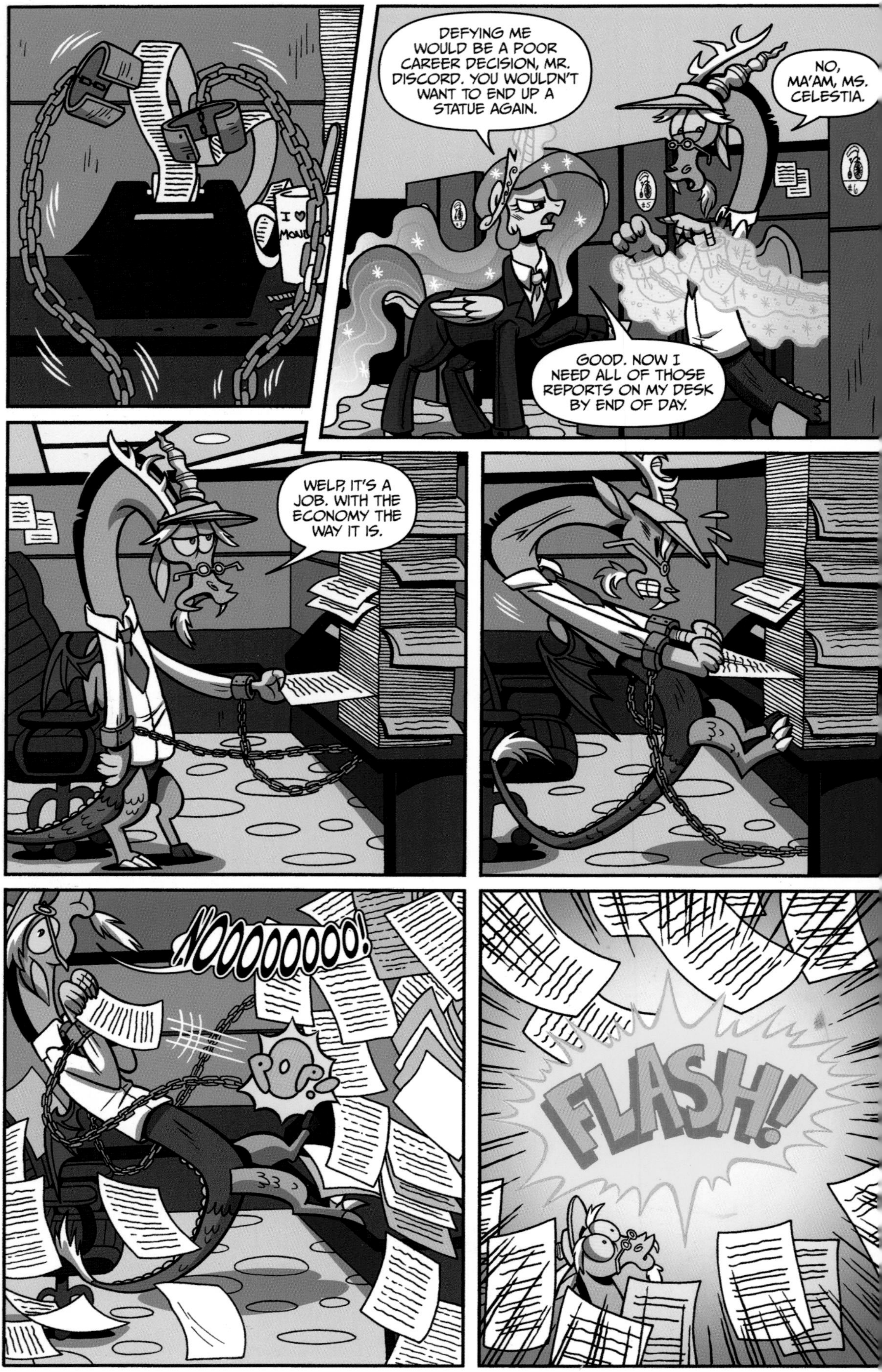
I ♥ MON
DEFYING ME WOULD BE A POOR CAREER DECISION, MR. DISCORD. YOU WOULDN'T WANT TO END UP A STATUE AGAIN.
NO, MA'AM, MS. CELESTIA.
GOOD. NOW I NEED ALL OF THOSE REPORTS ON MY DESK BY END OF DAY.
WELP, IT'S A JOB. WITH THE ECONOMY THE WAY IT IS.
NOOOOOOOO!
POP!
FLASH!

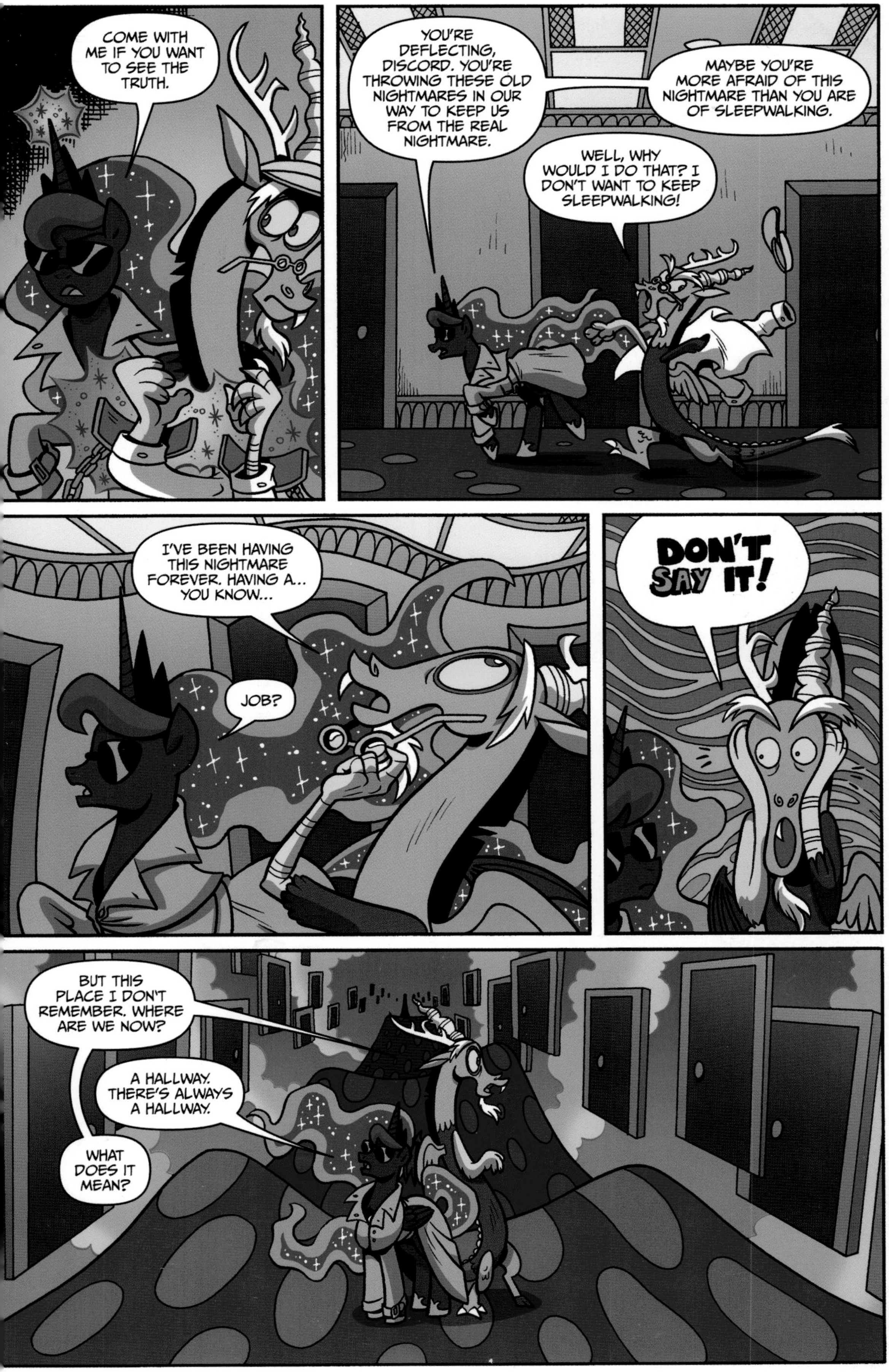
COME WITH ME IF YOU WANT TO SEE THE TRUTH.
YOU'RE DEFLECTING, DISCORD. YOU'RE THROWING THESE OLD NIGHTMARES IN OUR WAY TO KEEP US FROM THE REAL NIGHTMARE.
MAYBE YOU'RE MORE AFRAID OF THIS NIGHTMARE THAN YOU ARE OF SLEEPWALKING.
WELL, WHY WOULD I DO THAT? I DON'T WANT TO KEEP SLEEPWALKING!
I'VE BEEN HAVING THIS NIGHTMARE FOREVER. HAVING A... YOU KNOW...
JOB?
DON'T SAY IT!
BUT THIS PLACE I DON'T REMEMBER. WHERE ARE WE NOW?
A HALLWAY. THERE'S ALWAYS A HALLWAY.
WHAT DOES IT MEAN?

THE INFINITE HALLWAY IS A METAPHOR FOR CHOICE. EACH DOOR REPRESENTS ANOTHER CHOICE YOU MIGHT MAKE AND ANOTHER FUTURE IT WOULD CREATE.

HOW DO WE GET OUT?

YOU MUST CHOOSE A DOOR

THIS ONE HAS DIAMONDS. THAT MUST BE A GOOD SIGN, RIGHT?

THAT HARDLY SEEMS LIKE THE BEST BASIS TO CHOOSE.

WHAT ABOUT THIS ONE? IT LOOKS IMPORTANT.

NONSENSE, THIS IS CLEARLY THE BEST CHOICE.

CAUTION CAUTION CAUTION

STOP

CAUTION CAUTION CAUTION CAUTION

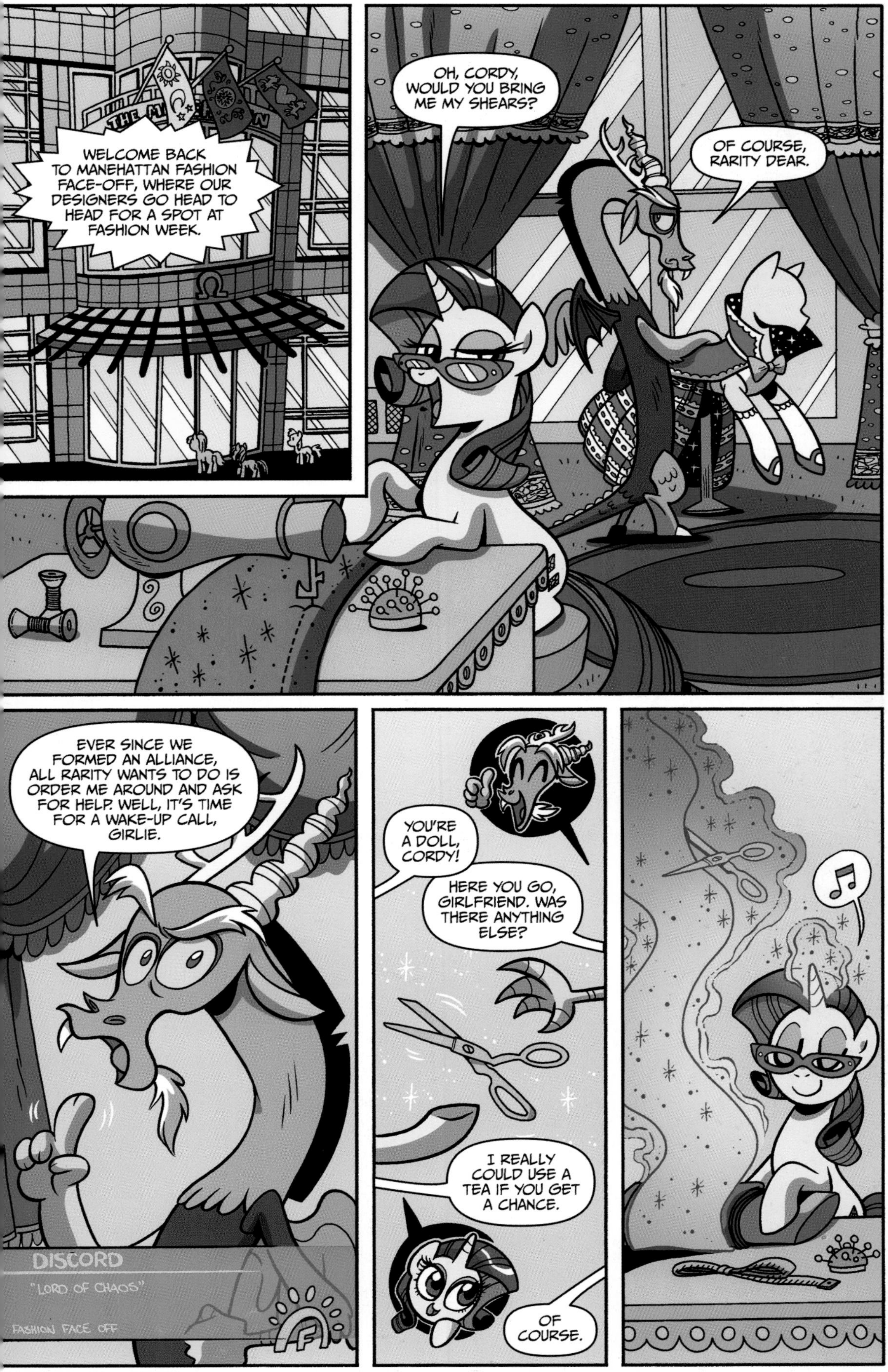
WELCOME BACK TO MANEHATTAN FASHION FACE-OFF, WHERE OUR DESIGNERS GO HEAD TO HEAD FOR A SPOT AT FASHION WEEK.
OH, CORDY, WOULD YOU BRING ME MY SHEARS?
OF COURSE, RARITY DEAR.
EVER SINCE WE FORMED AN ALLIANCE, ALL RARITY WANTS TO DO IS ORDER ME AROUND AND ASK FOR HELP. WELL, IT'S TIME FOR A WAKE-UP CALL, GIRLIE.
DISCORD
"LORD OF CHAOS"
FASHION FACE OFF
YOU'RE A DOLL, CORDY!
HERE YOU GO, GIRLFRIEND. WAS THERE ANYTHING ELSE?
I REALLY COULD USE A TEA IF YOU GET A CHANCE.
OF COURSE.

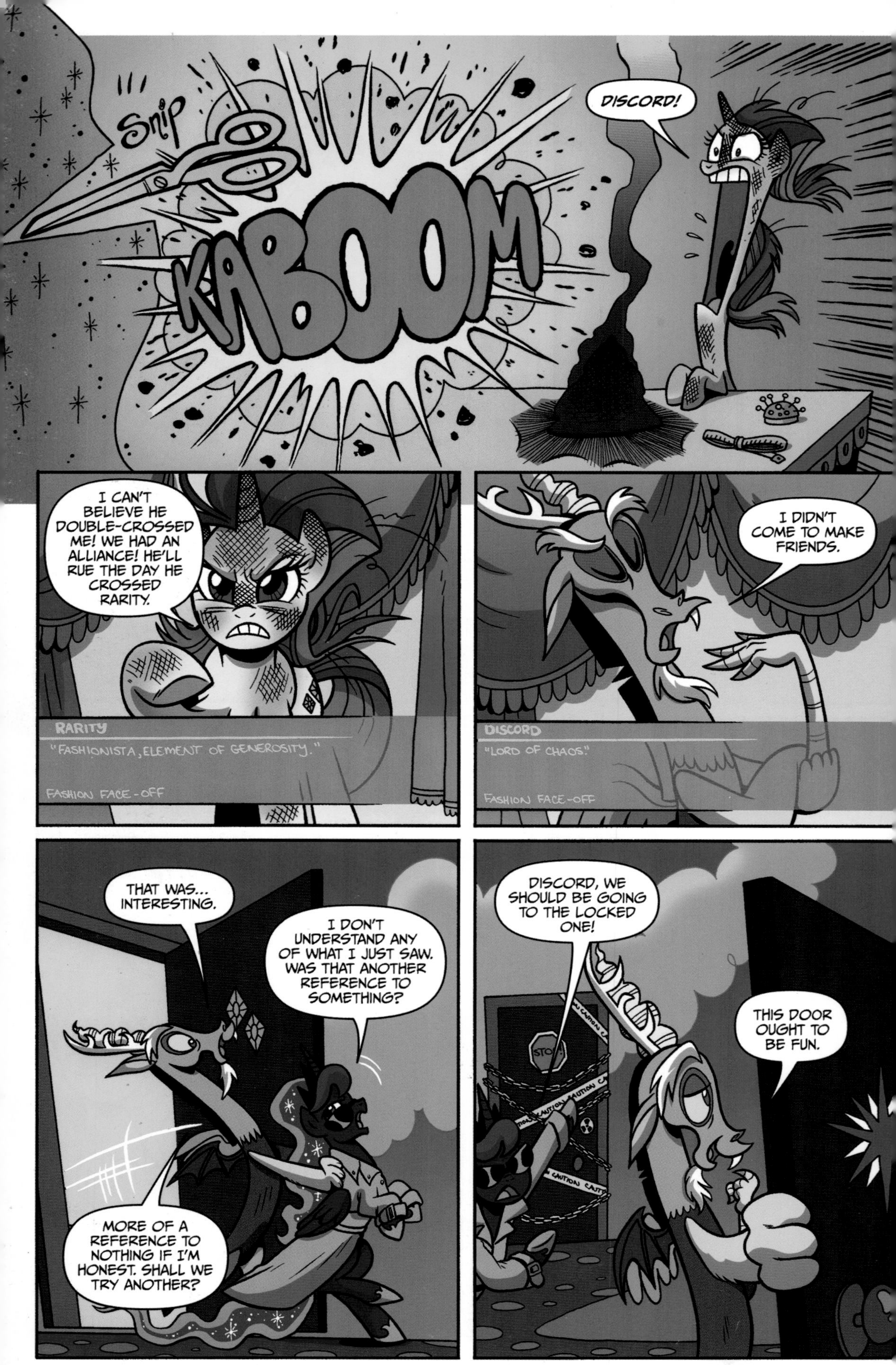
SNIP
KABOOM
DISCORD!
I CAN'T BELIEVE HE DOUBLE-CROSSED ME! WE HAD AN ALLIANCE! HE'LL RUE THE DAY HE CROSSED RARITY.
RARITY
"FASHIONISTA, ELEMENT OF GENEROSITY."
FASHION FACE-OFF
I DIDN'T COME TO MAKE FRIENDS.
DISCORD
"LORD OF CHAOS."
FASHION FACE-OFF
THAT WAS... INTERESTING.
I DON'T UNDERSTAND ANY OF WHAT I JUST SAW. WAS THAT ANOTHER REFERENCE TO SOMETHING?
MORE OF A REFERENCE TO NOTHING IF I'M HONEST. SHALL WE TRY ANOTHER?
DISCORD, WE SHOULD BE GOING TO THE LOCKED ONE!
STOP
THIS DOOR OUGHT TO BE FUN.

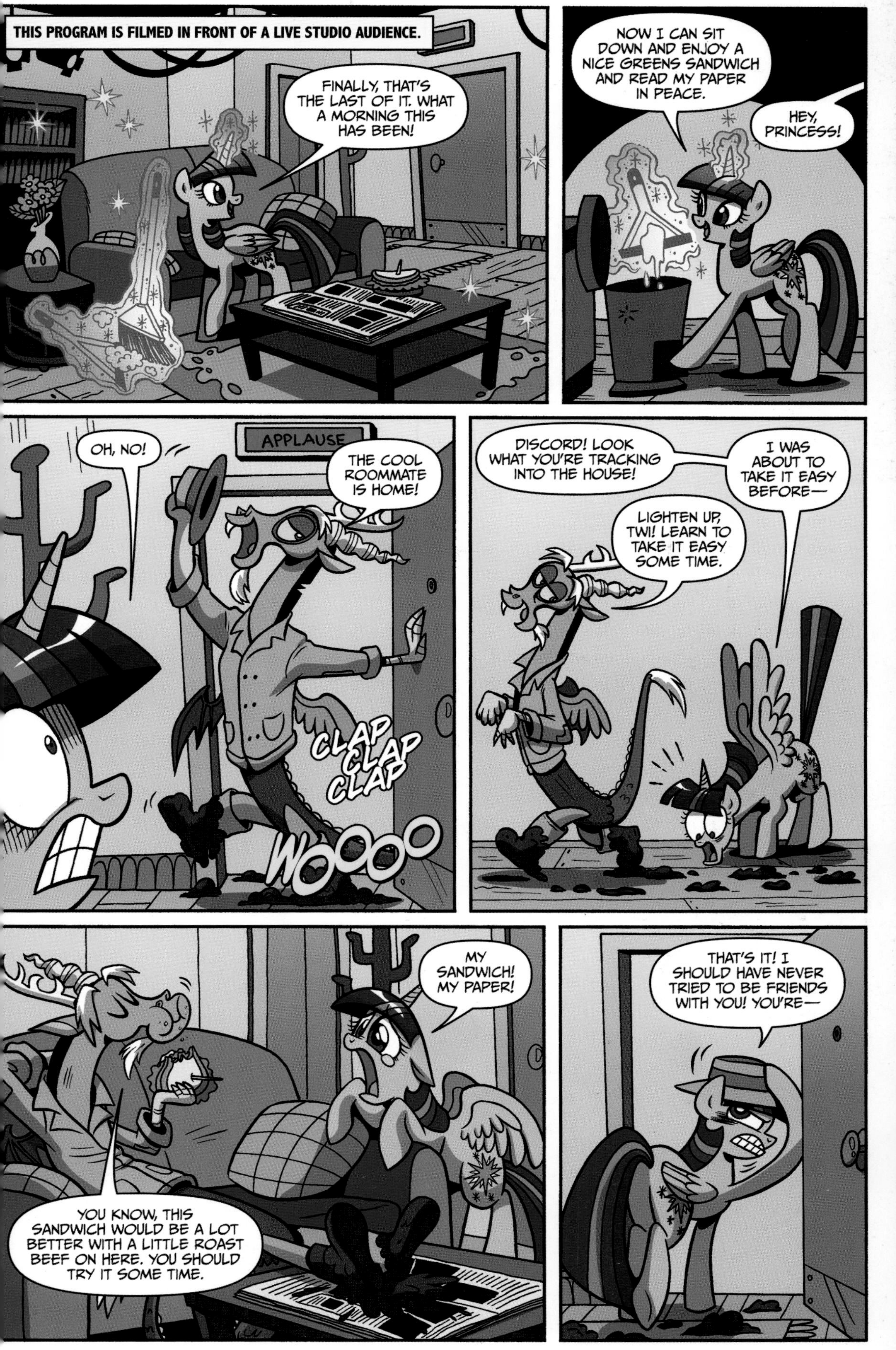
THIS PROGRAM IS FILMED IN FRONT OF A LIVE STUDIO AUDIENCE.
FINALLY, THAT'S THE LAST OF IT. WHAT A MORNING THIS HAS BEEN!
NOW I CAN SIT DOWN AND ENJOY A NICE GREENS SANDWICH AND READ MY PAPER IN PEACE.
HEY, PRINCESS!
APPLAUSE
OH, NO!
THE COOL ROOMMATE IS HOME!
CLAP CLAP CLAP
WOOOO
DISCORD! LOOK WHAT YOU'RE TRACKING INTO THE HOUSE!
LIGHTEN UP, TWI! LEARN TO TAKE IT EASY SOME TIME.
I WAS ABOUT TO TAKE IT EASY BEFORE—
MY SANDWICH! MY PAPER!
YOU KNOW, THIS SANDWICH WOULD BE A LOT BETTER WITH A LITTLE ROAST BEEF ON HERE. YOU SHOULD TRY IT SOME TIME.
THAT'S IT! I SHOULD HAVE NEVER TRIED TO BE FRIENDS WITH YOU! YOU'RE—

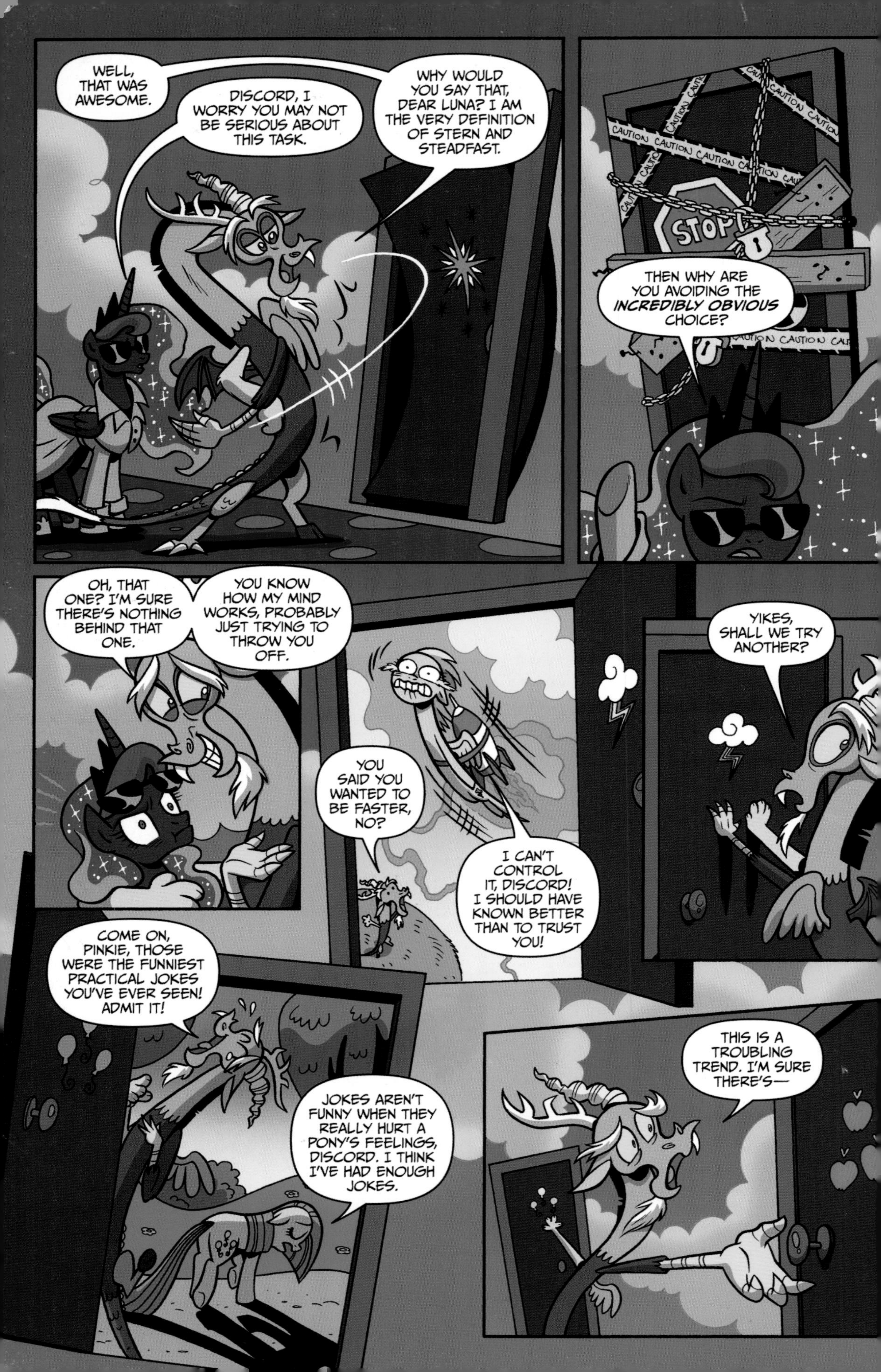
WELL, THAT WAS AWESOME.
DISCORD, I WORRY YOU MAY NOT BE SERIOUS ABOUT THIS TASK.
WHY WOULD YOU SAY THAT, DEAR LUNA? I AM THE VERY DEFINITION OF STERN AND STEADFAST.
CAUTION CAUTION CAUTION
STOP
THEN WHY ARE YOU AVOIDING THE *INCREDIBLY OBVIOUS* CHOICE?
OH, THAT ONE? I'M SURE THERE'S NOTHING BEHIND THAT ONE.
YOU KNOW HOW MY MIND WORKS, PROBABLY JUST TRYING TO THROW YOU OFF.
YOU SAID YOU WANTED TO BE FASTER, NO?
I CAN'T CONTROL IT, DISCORD! I SHOULD HAVE KNOWN BETTER THAN TO TRUST YOU!
YIKES, SHALL WE TRY ANOTHER?
COME ON, PINKIE, THOSE WERE THE FUNNIEST PRACTICAL JOKES YOU'VE EVER SEEN! ADMIT IT!
JOKES AREN'T FUNNY WHEN THEY REALLY HURT A PONY'S FEELINGS, DISCORD. I THINK I'VE HAD ENOUGH JOKES.
THIS IS A TROUBLING TREND. I'M SURE THERE'S—

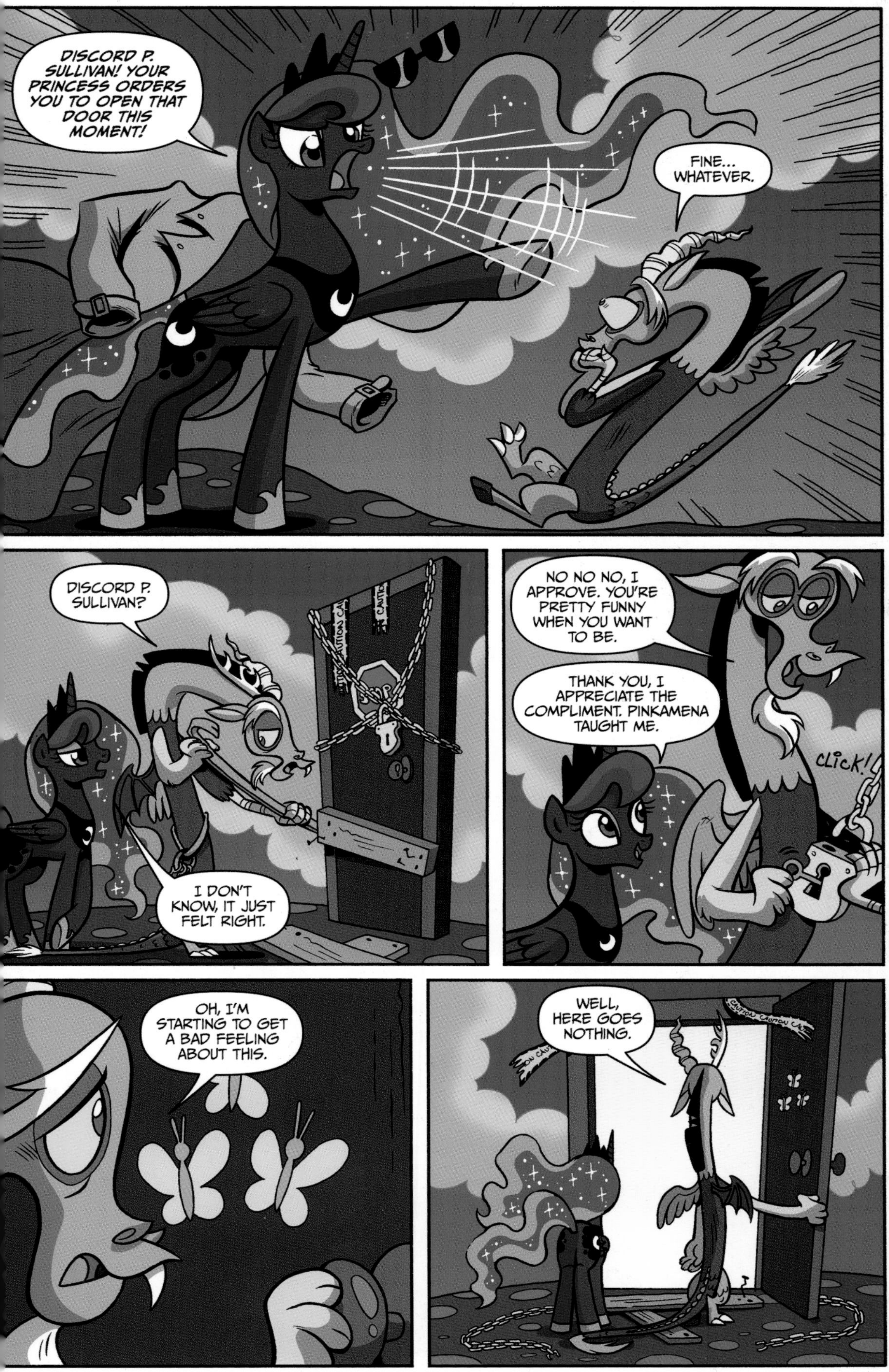
DISCORD P. SULLIVAN! YOUR PRINCESS ORDERS YOU TO OPEN THAT DOOR THIS MOMENT!
FINE... WHATEVER.
DISCORD P. SULLIVAN?
I DON'T KNOW, IT JUST FELT RIGHT.
NO NO NO, I APPROVE. YOU'RE PRETTY FUNNY WHEN YOU WANT TO BE.
THANK YOU, I APPRECIATE THE COMPLIMENT. PINKAMENA TAUGHT ME.
CLICK!
OH, I'M STARTING TO GET A BAD FEELING ABOUT THIS.
WELL, HERE GOES NOTHING.

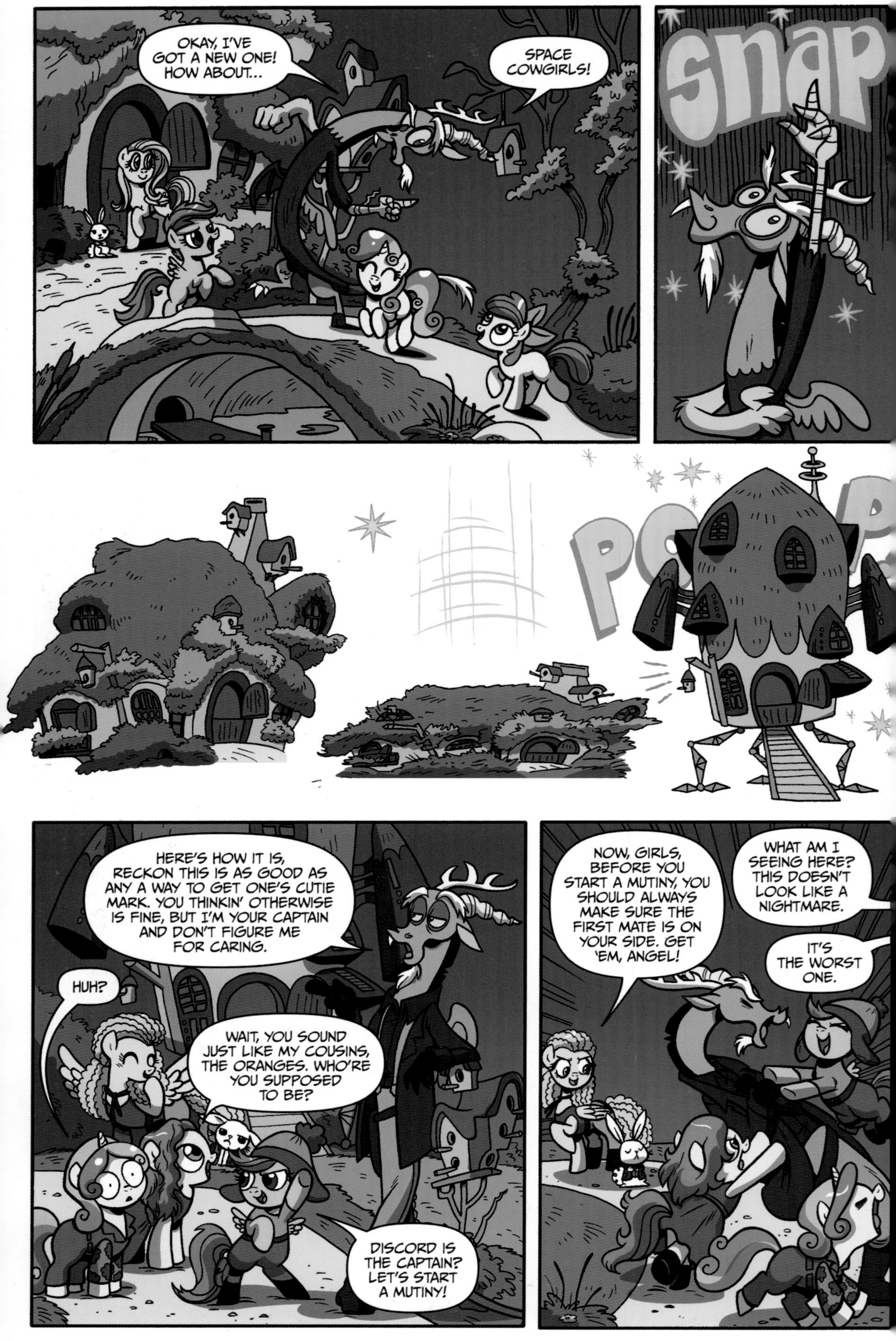

OKAY, I'VE GOT A NEW ONE! HOW ABOUT...
SPACE COWGIRLS!
SNAP
POP
HERE'S HOW IT IS, RECKON THIS IS AS GOOD AS ANY A WAY TO GET ONE'S CUTIE MARK. YOU THINKIN' OTHERWISE IS FINE, BUT I'M YOUR CAPTAIN AND DON'T FIGURE ME FOR CARING.
HUH?
WAIT, YOU SOUND JUST LIKE MY COUSINS, THE ORANGES. WHO'RE YOU SUPPOSED TO BE?
DISCORD IS THE CAPTAIN? LET'S START A MUTINY!
NOW, GIRLS, BEFORE YOU START A MUTINY, YOU SHOULD ALWAYS MAKE SURE THE FIRST MATE IS ON YOUR SIDE. GET 'EM, ANGEL!
WHAT AM I SEEING HERE? THIS DOESN'T LOOK LIKE A NIGHTMARE.
IT'S THE WORST ONE.

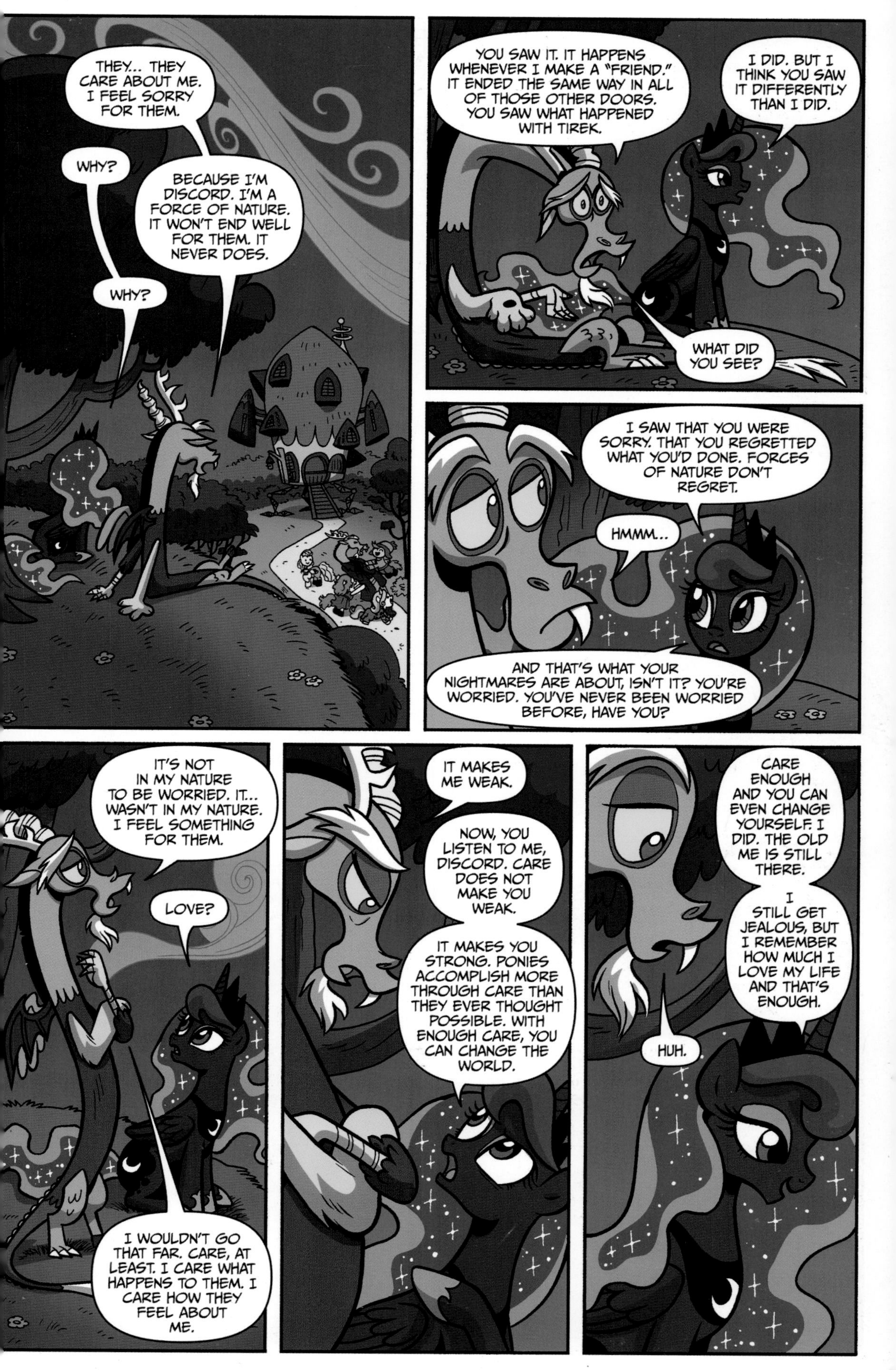

THEY... THEY CARE ABOUT ME. I FEEL SORRY FOR THEM.
WHY?
BECAUSE I'M DISCORD. I'M A FORCE OF NATURE. IT WON'T END WELL FOR THEM. IT NEVER DOES.
WHY?
YOU SAW IT. IT HAPPENS WHENEVER I MAKE A "FRIEND." IT ENDED THE SAME WAY IN ALL OF THOSE OTHER DOORS. YOU SAW WHAT HAPPENED WITH TIREK.
I DID. BUT I THINK YOU SAW IT DIFFERENTLY THAN I DID.
WHAT DID YOU SEE?
I SAW THAT YOU WERE SORRY. THAT YOU REGRETTED WHAT YOU'D DONE. FORCES OF NATURE DON'T REGRET.
HMMM...
AND THAT'S WHAT YOUR NIGHTMARES ARE ABOUT, ISN'T IT? YOU'RE WORRIED. YOU'VE NEVER BEEN WORRIED BEFORE, HAVE YOU?
IT'S NOT IN MY NATURE TO BE WORRIED. IT... WASN'T IN MY NATURE. I FEEL SOMETHING FOR THEM.
LOVE?
I WOULDN'T GO THAT FAR. CARE, AT LEAST. I CARE WHAT HAPPENS TO THEM. I CARE HOW THEY FEEL ABOUT ME.
IT MAKES ME WEAK.
NOW, YOU LISTEN TO ME, DISCORD. CARE DOES NOT MAKE YOU WEAK.
IT MAKES YOU STRONG. PONIES ACCOMPLISH MORE THROUGH CARE THAN THEY EVER THOUGHT POSSIBLE. WITH ENOUGH CARE, YOU CAN CHANGE THE WORLD.
CARE ENOUGH AND YOU CAN EVEN CHANGE YOURSELF. I DID. THE OLD ME IS STILL THERE.
I STILL GET JEALOUS, BUT I REMEMBER HOW MUCH I LOVE MY LIFE AND THAT'S ENOUGH.
HUH.

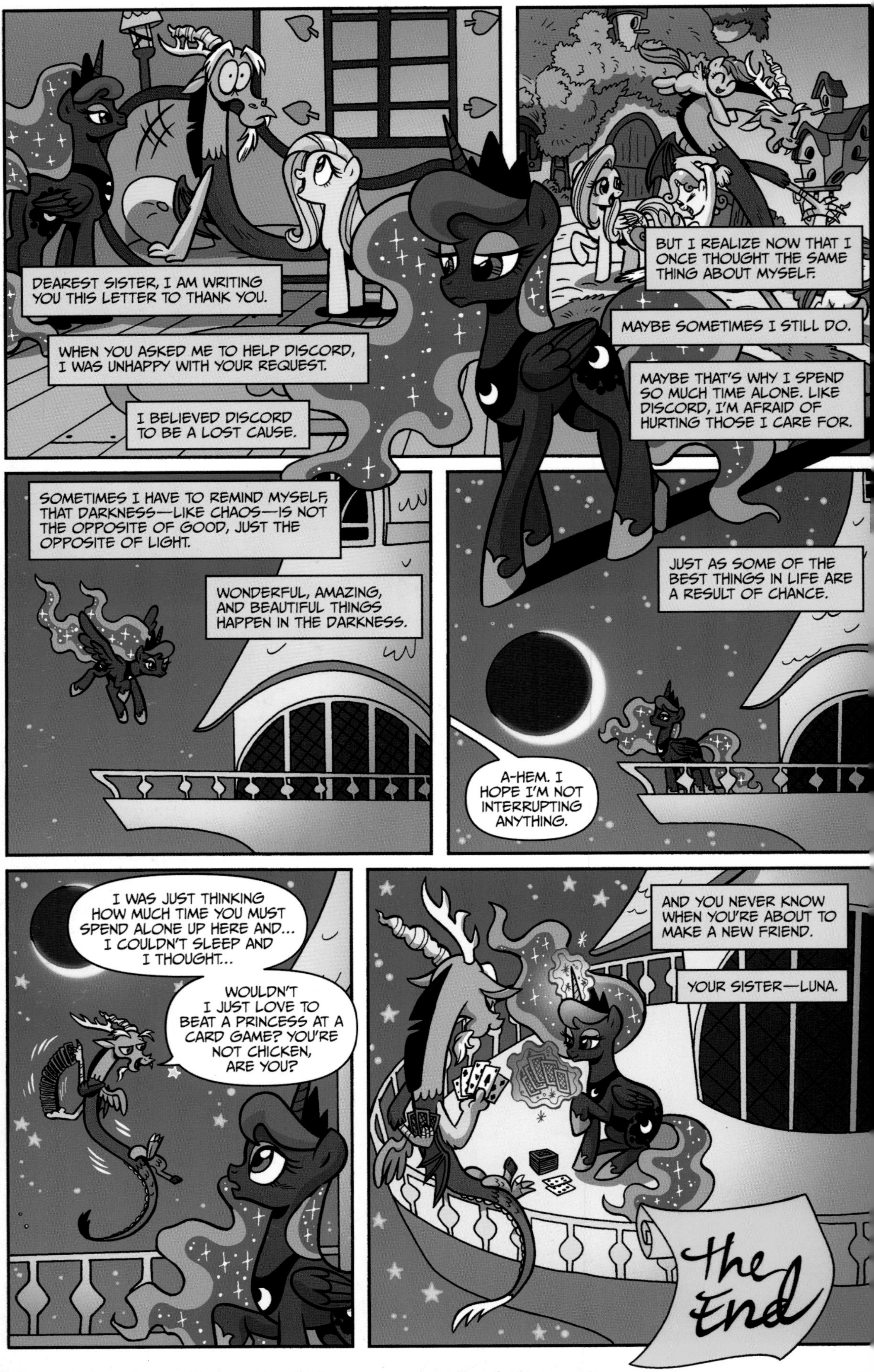
DEAREST SISTER, I AM WRITING YOU THIS LETTER TO THANK YOU.
WHEN YOU ASKED ME TO HELP DISCORD, I WAS UNHAPPY WITH YOUR REQUEST.
I BELIEVED DISCORD TO BE A LOST CAUSE.
BUT I REALIZE NOW THAT I ONCE THOUGHT THE SAME THING ABOUT MYSELF.
MAYBE SOMETIMES I STILL DO.
MAYBE THAT'S WHY I SPEND SO MUCH TIME ALONE. LIKE DISCORD, I'M AFRAID OF HURTING THOSE I CARE FOR.
SOMETIMES I HAVE TO REMIND MYSELF, THAT DARKNESS—LIKE CHAOS—IS NOT THE OPPOSITE OF GOOD, JUST THE OPPOSITE OF LIGHT.
WONDERFUL, AMAZING, AND BEAUTIFUL THINGS HAPPEN IN THE DARKNESS.
JUST AS SOME OF THE BEST THINGS IN LIFE ARE A RESULT OF CHANCE.
A-HEM. I HOPE I'M NOT INTERRUPTING ANYTHING.
I WAS JUST THINKING HOW MUCH TIME YOU MUST SPEND ALONE UP HERE AND... I COULDN'T SLEEP AND I THOUGHT...
WOULDN'T I JUST LOVE TO BEAT A PRINCESS AT A CARD GAME? YOU'RE NOT CHICKEN, ARE YOU?
AND YOU NEVER KNOW WHEN YOU'RE ABOUT TO MAKE A NEW FRIEND.
YOUR SISTER—LUNA.
the End

my LITTLE PONY

FRIENDS FOREVER

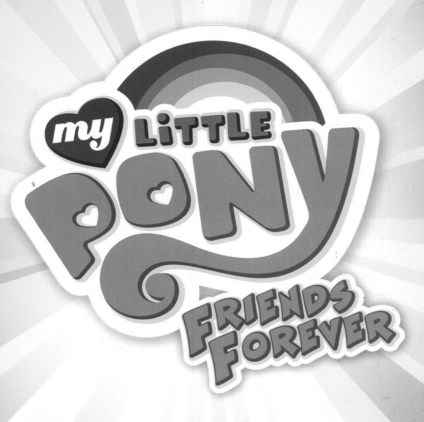

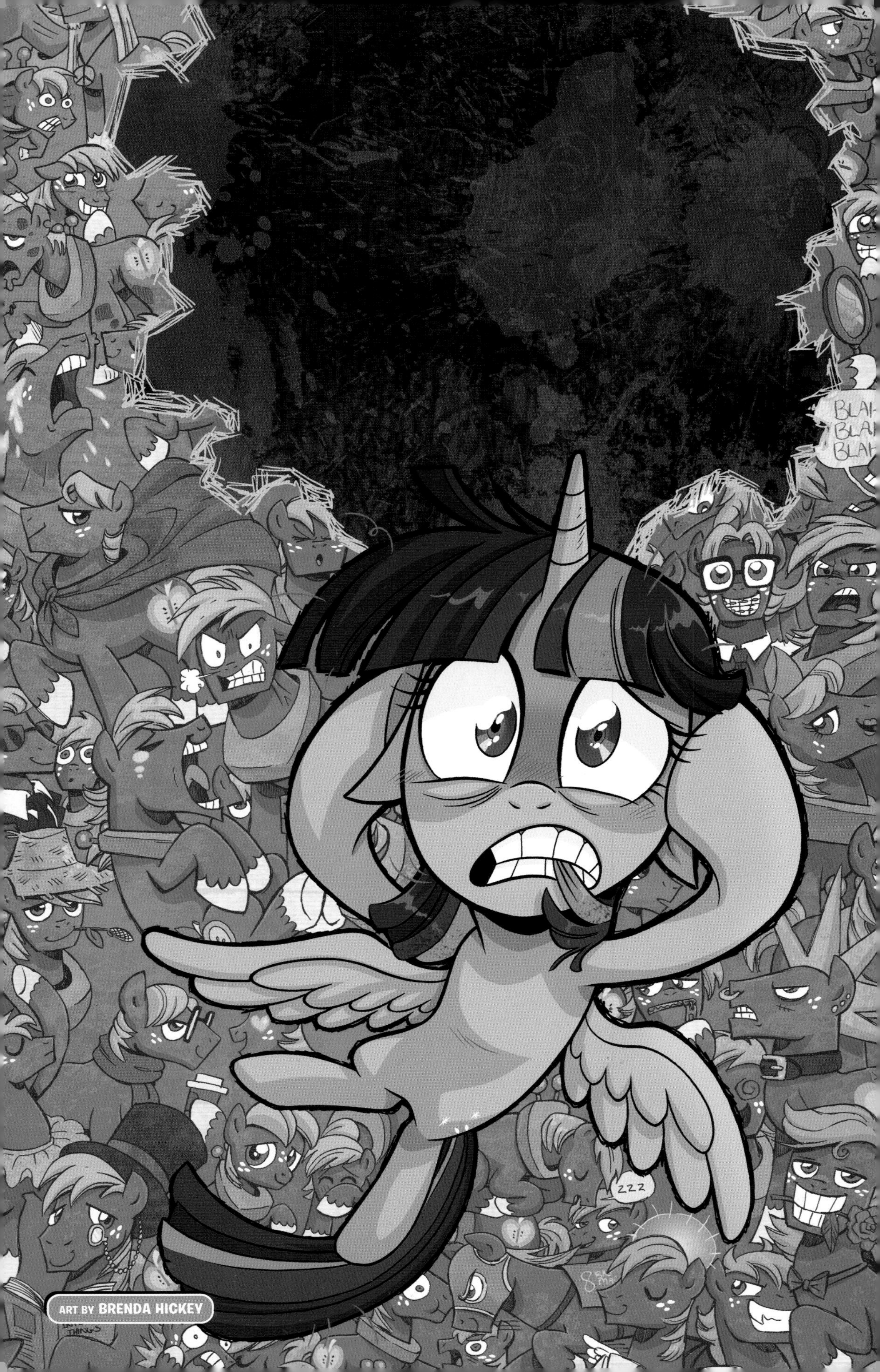
ZZZ
ART BY BRENDA HICKEY

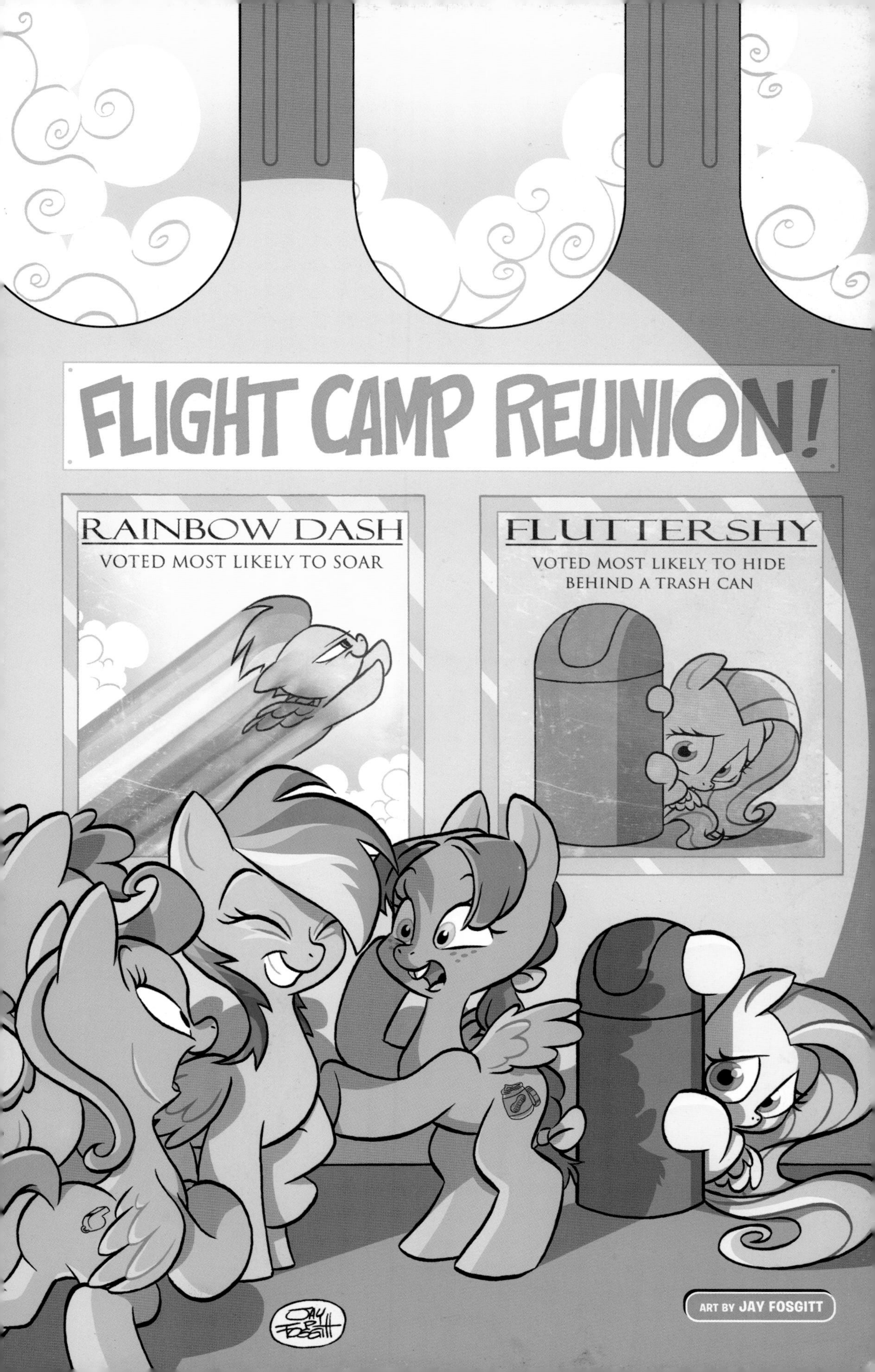
FLIGHT CAMP REUNION!
RAINBOW DASH
VOTED MOST LIKELY TO SOAR
FLUTTERSHY
VOTED MOST LIKELY TO HIDE
BEHIND A TRASH CAN
ART BY JAY FOSGITT

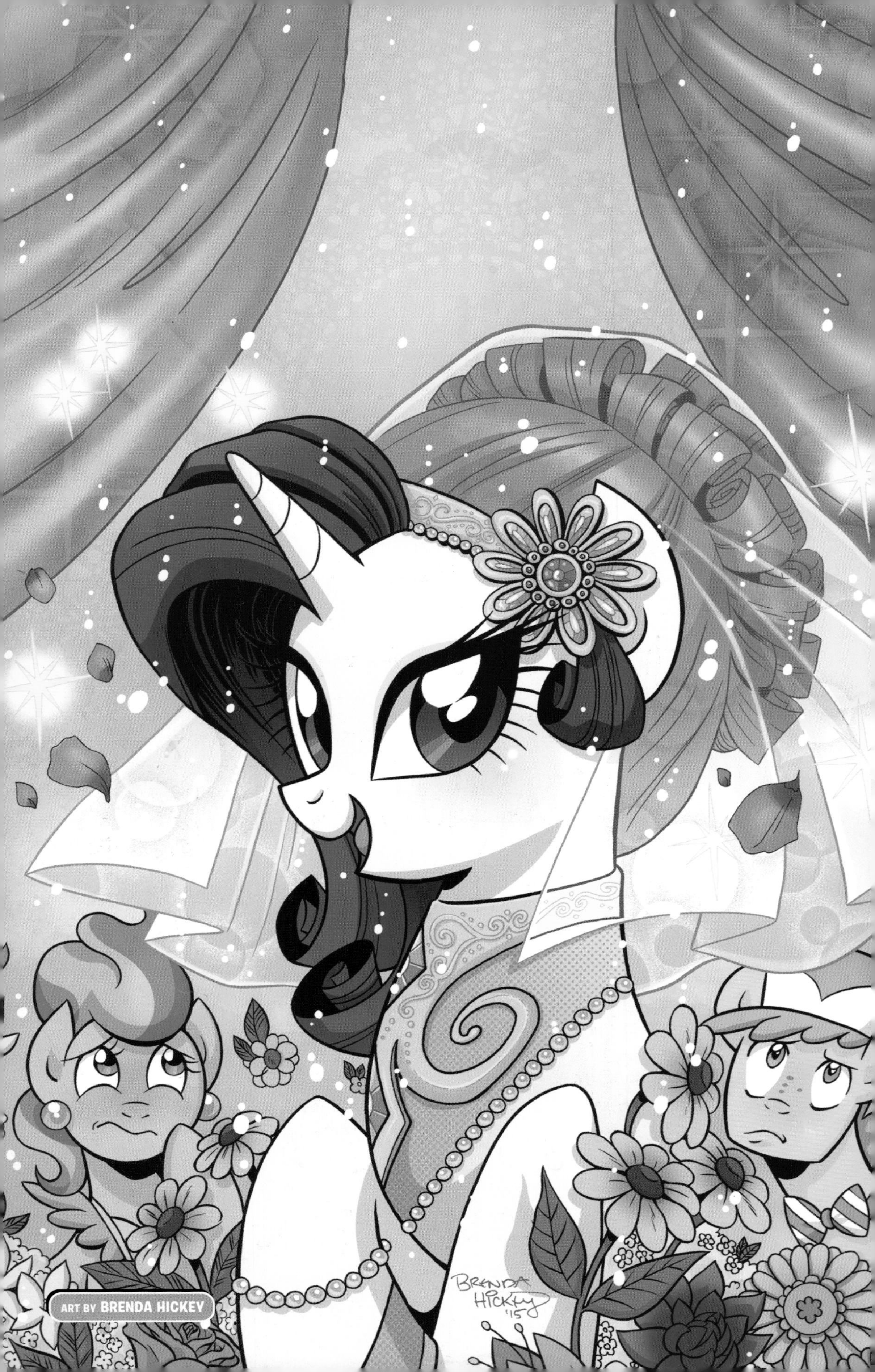
ART BY BRENDA HICKEY
BRENDA HICKEY '15

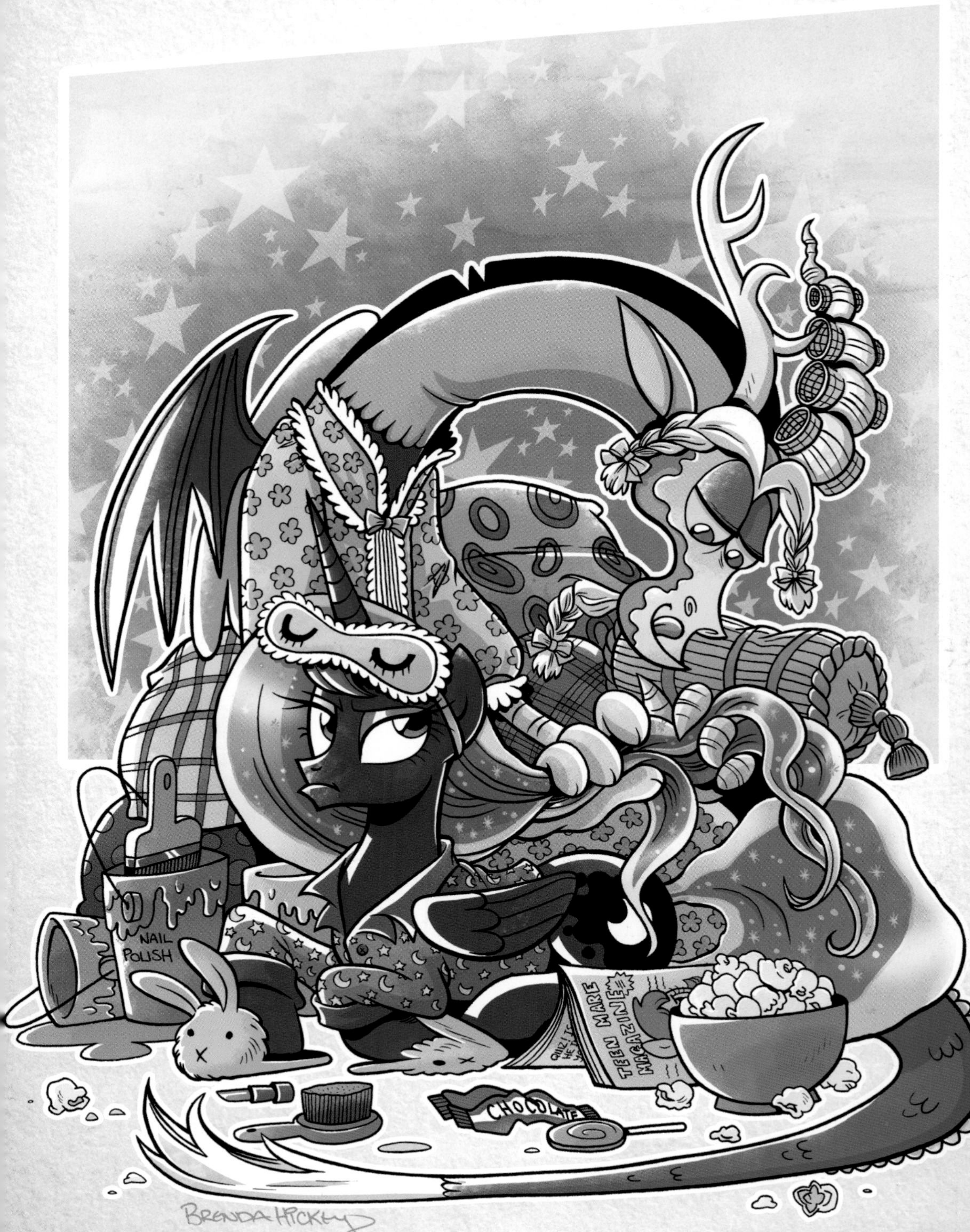
NAIL POLISH
TEEN MARE MAGAZINE
CHOCOLATE
BRENDA HICKEY

ART BY BRENDA HICKEY